FRACTURED FEAR
THE DEVILS OF NEW YORK

IVY KING

HEARTLEAF PUBLISHING LLC

Fractured Fear
The Devils of New York, Book 1
Published by Heartleaf Publishing LLC
Copyright © 2024 by Ivy King
All rights reserved.

Editing by Mara Montano - Mara's Editorial Services
Cover Design by Echo Grace - Wildheart Graphics

No part of this publication may be reproduced, distributed or transmitted in any form or by any means, including photocopying, recording, or electronic or mechanical methods, including information storage and retrieval systems, without written permission from the author, except in brief passages for review purposes only. To obtain permission to excerpt portions of the text, please contact the author at ivykingromanceauthor@gmail.com

This is a work of fiction. All characters, places, incidents, and dialogue were created from the author's imagination. Nothing in this story should be construed as real. Any similarities between person living or dead are entirely coincidental.

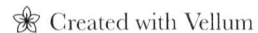

❀ Created with Vellum

To my real life book husband. From day one, you've always made me feel safe. Thank you for supporting me and loving me through all my crazy, anxiety-filled moments. I love you.

TABLE OF CONTENTS

Playlist — vii
Tropes & Content Warnings — ix
Spanish Translations — xi

Prologue — 1
Chapter 1 — 5
Chapter 2 — 13
Chapter 3 — 25
Chapter 4 — 31
Chapter 5 — 42
Chapter 6 — 50
Chapter 7 — 58
Chapter 8 — 64
Chapter 9 — 72
Chapter 10 — 82
Chapter 11 — 88
Chapter 12 — 94
Chapter 13 — 99
Chapter 14 — 109
Chapter 15 — 113
Chapter 16 — 118
Chapter 17 — 125
Chapter 18 — 132
Chapter 19 — 141
Chapter 20 — 146
Chapter 21 — 159
Chapter 22 — 167
Chapter 23 — 172
Chapter 24 — 177
Chapter 25 — 183
Chapter 26 — 187
Chapter 27 — 194

Chapter 28	199
Chapter 29	203
Chapter 30	206
Chapter 31	213
Chapter 32	217
Chapter 33	222
Chapter 34	230
Chapter 35	236
Chapter 36	246
Chapter 37	252
Chapter 38	264
Chapter 39	270
Chapter 40	280
Chapter 41	288
Chapter 42	294
Chapter 43	299
Chapter 44	306
Chapter 45	314
Acknowledgments	321
Stay Connected	325
About the Author	327

PLAYLIST

Voices - Hidden Citizens & Vanessa Campagna
Psycho - AViVA
Call You Mine (feat. Bebe Rexha) - The Chainsmokers
PILLOWTALK - Zayn
Paint the Town Red - Doja Cat
Human - DJ Goja & Vanessa Campagna
Starving (feat. Zedd) - Hailee Steinfeld & Grey
Summer Days (feat. Macklemore & Patrick Stump) - Martin Garrix
Idgaf - Besomorph & Silent Child
Free Me - NEFFEX
Into You - Ariana Grande
Close (feat. Tove Lo) Nick Jonas
I Ain't Worried - OneRepublic
Goodbyes (feat. Young Thug) - Post Malone
Stay - Zedd & Alessia Cara
Monsters (feat. blackbear) - All Time Low
Wicked - AViVA
Nothing Is As It Seems (feat. Ruelle) - Hidden Citizens

TROPES & CONTENT WARNINGS

Tropes
Why choose romance, age gap romance, he falls first, stalker romance, touch her and die, morally gray characters, forced proximity, one bed

Content Warnings
Death of a family member (off page)
Physical and Emotional Abuse (mentioned)
Violence
Anxiety/Panic Attacks
Stalking (the bad kind and the morally gray kind)
Sexual Assault (mentioned)
Torture
Assault
Drugging of the FMC
Body shaming

*This book also contains MM, MF and MMF scenes

SPANISH TRANSLATIONS

Ay dios mío – Oh my God
Cabrón – bastard
Cállate – shut up
Cerdo – pig
Compa – dude
De todas formas cambiaré el nombre – I'll still change the name.
Dios mío, dame paciencia – Dear God, give me patience.
Ella no está equivocada – She's not wrong.
En serio – seriously
Eres la criatura más bella. Por favor, ten mis hijos – You're the most beautiful creature. Please have my babies.
Es solo un niño – He's only a boy.
Estás gordo – You're fat.
Estás más loca de lo que pensé – You're crazier than I thought.
Este maldito niño – this damn kid
Gruñón – grumpy man
Hijo de puta – son of a bitch
Intenta correr. A ver qué pasa. – Try and run. See what happens.
Mara – gang

SPANISH TRANSLATIONS

Métete a la cama, idiota – Get in bed, idiot.
Mierda – shit
No hay lugar donde prefiera estar – No place I'd rather be.
No te diré ni mierda – I'm not telling you shit.
Palabrero – slang for MS13 clique leader
Pendejo – asshole
Puto/Puta – bitch
Qué pasa, hermano – what's up, brother
Segundo palabrero – slang for MS13 second in command
Tan bella – so beautiful
Tus gustos musicales son una mierda – Your taste in music is shit.

PROLOGUE

SPENCER

I don't know when he'll be back, and I don't have the luxury of guessing. Guesses don't keep me safe. Guessing didn't save me last night.

I stumble naked through the home where I have become a prisoner. I may have food in the fridge and clothes in the closet, but I've never felt so empty. So broken.

My head pounds and blood mattes my hair, but I can't worry about that now. I'll take care of it when I'm gone. When I'm safe.

Darting into our closet, I throw on jeans and a T-shirt from my alma mater, University of Houston. Bruises cover my skin and my body aches, but that's another problem for later. I cover my bloody hair by throwing it up in a ponytail and adding a baseball hat.

As I pack a bag, my mind floats over my choices. Choices that brought me *here*. I don't know why being alone used to be my worst fear. Now that I know, I'd rather be alone than feel like this. Terrified and damaged.

Then there was last night…I should have stayed in my

studio above the garage. I never should have left that space to make dinner. He hates it up there. He doesn't like getting the clay dust on his shoes. My studio is safe.

Was safe. Not anymore.

I never should have gone into his office. I rarely go in there. The little voice at the back of my mind always told me not to. Now I know why. Nothing good ever happens in that room.

I dig through our bedroom to find my essentials.

Dresses? Leave them. I can buy new ones when I get where I'm going.

My favorite set of graphite pencils? No brainer.

The shoebox of photos of Abuela and I? Definitely take. I hid them on the top shelf behind some T-shirts and never knew why I did. But now I understand. This box contains important memories and the key to my new life.

My heart pounds with the unknown. I don't know how much time I have. I don't know how I'll get out of town without him or one of his men, like Pierce, spotting me.

I'm surprised when I find the front door unlocked, but don't take the blessing for granted. I was prepared to throw a chair through the window; an unlocked door is pure luck. I guess he thought I wouldn't dare leave.

As I walk out on trembling legs, I don't look back. I don't have the time, and I don't need another glance at the house that will haunt me for years to come. The upscale home whose halls will forever plague me. Where my screams echoed off the walls and no one came to my aid. Instead, the only other person present stood by and watched. Now I'm left with aches and pains I've never endured before.

After throwing my bag in the back of my Jeep, my hands shake as I shift my car into reverse and peer over my shoulder. I glimpse the bag, shoebox, and urn of Abuela's ashes. I couldn't just leave her there. Never there.

I back down the driveway, past the perfectly manicured lawn, and I force myself to go the speed limit. I don't want to get pulled over in town and risk him seeing me or someone telling him they saw me.

As I merge with the steady flow of traffic down main street, my focus darts around looking for his car. When I don't see him right away, I allow myself to relax a fraction.

I'm okay. I will be okay.

I pass a police car sitting in a fast-food parking lot and hold my breath, tugging my hat down to cover my face. I don't know who it is, but I can't risk it if the cop is one of his friends.

The journey to the freeway is long and my stomach is in knots the entire time. But when I make it to the 10 and head east, I finally let out a breath.

I did it. I actually left, and I'm not going back.

But before I reach New York, I need to stop at a pharmacy for a morning after pill.

CHAPTER 1

SPENCER - THREE YEARS LATER

Footsteps echo down the hall and I force myself to think fast. I open the closet, the bathroom door, and curtains. Hopefully it'll make them think I searched the room and moved on.

Praying I fit, I lay flat on my stomach and squeeze under the wood bed frame. My ass barely makes the cut, but now I'm tucked away with my head at the foot of the bed. Laying my cheek to the carpet so I can see in the two inches of space between the bed skirt and the floor, I cover my mouth with my hand and attempt to slow my rapid breathing. It seems impossible, but I have to try or they'll hear me. If they find me, who knows what will happen next.

I don't want to find out.

A pair of brown leather Oxfords come into view and stroll into the bedroom. The shoes pace about the room and stop right in front of my eyes. "Spencer, dear. Come out, come out wherever you are."

My phone alarm goes off and I jolt upright in bed. I'm covered in sweat. Again.

Shaking off my nightmare, I glare at my alarm.

What idiot thought waking up at five a.m. to go to the gym was a good idea?

5

Yeah, that was me.

I knew I would fall back asleep if I left my phone next to me on my nightstand, like usual, so I set it on my dresser on the other side of my room. Even though it feels like I just fell in bed five minutes ago, I realize I need to start crawling to my phone across the room to turn my alarm off and get my ass in gear.

Damn Yesterday Spencer. She outsmarted Today Spencer.

After I make my way across my room, I stumble into the attached bathroom and catch my morning glow in the mirror. More like morning disaster. Rat's nest for hair and dark circles under my eyes. Definitely looks like I got five minutes of sleep. Constantly waking up from nightmares throughout the night will do that to a person.

I wash my face, brush my teeth, and throw on a pair of leggings and a sports bra. Yesterday Spencer set out Today Spencer's clothes, so I'll let her slide with the phone on the dresser stunt.

Shoes on and hair up, I'm ready to go and I can't think of any more excuses to delay the start to my day.

I put my headphones in, press play on my running playlist, and head out the door. I lock up behind me because this is New York, not the Houston suburb where I'm from. You don't leave your front door unlocked here like Mom always did growing up.

I head down the stairs, out the shared door that's wedged between my studio, Clay Creations, and the coffee shop, The Mudhouse. Warm, humid air blankets me with a comforting familiarity.

Bringing my ankle to my ass with my opposite hand, I allow myself only a few minutes to stretch. If I go any longer, I'll fall back asleep right here on the sidewalk. There's an unknown substance a few feet away that made an appearance last week and has yet to wash away even with the two rainy days we have had since then, but I would still curl up on my side and catch some Z's on the pavement.

After stretching, I start off with a jog.

I used to run when I was younger. I was pulled aside in gym class in seventh grade and the cross-country coach tried to convince me to join the team. But I was never a competitive person; I'm still not. Competing would have taken the joy out of running and it did. Mom made me join the cross-country team the next day.

Now I run for myself again. I run because I want to, but also because I have to. I never want to feel stuck and helpless like I did that night.

As *Lion* by Saint Mesa blasts through my headphones, I turn left a few blocks down onto Ninth Ave. I don't like to take the same route every morning in order to keep things interesting.

More like I don't want to make it easy for some psycho to snatch me up. I'm cautious like that.

My first week in New York, three years ago, there was a woman kidnapped and killed just three streets over from where I live. Her name was Natalie Cabrera. She was just living her life carefree and happy, but it was stolen from her. She was only twenty-four years old.

So here I am, like a crazy person, running at five thirty in the morning on my way to the gym. Just like I have done almost every day for the last two and a half years. I used to go at night, but my trainer told me that wasn't the best idea and that women are more likely to be abducted at night. Thus, the masochistic ritual of early morning workouts began.

Adjusting to my new life was…well, an adjustment. Busy sidewalks, jam-packed streets, pushy street peddlers, the smell of urine and decay, an alternating chorus of "get out of my way" and cat calls being hurled my direction every few minutes.

My mind wanders back to my first moments in New York, like the first time I was using the subway and someone asked me if I wanted to see snow. My social anxiety shoved me out of the seat and responded, "no, thank you" to the man with greasy hair who reeked of cigarette smoke. I stared across to the other window the rest of the ride. I convinced myself that if I didn't make eye contact, he wouldn't ask me again. He didn't. Then I went home and searched on the internet what "snow" could mean. Cocaine. It means cocaine.

There was another time when I decided to brave Times Square to go to the M&M store. I saw a man in a brown robe walk across the street, he then began to untie the knot at his waist, and I was too shocked to look away. It's like when you know a car accident is about to happen and no matter how much your mind screams at you to avert your gaze, you can't. That was me. Thankfully for the sake of my eyes and memory, an officer was right there and stopped the man before he could *disrobe* himself.

And then there was the time I decided to explore Chinatown. I wanted to see if the knock-off purses were actually as great as everyone says. Newsflash! They weren't. I was approached by strange men with Bluetooth earpieces on every corner asking if I wanted to buy everything from Gucci to Prada. I said no every time. I wasn't going to be that girl that disappeared into a back room and never came out.

Running in the morning means less people out and about. Plus, there's something peaceful about being awake before everyone else when the sun is rising. Less noise, and no one to tell you that you didn't make his over-easy eggs the way he likes. Just peace.

My mind wanders as I continue my run. Unfortunately, my mind has a mind of its own and goes down the path of last night's dreams. It's a scene that has played out many times in my mind. I lived it and my mind won't let me forget what happened the night before I left.

I wasn't supposed to see, and I wish I never did, but I can't take back what happened. I can wish on all the stars in the sky and not a damn thing will change.

I never should have agreed to go on that first date with him. I was only seventeen when I met my ex. He was twenty-seven. My mom was so excited when I bumped into him at my first art show. A gallery in town was accepting small artists' work and somehow a few of my pots and sculptures were chosen. He was charming and attentive; he asked thoughtful questions and seemed genuinely interested in my work.

Just the thought of that night has me steaming with anger. Anger towards him for lying. Anger towards myself for falling for his act.

He knew exactly how to build me up only to tear me down himself a few hours later. He was an expert at it.

He broke me down lie by lie with each strategic word. Then he rebuilt me so many times that eventually there was nothing of me left. I was the doll he wanted, the perfect image of an obedient little servant, and I stayed through all of it. I never once tried to leave, I didn't even threaten it.

I shake my head to give myself a reset. I can't remain a passenger on this thought train, it'll send me into a panic. That's not something I want to do today. Instead, I focus on putting one foot in front of the other and lengthening my stride. I embrace the burn in my legs and the sting in my lungs. The pain brings me back to the present rather than letting me journey through my upsetting past.

As I arrive at Joey's Gym I try and fail to take deep breaths, relieved I don't have to battle my own brain anymore. This place has been a sanctuary since the first time I walked through the doors. As I walk inside, my mind is cleared of the fog that is always present after a nightmare.

Here, no one looks down their nose at me. Here, I am powerful. Here, I am in control.

"You look like shit," a gravelly voice says to my right.

I look and see sweet old Joey standing behind the front desk. The white haired man always says that. It's like his way of saying "Good morning, beautiful. Aren't you just a glorious ray of sunshine on this otherwise dreary morning?"

Ha. Yeah, the charming lightweight champion from 1979 would never let those words leave his mouth.

The first time I met him he came off as harsh, but he quickly changed his tune.

"What do you want?" he asks gruffly when I approach the front desk. There's that New York charisma.

"Umm. I saw in the window that you offer self-defense classes," I say without looking him in the eye, keeping my gaze cemented on the floor.

"Hey." His voice grows soft.

I glance up and see that look in his eyes. Pity. I hate pity. I don't need to be pitied. "I just need classes," *I say in an attempt to sound firm.* "If you don't have any open spots, just let me know and I'll be on my way." *My tone gets stronger as I speak each word.*

He returns to his brash self but still not as rough as when I walked in. "I got a spot for you. No need to get your panties in a twist."

And that was that. I signed up for classes and now he trains me one-on-one. Every morning he tells me I look like shit and I respond with…

"And you look like a shriveled up dick."

It's our way to check in with each other. If he ever greeted me differently, I'd be worried he finally lost his mind and succumbed to old age.

"Get some water and go stretch. You'll be no good if your muscles lock up ten seconds in."

I walk over to the dinged-up fountain attached to the wall, take a sip, then stretch on the mats. As much as I love to hit inanimate objects, stretching also calms my mind. There's no room for anything else in my brain when I feel the pull of my muscles as I fold forward and reach for my toes.

Once I'm all stretched out and ready to go again, Joey sets a grueling pace. Burpees, jump rope, back squats, and leg lifts. He says we're not getting in the ring today because I went too hard yesterday, but we both know it's because he can see the shadows under my eyes, so today is just strength training. Weights mixed with cardio. Basically death.

He's never asked why I'm here and I've never told, but he knows. Joey knows when to push and when to back off. On occasion, I've cried during workouts. Usually after a terrible nightmare while I'm at the punching bag.

One day in particular was especially difficult. In my dreams, I had relived the worst part of my last night in Texas, and I couldn't shake my body's natural responses. Joey made me stop sparring when my tears blurred my vision and involuntary bursts of noise started to escape my throat. He pulled me into his office, sat me on the couch, and didn't say a word. I wailed from the agony I felt. Not only did my ex break my body that night, but he also broke my heart.

Joey sat next to me and pulled me into his arms as my tears puddled onto his shirt.

"It'll be okay. It's just for now. This pain isn't forever."

"But it hurts so bad," I expressed through the haze of relived trauma.

"I know, kid. I know." He didn't let go until the sobs had subsided. Then he called a cab and took me to The Mudhouse. We sat for hours, conversing over cups of lukewarm coffee.

Not once did Joey ask what had happened or what I had been through, that's not him.

Now when those memories haunt me from sleep and into the light of day, I go straight to the punching bag. As I pound the leather with my wrapped fists, I imagine what I should have or could have done differently that night. I imagine punching *him* in the face. I imagine running sooner than I did.

I can't change it now, but I can prepare. I can train. I can continue to be stronger than the fear I'm fracturing one punch at a time.

CHAPTER 2

SPENCER

I all but limped out of the gym after my workout with Joey. Brutal as hell, but I know he loves me. Deep down in his tiny, cold heart…way down there.

Who am I kidding? I curse his name every day when I leave that place. Literally. My parting words are, "Fuck you, old man."

To which he responds, "See ya next time, kid."

I allow myself Sundays to sleep in and relax. It's not because Joey told me to rest on Sundays. It's not that at all. The studio and gallery aren't open so I usually laze around my apartment and watch Netflix.

On my way home, I stop by my favorite smoothie shop Starry Night Smoothies for a protein pick-me-up. A key part of my daily ritual that brings me joy because food is happiness, especially if it involves chocolate and peanut butter. Even better if I don't have to make it.

When I sit down at the table in the back, corner my phone vibrates with an incoming call.

"Hello?"

"Oh, sweetheart. It's so good to hear your voice." Mom expels a breath as if she'd been holding it while waiting for me to answer. It's not like I made her wait long, but I guess she just misses me.

"Is everything okay? I thought we agreed *I* call *you*." My eyes dart around the shop searching for anyone who might be paying too close attention to me. I can't risk him finding me.

"I know, Spencer, but I missed you. I needed to hear your voice, and you never call me." Mom and I weren't especially close as I was growing up, but I'm sure she isn't used to not having me around.

"You're not supposed to call unless it's an emergency. We talked about this. It has to be this way." I reaffirm.

"But why? You won't tell me why." It's the same argument every time.

I let out a sigh through my nose. "It's best if you don't know that either."

"Just tell me where you are. Please. I can come be with you wherever you are," she pleads.

"I can't. It'll only put you in danger."

"Please, sweetheart. Maybe I can help." Her begging is almost enough to make me cave. I don't want to hurt her, but I have to keep her safe. The less she knows, the safer she will be.

"No, Mom. I'm sorry."

"Fine," she lets out a long sigh that crackles through the phone. "I have to go. I just wanted to check in. I'll talk to you in a few weeks." She hangs up before I have a chance to make it up to her or even say goodbye.

When I set my phone down on the table, I notice a new text. I already know who it's from. Or at least, I suspect. The police have told me since the number is from a burner phone, it's untraceable. My hands shake a little as I open the message. I don't want to read it, but I need to know.

Maybe I really am a masochist.

> Unknown: You never should have left. The longer you're gone, the worse it will be when you inevitably come home. Make no mistake, I'll be seeing you soon.

Breathe in—one, two, three, four—breathe in the fear. Breathe in the panic.

Hold it—one, two, three, four—let myself feel what I feel.

Let it out—one, two, three, four—breathe out the pain. Breathe out the lies.

The technique I learned from a self-help book doesn't always "help," but it makes getting through the next twenty-four hours easier.

Focus on the truths, Spencer.

It's not the worst text he's sent. I don't for sure know it's *him*. It's just a text. It could be anyone. He didn't openly threaten me and gave no indication he knows where I am. I'm safe.

He can't touch me. He's not here.

I read over the text again and allow my blood to simmer. *The fuck you will, dickhead. You won't be seeing my face ever again.* I don't send my words. I won't give him the satisfaction.

In my first year here, I changed my number five times. I don't know how he keeps getting it, but I have given up trying. At least this way I can determine if he has found me by what he says. As of right now, I live under the assumption he doesn't know. *Yet.* The premise could be a dangerous one, but my options are limited.

I set my phone down, finish my smoothie, and go over what needs to be done today. Focusing on the things I can control because I can't control this fucking creep texting me.

I need to order more clay, take inventory, figure out what's wrong with pottery wheel number three, contact my agent about my next show to see what she needs from me, check in with Iris at Abstract Dreams, my gallery, and see what has sold and what needs to sell.

Okay, maybe thinking about my to-do list was a bad idea.

Deciding I need to clear my head, I get up from my table, throw away my cup, and make my way outside.

Headphones in, *Gold* by Kiiara playing, I begin my run home. This time around, my mind still isn't clear.

I miss Abuela.

Abuela spent her life living and breathing art. She studied and traveled all over the world to learn different painting styles and techniques from whoever would teach her. She said there was only so much she could learn in a classroom and the best way to learn was to go out there and try. After her travels, she settled in New York. Chelsea to be exact. She bought a space with the money she earned selling her paintings, opened a studio, and lived in the apartment upstairs.

Traveling around the world with a child wasn't easy for Abuela, but she made sure Mom had everything she needed and was able to experience different cultures. Mom tells the story differently, she says Abuela is too flighty. *Was* too flighty. Mom describes her childhood as chaotic, but I think it sounds like a dream. Different countries, online school, art all day, different foods. Sign me up.

Once Mom was old enough, she cut off contact with Abuela and settled in Houston, where I grew up. Then Mom had me and as soon as I was old enough, she would send me off to wherever Abuela was at the time. I wanted to stay with her year-round, but Mom wouldn't allow it.

My father was more of a ghost than a man. Never met him. Never saw him. I don't think my life would have been better if he was present. He clearly didn't want me, and all I got from him was my last name, but even that wasn't given to me by his choice.

I can't ever tell Mom where I am. If Abuela had left Mom the studio then she could have sold it and kept the money; I know she would be pissed if she knew she lost out on a large payday. Mom didn't know where Abuela ended up before she died, and now I intend on keeping it that way.

※ ※ ※

When I get back, I pass Abstract Dreams and go through the glass door of Clay Creations, my studio. I take in the space that has seen me through these last three years. The entire front is made up of windows which let in as much natural light as possible, and white walls to help reflect the luminescence and make the space feel bigger. Unstained, floating wood shelves cover most of the walls, some filled with other artists' finished work, some contain pieces that are still wet or aren't quite done. Green pottery wheels are lined up in two rows on the right; three large canvas worktables and a wedging table on the left. It's early and no one has arrived to work on their pots, so all the stools are stacked by the worktables. In the back is the kiln room, damp room, an overflowing storage closet also known as "the abyss," and bathroom. I'm still in awe of how my vision has come together and that I get to be here every day.

Abuela's studio used to be one big space, but I cut it in half and made one side the gallery. I also renovated the apartment upstairs at the same time. Abuela left me an overabundance of money from the sale of most of her final paintings. Her attorney said she knew I wouldn't be able to part with her paintings after she passed so she did it for me which made me feel even more guilty. I didn't see her in her last few years of life. We talked weekly, but I didn't make the trip out here. I let *him* convince me to not visit.

Another thing he took from me.

"Hey, boss!" Hayes greets me. A little too chipper this early, but that's Hayes. He's a sweetheart to the core. He's only eighteen-years-old, just graduated, and comes in early on Saturdays even though I always tell him he can sleep in. His birthday is at the end of the summer and I plan on having a little celebration for him with the other artists and Iris. I know he likes her and is too afraid to make a move. He's still trying to get comfortable with his growing teenage body. I swear he shot up six inches over the last few months. He has that boy next door, blonde hair, blue eyes look going for him. I may have given up on relationships for myself, but dammit this boy deserves happiness.

"Morning, Hayes! What're you doing here so early?" I try to smile and sound excited even though I'm dead tired and need more food after my second run.

"I wanted to get a head start on counting inventory and cleaning the studio. I swept last night but you know how it is. Nonstop clay dust."

My shoulders instantly sag with overwhelming relief. I can check those off my list.

"You're a godsend! Seriously. Where do you hide your angel wings?" I tease.

He blushes and tries to hide it with a snigger. Poor kid isn't used to being appreciated. He's never confirmed or specifically said, but I assume his parents aren't supportive of him working here. Knowing what that's like, I do my best to encourage him. I hope he's happy here. I want Clay Creations to be a safe place for other people as well as myself.

"Nah. I hide my horns under my halo," he jokes.

I chuckle and shake my head at him. Hayes doesn't know how to take a compliment.

"I'm going to head upstairs for a bit. I have to spend half the day next door with Iris. Want me to bring down a cup of coffee when I come back?"

He lights up at my offer. "Yes, please. I'll wipe down all the wheels for a cup."

"You got it." I smile back at him and head out of the studio. When I approach the stairs just a few feet away, I groan and contemplate crawling up to my apartment.

When I signed the papers Abuela's lawyer gave me, I had mixed feelings about renovating the apartment, but renovations are just what I needed. A clean slate. It used to be just like downstairs, one big open space, I converted it into a three-bedroom, two-bathroom apartment. The front door opens to a large kitchen that I rarely use, and a spacious living area. The cozy, light gray sectional might be my favorite part about the room. The floor to ceiling windows give the room an inviting feel as well.

I wanted to keep things simple, but the designer convinced me that I deserved a nice space where I can relax. I caved to some of her ideas like the marble countertops, the over-the-top en suite, and the obnoxious walk in closet to the master bedroom. I admit that the luxuries have made this place feel more like a place I can call "home."

Once I'm through the front door, I strip my clothes on my way to the bathroom, not caring where they land. Tomorrow Spencer can deal with that shit. I let my hair down, walk straight into the shower, and turn it on not caring that the water will initially freeze my tits off. Just another way to wake myself up. Again.

After going through the motions for the rest of my routine, I get to the annoying part of picking out an outfit. I try not to care and just grab and go, but I can't. Sometimes I still think I need to look a certain way, but I remind myself that *he* isn't here.

He always said that my hips were too wide, my bra made my back look pudgy, my legs were too long, or my gut was too pronounced. At the time I told myself that *he* just didn't want me to feel embarrassed, but now I see his comments for the ugliness that they were.

Fuck him and the pole up his ass.

I may workout but I love carbs; I have *natural* wide hips and an ass that isn't leaving anytime soon.

Peering at my shelves, I snag three items without giving it a second thought. Dark green blouse, black pencil skirt, and black pumps. I shove my arms into the sleeves, shimmy the skirt up and over my ass, and ram my feet into the onyx torture devices.

There, that wasn't so hard. I just had to get a little angry first.

Anger makes the fear go away, but only for a bit. It's a band aid, not a cure, but I'll take it right now.

I do a quick swipe of makeup to keep things simple and cover up the dark circles under my eyes. After I meet with Iris, I'm heading right back to the studio. No need to do a full face when it isn't necessary.

Staring at my reflection, I note that I don't look like I did when I arrived in New York. My hair was dull and lifeless. My skin was pale for its tone. Now my hair is rich and full, and my skin is a nice tawny gold.

But my eyes are still haunted. Will that ever fade?

Walking away from my reflection, I begin to leave but remember Hayes' coffee and run back to my kitchen to make it. More like I do a weird clomping shuffle. It's impossible to run in heels. I don't care what anyone says.

It's. Not. Fucking. Possible.

I warm up a frozen breakfast sandwich while I make one coffee for Hayes and one for myself. I hate cooking because of *him*, but I splurged on a fancy espresso machine just over a year ago. I figured it would save me money because I wouldn't go to the coffee shop next door as much.

Yeah, that's a lie. It was on sale and then I justified the purchase. Girl math. The purchase didn't do its job anyways. I still go to The Mudhouse more than is socially acceptable.

Coffees in hand and breakfast sandwich scarfed down, I head out my door and back down to the studio.

Hayes is almost done counting inventory, so I discreetly set the to-go cup next to him. It's called being considerate, everyone hates it when they have to start over counting.

I wave at a few artists who have come in while I was upstairs.

"Alma! How are you? How are the kids?" I love this woman. She's a stay-at-home mom and now that all her kids finally go to school during the day, she likes to spend her free time here. In the summer, she only comes when she gets a babysitter.

"Giving me hell as usual," she says with all the love a tired mother can muster. "Oh, and I put the kids in that day camp you had in here the other day. It's a life saver!"

We laugh together as I remember the elementary and middle school-aged kids Alma is referring to. I like showing kids how fun art and clay can be, but this group had more than a few wild spirits.

I turn to Paul and give him a wave. Paul's wife died right before I moved to New York. He retired when she got sick so he could be with her. He said they spent her last days doing all of her favorite things. A trip out to Ellis Island, watching the sunset at the Empire State Building. They were never able to have children, and I know he's lonely, so I like to give him my time when I can.

"Hi Paul! How's the teapot coming?" I ask with a genuine smile on my face.

"Good, but I'm struggling with the spout," he answers without looking at me, staring at the piece on his wheel which I assume is the spout.

"Those are the worst. I'll help you out after my meeting next door." I pat his shoulder and head over to Abstract Dreams.

"Thanks, Spencer," he says, still without looking at me.

I stop at the door that connects the studio and the gallery, it always gets stuck and I have to use my hip to push it open.

Add 'fix the door' to my to-do list.

When I walk in, Iris is already at the computer behind the half-circle front desk that sits right by the entrance. The sun shining on her through the windows that cover the entire front of Abstract Dreams. All that glass wasn't cheap when I remodeled, but it was well worth it.

I added the gallery so smaller artists had a space to display their hard work. I have bigger exhibits here from time to time thanks to my curator. We don't only showcase ceramics and pottery, we also have watercolor, oil, and other paintings on the walls. I love that the artists who find peace at Clay Creations have a place to show off their work.

I stroll past the pedestal display cases and make my way to Iris. She's a gorgeous girl with chestnut hair and sun-kissed skin. Iris is a year older than Hayes and is working a few different jobs while she figures out what she wants to do with her life. I'm more than happy to be her introduction to the art world.

She always comes to work dressed to impress. I told her she doesn't have to do it up so much, but she said she wants to see how it feels dressing up for work every day. I'm quite positive the get up is to impress a certain employee next door.

"Playing solitaire?" I tease.

"Ha. Ha. Good joke, grandma," she responds quickly. I swear this girl is too witty for her own good sometimes.

"Hey! I'm only five years older than you."

"Whatever you say, babe." She smirks as she continues to stare at the screen and type away.

I sit down with my coffee and we get to work going over spreadsheets. Thank you, God for sending me this girl who knows how to make a spreadsheet her bitch. I'm hopeless with technology. I can do the basics like send a text, make a phone call, write an email.

Oh lord. Maybe I am a grandma.

After I'm done meeting with Iris, I take notice of a few patrons who have made their way into the gallery and strike up conversation about the pieces they're viewing.

Someone's gotta pimp the art.

Once I'm all talked out, I change into studio clothes. An old, ratty T-shirt will do the job so that I can head back to Clay Creations and finish out my day there. I barely stop to eat lunch.

Paul is the last to leave, as usual, and I lock up behind him. I give myself a moment to look around.

Paul's completed tea pot is out and drying on a shelf. His wife loved to drink chamomile tea, so now he makes tea pots he thinks she would have loved and sells them in small coffee shops here and there.

Hayes' massive, three-foot vase that he's been working on for the last month is covered with plastic bags and wet paper towels, waiting for further progress on Monday. He's enjoying the challenge. He said his goal is to one day make a pot taller

23

than himself. He's six feet tall. I've never taken on that kind of endeavor, but I know he'll succeed, he has natural talent.

Alma's set of plates are glazed and waiting to be fired. She was commissioned to make them and came into the studio squealing with excitement. We ordered her cupcakes and a bouquet of roses—her favorite—to celebrate. It's her first commission and she is determined to get them right so we're all pitching in where we can. She's killing it.

Then there's a couple shelves that hold the pinch pots made by the day camp kids who took a field trip to the studio. It was complete chaos, but the smiles on the kids' faces made the frantic energy in the studio worth it.

A shelf towards the back holds some of my works in progress that need to be done for my next show. My agent and I decided to push the date back because I'm feeling stuck and I can't figure out why.

Iris said I need to "get out there" and find inspiration.

Where the fuck is "there?" If I knew, I'd go. I don't like feeling stuck. I got away from *him* so I'd never feel that again.

When I'm done looking everything over, I grab my keys, sketchbook, and purse then leave the studio behind to catch some sleep.

CHAPTER 3

SPENCER

Saturday night's sleep was a joke. A big fucking joke, but no one is laughing.

Well, I'm not. Maybe my demons are.

Thank the powers that be I gave myself Sundays off. I spent the day lounging around in an oversized All-American Rejects tee and my boyshort underwear. No bra. Because no bra equates to ultimate comfort. I watched some Netflix and ate Chinese takeout.

However, the self comfort did nothing to calm my racing heart. Every noise had me ready to grab my bag and go. Even my eyes were messing with me. A few times I thought I saw someone standing in my doorway, but every time I looked, there was no one there. I chalked it up to a trick of the light.

When Monday rolls around, Joey decides after my day of rest that I could take a hit…or twenty. He kept barking at me because I was leaving my left side vulnerable. He proved his point and now I'm sore as hell.

After a soothing shower and devouring the hell out of a quick breakfast, I'm down in Clay Creations doing what normally makes me happy. But right now, I would give anything for a distraction from my inability to come up with an idea.

As I massage my temples with my fingertips, the front door opens and in walks…a man. A very attractive man.

His thick, dark curls hang perfectly, framing his face. His jade-green eyes viciously suck me in; and his strong jaw and sharp cheekbones are what every model dreams to be born with. Flawless couldn't begin to describe his ivory skin. With how much I'm staring I am sure that if there was a flaw, I would have discovered it by now, or it's covered by his sexy layer of stubble.

He's wearing a dress shirt, but it doesn't hide his broad chest and firm muscles. He's tall. Definitely taller than my five feet eight inches. He's the perfect height for me to go up on my toes and run my lips down his strong neck.

Nope. We're not going there.

Iris and Alma tried taking me out one night. They said I needed to have my donut hole glazed. I told them I'd go if they stopped phrasing it like that. Iris brought over a few dresses for me to try on, forgetting she's a size smaller than me. I ended up wearing the dress that Iris said gave my girls "a killer lift." It was an off-the-shoulder, bodycon, short black dress. Alma curled my hair into waves and Iris applied the perfect smokey eye. I looked hot. Unfortunately, every douche in a five-mile radius noticed as well. Needless to say, the "hooking up" part of the evening was a disaster.

We were at Moonlit when a guy thought that sitting next to me at the bar and telling me that I was "easy on the eyes" meant he had the right to grab my ass. I got up to head to the small dance floor when the asshole made his move. I punched him in the face on instinct. I was embarrassed and ready to leave, but the owner, Jerry, stopped me and ended up kicking out Mr. Grabby Hands. Our drinks were free the rest of the night. Now the three of us go back to Moonlit once a month.

Something tells me this man isn't the kind who thinks he has the right to touch me.

"Hi, I'm looking for the owner. Spencer, I believe." A kind smile graces his face. I practically melt, and the instinct to run the other direction when a beautiful man comes within a few feet of me starts to kick in.

The attractive man holds up a flier in his hand. A flier I recognize as one of the many I had printed on neon yellow paper and hung up in various small businesses.

Hayes and I make eye contact, and he smirks. We both know how this is going to go. I've found myself in this situation more than once where someone walks in and wants to speak to the owner. No one ever expects Spencer to be a woman, let alone a business owner. Art may seem feminine, but it's still a male dominated industry. I have had people walk out when they see I'm a human with boobs and not a stocky person who can grow a beard.

I stand from the small eighteen-inch stool and greet the beautiful stranger. "That's me. What can I help you with?"

He doesn't look shocked—like every other man does—when I introduce myself. Instead, his eyes trail up and down my frame, taking in my plain black leggings, crusty All-American Rejects shirt, and messy bun. His eyes alight when they reconnect with mine.

Is this man checking me out?

"Zane Kingston," he states and stretches his hand towards me.

"Spencer Gray. What can I do for you?" I take his hand and do my best to seem unaffected by his touch. His hand is warm and calloused. Deliciously so.

Still not going there. But maybe later.

Wait. WHAT! Down, Spencer!

"I was hoping to purchase some pottery classes for my friend for his birthday," Zane answers as he pulls his hand away and places it in his pocket, naturally falling into a hot guy pose. I would bet big money he doesn't even realize what he's doing.

His answer is not at all what I was expecting to come out of his mouth. It takes a minute before I'm able to reply, "I can help you out with that." I walk over to one of the work tables and grab my tablet. When I turn, he's right there behind me. "Oh. Umm. How many classes were you thinking? Does your friend have any experience?"

"He doesn't. I saw on the flier that you offer one-on-one classes. Who teaches them?"

"I do."

He flashes his tempting smile at me and says, "Definitely one-on-one classes then."

My face heats at his implication and I do my best to not look him in the face anymore. If I peek at his angelic features again, I'm sure I'll do something completely unlike me and ask him to take me upstairs so he can do some glazing on my donut hole.

We get the classes set up for his friend and I stand there uncomfortably waiting for him to leave the studio…and my life. I'm the awkward one. He stands there as if Michelangelo sculpted him from marble and placed him smack dab in the middle of my studio.

"How long have you owned this place?"

Is he making small talk? With me?

"Oh. I—uh—" Of course I can't even form a single coherent sentence right now.

"I work near here, but I don't come by this area often."

I get my shit together and answer, "I've owned the space for the last three years, but my abuela owned it before me. I did some renovating which took six months. It used to be one big studio, but I cut it in half and made the gallery next door."

"Abstract Dreams?" He tilts his head to the side causing a curl to fall across his forehead. My hand itches to sweep it back, but I refrain by white knuckling my tablet.

"Yeah, have you been in?" My question comes out all squeaky.

Real smooth.

"Not yet," he responds, and I glimpse that smile again.

Stay strong, Spencer. Stay strong. This man is a literal stranger.

Where the hell was he on my ladies' night out? I would've let him take me home in a heartbeat.

Stay. Strong.

"Well, it was nice meeting you, Mr. Kingston," I say, making it clear this embarrassing chat is over.

"Please, call me Zane." Another smile. Does he ever put that thing away?

"Zane. It was nice meeting you."

He turns to leave, and I involuntarily note his firm ass. You know a man with an ass like that doesn't skip leg day.

When the door finally closes behind him, I let out a breath I didn't realize I was holding.

"You okay there, Boss?" I hear from behind me.

I turn and Hayes is doing his best to hold in his laughter.

"Oh, shut up," I retort and fan my face. I have a tendency to get cherry-red cheeks, and I know I'm turning a shade of crimson now.

I set my tablet down and use both hands to fan myself. Hayes can't hold it in any longer and busts out a barking laugh. I just shake my head at him and remind myself to be grateful he's the only one here right now. I would die of embarrassment if everyone was present to witness how I almost jumped into Zane's muscular arms.

I know Hayes will inevitably tell Iris and then it'll spread like wildfire.

I'm so fucked.

On the bright side, I'll probably never see Zane again.

Is that a bright side?

Yes, yes, it is. I have done my best to rebuild everything my ex-fiancé broke, and I don't need another man to complicate things.

CHAPTER 4

ZANE

Another day, another case—or ten.
I've been at the tenth precinct for the last five years or so. It's cramped and the building is old, but the people are nice to work with for the most part, which is more than I can say about my last assignment. If you look hard enough you can find bad apples anywhere, but the bad apples were plentiful at my last precinct.

I caught one officer sneaking coke from the evidence room. Come to find out he was being paid to make evidence disappear. His wife mysteriously found out about his arrangement the next day and left with their kids. She was eager to go, especially after she realized her and the kids weren't seeing any of the extra money he was making. That piece of garbage had a mistress in Queens that got to live a lavish lifestyle from his secret paydays.

Another officer would trade "special favors" with sex workers in lieu of being arrested for solicitation. Turns out not all of them were willing to participate in that little trade, and he may have found himself at the bottom of the Hudson for that one.

The biggest discovery was when a certain lieutenant got popped for installing cameras in the female officer showers and live streaming it on the dark web. That particular incident took some digging, but we went about his justice a different way. The legal way. That lieutenant is now serving his sentence at Attica Correctional. It helped further convict him that one of the women filmed was the granddaughter of the Police Commissioner.

All in all, even though the walls here are more gray than white, I'm happier here.

As I stand in the break room waiting for my coffee, I think of all the other things I could be doing today. Hanging out with Rio at his mom's house while she makes us empanadas, getting drunk at the Black Horse, lazing about on the couch, or getting to know a gorgeous pottery teacher.

Pinching the bridge of my nose, I set down the file on the warped laminate counter and think through the details of another missing person's case I was assigned when I walked in.

Ava Thomas, sixteen-years-old, last seen at Sunny's Market, three blocks from her home.

This is the fifth missing person's case this month. I can't legally prove it, but I know what it means. They're taking more women and children, and they are not slowing down any time soon.

Bracing my hands on the counter, I drop my head forward. My mind instantly going back to *her*.

What the hell happened this morning?

Putting one foot in front of the other towards the door was more than a chore. It was damn near impossible. I just about turned right around, went back into Clay Creations, and kissed the hell out of that woman. If I didn't have to get to work, I would have considered doing it right then.

I mean, kissing her is definitely going to happen one day because *holy shit*. Why was I so grossly underprepared for the beauty that is Spencer Gray?

Her gaze ignited something in me, and I know I never want to lose it. Her beauty alone commands attention, but those eyes. The depths of sorrow and pain. I want to dive in and discover the cause then erase it for her so she knows nothing but joy.

Her smooth, golden oak skin shined just like I'm sure it would at any time of day. I mull over the way her cheeks heated when she caught me checking her out. I was eager to see if that color made its way across her chest. Her long dark hair looked like swirls of coffee as it sat in waves pushed forward over her shoulder.

If she thinks she's hiding under those clothes, she needs to think again. You can't hide a body like hers under a baggy shirt. Nothing could hide the swell of her tits or the way her hips flare out in a way that has me longing to use them to pull her close. And her long, lean legs in those damn leggings, perfect for wrapping around my waist—or my head.

My dick twitches at the thought. Thank you to whoever brought leggings into women's fashion. Considering I'm at work, right now probably isn't the best time to sport a semi.

I have never felt the urge to be around someone all the time, especially within minutes of meeting, but with Spencer, I would happily bask in her light every day. It's clear she has her own strength. I only want to add to it.

I already know I'll go back to her later, just to check on her and do my neighborly duty. That's all it is. No big deal. Doesn't matter that I live in the Bronx, Spencer and I are basically neighbors.

It has nothing to do with the fact that when we touched, I wanted to throw her over my shoulder and take her home where I could fuck her all day and night.

Nope. Not the reason.

Shitty coffee brewed and file in hand, I head back to the mountain of case files also known as my desk.

The movies got one thing right, police station coffee sucks ass. You would think after the first year of drinking this shit, I would go to Starbucks instead. But no, here I am ten years later still consuming this sad brew, willing it to get tasteful with each gulp.

Who was it that said the definition of insanity was doing the same thing over and over and expecting a different outcome? Well, that's me. Insane.

I take another sip from the chipped white mug.

Yeah, it's still shit.

Looking over the file, I'm stopped in my path to my desk.

"Hey! I'm Liam James."

He's young, probably in his early twenties, with ash brown hair, brown eyes, and pale skin. Very average looking. Even his clothing is plain. The good news is we don't have Crazy Sock Day here at the precinct.

I glance at the man's expectant outstretched hand. I don't touch others, not even something as simple as a handshake. The feeling makes me want to crawl out of my skin. I get this buzzing in my ears and feel like I'm going to explode at any moment. I get plenty of sneers and odd looks when I don't reach my hand back. But I don't want to, so I shouldn't have to. Some think I'm being a snob, but it's more like saving those around me from potential mass murder.

Very few people are allowed to touch me. Two to be exact. Rio, because he's always made me feel comfortable, his eyes never contain judgment and always remain soft when gazing at me. And Asher, but we've only hugged a handful of times. That's it, no one else.

Now, I should add Spencer to that list. I didn't even think twice about shaking her hand earlier. All I knew was that I needed to feel her.

Now is not the time, Kingston. No semis.

Ever since I survived my foster parents, Teresa and Michael Brunson, I can't stand the brush of another's skin against mine. I can handle the whispers about the strange detective, they don't bother me.

Liam drops his hand and awkward silence ensues. I don't know what he expects from me here. It's not like we're partners.

Oh shit. Did Captain Abrams get me a new partner?

"Zane Kingston." I give him a simple head nod and step around him.

Liam recovers quickly and follows me. "I know. I figured I would introduce myself since we're going to be working together."

Fuck. I get to train the new guy.

His energy is too bright. Too high. This job is going to kill that quick.

Sighing at my dismal desk, I unload my hands. My workplace is plain and standard. I have no need for photos or anything like that, plus there's no room for personal effects when the hunk of metal is covered in case files.

I peer at the desk in front of mine. It's been empty since I transferred, but now there's a cardboard box that no doubt contains Liam's things.

Liam continues, "I'm excited to work together. It's going to be great. I have so many questions. Like how did you catch the Midnight Rose Rapist?"

That case was actually more simple than people know. I narrowed down his comfort zone, staked out the bar I was sure he would hit next, and boom. There he was pretending to help a woman he drugged. Of course, the resources I used to find him will never become public knowledge since it wasn't exactly legal. What happened after I followed him home didn't follow the letter of the law either, but no one questioned when I brought him in and the bastard had two black eyes. Once he was taken care of, I made sure the evidence I logged was obtained by legal means.

I don't answer Liam. I just lean back in my crappy desk chair and let him ramble, and ramble away he does.

I catalog each detail he gives me. The facts he's sharing will help when I look into him later.

Two kids, married six years, his wife was his high school sweetheart, grew up in Brooklyn. It's a cute story.

Honestly, this guy really should be careful about who he gives this information to.

"Kingston!" Captain Abrams calls and stops next to me before I get my next sip of my sad excuse for coffee.

"Yes, sir?" I sit up in my chair as it creaks.

Captain William Abrams is stout and just a few inches shorter than me. The only sign of aging on the man is the white hair peppering the sides of his head and small beard. Captain Abrams is a good man. I would know, I checked him out when I started working here. He's close to retirement, but you can't tell. He doesn't know how to slow down. Abrams is a native, he grew up here and is passionate about keeping the people safe. He's been especially worked up about the recent increase in missing women and girls. He's a father and a husband. I can't imagine what it's like to worry about the women in his life on a daily basis.

Whoever is abducting people off the streets, doesn't have a type. Captain thinks we just have some crazies out and about right now, but I know the real answer.

"Meet your new partner." Captain tilts his head towards Liam.

"Already done, sir."

"Good. The missing persons case you got this morning. The girl's sister witnessed it. Go talk to her and see if she can remember anything. I want to know what the hell is going on here and I want that information yesterday."

"I'm on it, Captain," I reply dutifully.

"Take James with you."

"Come on, newbie. I'm driving." I nod at Liam, set down my lousy coffee on my pile of casework, and head out.

Time to break in the new guy.

Rolling up to Central Park, I turn to Liam. "Stay here."

"What? Why? Shouldn't I come with you as back up?"

"Hank spooks easily. If he sees you, he'll bolt," I raise my eyebrows to emphasize my point that we can't lose Hank and the leads he may give us. "Stay."

I exit my car with the hotdog, no ketchup with mustard, and the can of coke I made Liam buy earlier. I ignore my partner's protests and stalk off into the park. Food always softens Hank up a bit. Leisurely walking down the path, I easily blend in with office workers enjoying lunch in the park.

While looking for Hank, I think back to what we learned from Ella Thomas, Ava's sister. Ella is a few years younger than Ava and idolizes her sister. Which is why she was following Ava to Sunny's Market yesterday. Ella saw a white van with no windows speed down the street right towards Ava. They stopped and two men with ski masks, dressed in black, jumped out of the sliding door, and snatched Ava. Ella said the guys put a hand over Ava's mouth and that she didn't fight long. Before she was even in the van Ava "went to sleep," which means the kidnappers used chloroform.

Ella's statement is huge. We finally have a fucking idea how these guys operate.

I spot Hank leaning against a sycamore like some bad boy that suburban moms warn their daughters to stay away from, which I guess he is. He's only twenty-one-years-old with shaggy, dark blonde hair and gray eyes. His skin is covered in freckles from hanging out in the streets all hours of the day every day. He's only a few inches shorter than me and skinny, but he's lean and packs a punch.

I busted Hank eight years ago when he was just starting out as an errand boy for the annoying as hell MS-13. His mom was never home. She goes by Roxanne on her corner, but her real name is Alice. I don't judge her for doing what she has to in order to provide for her kid, but her absence didn't go unnoticed and left plenty of time for Hank's hands to get him into trouble. A lot of trouble.

When I need to find Hank, I know he'll be in this part of the park. He sells whatever he can to whoever he can. I understand his lack of morals when it comes to not caring who buys the shit he sells. When it's survival of fittest and a boy becomes a man at a young age, he doesn't give a fuck what he has to do to make sure he's breathing at the end of the day.

I wait a good twenty yards away, watching him finish his sale. He hands a man wearing a suit and tie a small bag with white powder and the man hands over some folded bills. As the man slinks away—I'm sure to find the closest bathroom so he can do a quick line before heading back to his boring as hell desk job—Hank nods at me indicating he's ready.

He tries not to eye the hotdog in my hands, but I don't miss the lick of his lips. Kid probably hasn't eaten today. I know some nights he doesn't even go home, and if he has to he will skip a meal choosing to feed his overworked mom instead.

Handing over the food, I wait for him to devour it. I make a mental note to bring him two next time. Maybe some fries or a bag of chips as well. Once he's done, I hand over the drink, but he takes his time sipping instead of chugging it.

"To what do I owe the pleasure?"

I keep my face blank. The little shit is always trying to get a reaction much like Rio does. He should know by now I'm not easy to rile up.

"Have you heard anything about Cain?"

He lets out a low whistle. "Still going for the big fish, huh? Mr. Hot Shot bagged himself a serial rapist and now thinks he has the balls to take on the head honchos?"

Still no reaction. I have perfected my poker face over the years. I had to at a young age. Reactions meant more pain, so I keep my face empty of emotion. Not even a blink.

Understanding that he's waiting for payment, I give it in terms of a promise. "I'll go pick up your mom and hold her for twenty-four hours." Hank doesn't fault his mom for her job, but he doesn't like that she has to do it. Hank has always seen himself as her protector.

Once when Hank was seventeen, I had to pull him off of Fat Bruno, Alice's pimp, after the dumbass backhanded Alice in front of Hank. Fat Bruno ended up with two black eyes, a fractured cheekbone, and some gnarly bruised ribs. I threw the kid a bone and shoved the pimp out the door and told him to forget it ever happened or I would bring him into the station and spread the word that he was a snitch. I knew Hank would be tried as an adult if charges were pressed. Thankfully, Fat Bruno left quietly, but he didn't leave Alice alone. She was back out on the street the next night.

Like I said, survival of the fittest.

Plus, who calls themself Fat Bruno? The guy's real name isn't even Bruno. It's Arthur.

Hank doesn't bite at my first offer. He never does. You don't survive the streets of New York without learning how to haggle.

I stick out my hand discretely slipping a hundred into his. He nods then offers up his info. "All I know is he's taking healthy women and kids." His eyes wander to the left a little so I narrow my gaze. If the foster system taught me anything, it's how to read someone. I had to if I wanted to avoid the wrath of Teresa and Michael.

"What else?"

The muscles in Hank's neck strain. "That's it, man." He's trying to hold out and be a tough guy, but he always caves. If he doesn't give me information, then he won't have me to help with his mom. So again, I wait. Some people will relent and all you have to do is wait them out, and I know Hank will give in. He needs me gone so he can see more customers.

Two minutes go by and Hank starts tapping his foot. I begin my countdown.

Three, two…

"I'm not sure if it's true. Probably just a rumor."

There he goes giving me just what I need. Good Hanky Boy.

I grunt, not giving anymore prompting than that to continue.

"Cain has some ink on his forearm. A skull with a snake coming out of its eyes surrounded by lilies."

Giving him a quick nod, I turn on my heel without any parting words. I may have a soft spot for the kid, but that doesn't mean I'll coddle him.

He's tough. He doesn't understand kindness. In Hank's world, no one gives without expecting reciprocation.

I slide back into my car and eye Liam's fingers drumming away rhythmically on the center console.

"So…what now?"

"We go arrest a prostitute."

Liam rears back and stares at me like I have lost my mind. He'll soon understand that I lost that over twenty-five years ago, along with my heart and soul in a two-story brick house in the suburbs of New Jersey.

CHAPTER 5

SPENCER

The rest of my day flies by uneventfully. Alma gets more plates done, Paul makes a set of teacups to match his teapot, Hayes adds more shape to his monster of a vase, and I teach the day camp how to make a coil pot. Still no progress on the pieces for my exhibit. I think if I bang my head against the wall, an idea will come to me.

I checked a few items off my to-do list. But, of course, there's more to add by the end of the day. By that time I'm tempted to fall asleep on a work table, but I force myself to lock up before I tumble into bed.

When that damned five a.m. alarm goes off, I'm ready to question my choices. Do I really need to go to the gym today?

The unfortunate truth is yes.

I once skipped a workout without calling Joey and he flipped his shit when I showed up the next day. The workout was twice as hard, and I could barely walk home afterwards.

As much as I love being prepared to punch a handsy man in the face, being sore is the absolute worst and I'm a whiny baby about it.

Surprisingly, my workout is easy today. Well, *easier*. I don't hobble out of the gym, so that's a plus.

Now it's just after lunch and in walks...another fucking sexy-as-hell man.

Is there a sign on my door offering discounts to hot men or something? Because what the hell? I normally get teachers looking for a field trip for their students, stay at home moms who want out of the house, artists who need a space to create. I do not get sex-on-a-stick men.

He's tall like Zane, but where Zane's skin is a beautiful ivory, this man has a rich tawny tone. His eyes are a deep chocolate I would happily drown in. His hair is cropped all around and looks to be a true warm brown. He's wearing a simple white henley, dark wash jeans, and work boots, but on him they are anything but simple. The shirt hugs his chest and torso in a way that showcases the solid muscles underneath. His rolled-up sleeves display his mesmerizing tattoos, and...oh my. Are those finger tattoos? Why is that so hot?

Pushing myself to be the professional business owner I am—who does not check out every man who walks in the door—I stand and greet the man in the only way I know how.

Awkwardly.

"Hi! Welcome to Clay Creations. How can I help you?" For good measure, I throw in a wave that can only be described as the imitation of a fish flopping on dry land.

Yep. Awkward as fuck. Apparently, that's me when a man is involved.

He looks at me and smiles.

Shit.

This is going to be a repeat of yesterday. Only this time Alma and Paul are here with Hayes. Well, I guess they don't need yesterday's story. They'll get to witness it all first hand.

"Hi, I'm here for a lesson my friend signed me up for."

Friend? Is he Zane's friend?

Of course, Zane's friend is as hot as he is. Hot men live in packs I swear. They all know each other and have some sort of hot guys club. I'm so fucked. Zane paid for three months' worth of classes. I'm going to be seeing Rio two days a week for the next nine weeks. Yep, definitely fucked.

"You must be Rio. I'm Spencer. I'll be your teacher." I reach out my hand to shake his.

But when he takes my hand, he pulls me close and says, "Actually my name is Navarro Juan Carlos de la Cruz Flores. But, Mama, you can call me Rio."

Oh. Hell. That shouldn't be as hot as it is, should it?

I realize I'm panting. *Fucking panting* while I'm less than a few inches away from this man. Could I be any more pathetic? He's just flirting. He probably does this with all women.

I go to pull my hand away, but he holds firm. Not in a painful way. It almost feels as if he doesn't want to let me go.

His hands are warm and soothing. How is that possible? It's just a handshake, but his touch speaks volumes, as if telling me a story. It tells me that he works hard. The scars on his knuckles hidden under the ink tell me he's fought before. More than once by the look of it. He's no stranger to pain, but instinctively I know he wouldn't turn that pain on me. I don't know how I'm so sure of that after only just meeting him, but I am.

"You never truly know someone" has been a rule that has kept me safe in recent years. I don't want to give Rio the opportunity to prove me wrong, but I get the feeling he'll show me whether I want him to or not. I shouldn't let him, but everything about him piques my curiosity.

After a moment I realize I haven't moved, but neither has he. He's watching me with a playful heat, a heat that warms me all the way down to my core, and I find that I don't hate it. I should hate it. I should turn his attention elsewhere, deflect his focus, but I can't bring myself to do it. His attention on me is addicting and I revel in the burn.

He slowly lets my hand slide from his. His fingertips graze down my palm making my heartbeat silently pound against my chest.

I make myself switch into work mode. "I'll give you a tour today and do some demos. Next time you'll be on the wheel. Before you leave, I'll need you to sign some paperwork. Sound good?"

"All good here, Mama." He flirts further while dragging his eyes from my dirty Chucks, up my dusty leggings, and over my large band tee.

"We The Kings?"

"Huh?" I glance down at my shirt. "Oh. Yes. Love them."

"Never heard of them."

"What? Okay. That has now been added to your classes. Music education."

He smiles as if he just won something. I'm not sure what he won, but I'd give him a gold medal for that smile alone.

A man with a nice smile will forever be my type.

"Follow me. I'll show you where you can put your stuff and where your pieces will be stored. Everyone has their own shelf space," I explain as I walk towards the back. "Your shelf is here. You're going to want to put your keys, wallet, and all that here while you're working with clay. It gets messy very quickly. On that note, next time, wear clothes you're okay with getting dirty. Some clay can stain, so be ready for that."

Rio looks down at himself and inventories his outfit. "Clothes I'm willing to get dirty. Got it." Then he winks. Fucking winks. My face heats at his implication, but I think I do a good job brushing off his comment.

"Um. Uh. Right. Yeah. Clothes you don't mind getting dirty."

Real smooth.

"And who is this handsome man?"

I internally groan and turn to Alma. "This is Rio. He's taking some pottery lessons," gesturing between Rio and everyone else, I make introductions. "Rio, this is Alma and Paul. They're both artists who come here often. And that's Hayes over there, he's my studio assistant."

"What's up, man? Nice to meet you." I turn to Hayes and he gives me a smug look. A look that says *I know you think he's hot.* I shoot him a glare in return.

"You too," Rio replies politely.

Paul just gives Rio a chin lift, but Alma gives him a huge megawatt smile.

"Well, hello there, handsome." She bats her lashes and practically makes googly eyes at him.

"*¡Hola, chica!*" Rio turns his winking power on Alma and the woman fucking swoons. Dampening Rio's effect on me would be a lot easier if everyone else didn't feel it as well.

Continuing with the tour, I show Rio the kiln room, damp room, and storage closet with clay and tools. Once he has his own set of tools, I begin the demo. I explain how men naturally build upper body strength easier because their center of gravity is in their chest. So centering the clay and shaping his pot on the wheel will look different from how I do it. A woman's center of gravity is in her hips, therefore I utilize the strength there to work clay on the wheel.

During the demo his eyes never leave me, making the fire he lit inside me burn hotter. I don't think he actually watched my hands at all. Well, maybe when I showed him what coning was. That always gets an adult male student's attention.

After I'm done with the demonstration I ask, "Do you have any questions?"

"Do you have a boyfriend?"

"What?" My mouth hangs wide open in shock.

"Do you have a boyfriend?" Rio repeats the question slowly, enunciating each syllable as if I didn't hear him the first time.

"Um. I meant, do you have any questions about the demonstration?"

"Yeah. That's my question. Do you have a boyfriend?"

"Well. No. But I don't see how it's related."

He smirks at me and says, "I'll explain it one day, Mama."

Why does it feel like there's a joke here I'm not getting?

I narrow my gaze and attempt to say threateningly, "If you say so, Rio."

He chuckles and I can't help but smile back. After a moment, I'm laughing myself. His laugh is infectious. A deep, rumbling laugh that makes me smile just to hear it; it's pure joy.

"Any other questions that actually pertain to pottery and not my relationship status?"

"Not right now." He winks. Again.

He really needs to cut that shit out or I'm going to end up in the hospital with an irregular heartbeat.

At that moment, my phone goes off and breaks the bubble Rio and I had unwittingly erected. I normally have my phone on silent while I'm in the studio, but I guess I forgot to turn it off. We have a landline here for any work calls, so I know this notification isn't work related.

I know. I'm ancient.

I wipe my hands off, pull out my phone, and freeze. There's a ringing in my ears and everything around me fades away as I read the text.

> Unknown: Remember. You're mine. If you let another man touch you, you'll regret it. I fucking swear, Flower, you better not.

Flower. That name. *He* always called me that.

After the first time he yelled in my face, he bought me a bouquet of flowers and begged me to forgive him. I gave in easily because he seemed so sincere and genuinely remorseful, but the next day the flowers were cut up and scattered all over my apartment for me to clean up. That's how it happened every time after that. We would argue, he would buy me flowers, and they would all be ripped to shreds the next day.

He's coming for me isn't he? Just when I feel like I'm actually making progress. Am I going to have to pack up and leave? Will I have to sell everything and run? Where would I even go? I don't think I can start over again. I'll never find another Alma or Iris or Paul or Hayes. To keep myself safe I would have to leave, wouldn't I?

My mind wanders to the duffle I have ready to go at the bottom of my closet. I could leave if and when I need to, but that would mean leaving this life I've built. This life I've worked so hard for.

If he really has found me, I don't have a choice. I have to go.

"Are you okay?"

I snap back to the present to see Rio peering down at my phone. I quickly hide it and shakily answer, "Yeah. Yeah I'm fine."

"Spencer, you're as white as a ghost."

"I'm okay. Must be low blood sugar or something." My voice still wobbles.

A gentle hand under my chin softly tilts my head upward. When I allow my eyes to follow, I'm looking directly into Rio's rich irises. The sincerity and concern shining from them is alarming. I'm not used to that kind of care. Why would he be so nice to me? He barely knows me.

"Who was that?"

"I don't know what you're talking about." I deflect, breaking eye contact.

"Okay. We'll play it your way for now, but promise me you'll tell me about it someday."

"Sure," I respond to get him off my back.

"Yes or no, Spencer." He says each word with such authority. It's not the type of authority that results in harm if not obeyed, this type of authority I'm unfamiliar with.

"Yes," I breathe out.

"Good girl. I'm going to go and I'll be back in on Thursday for my next lesson, okay?"

Fuckitty fuck fuck. *Good girl?* That should not make my panties wet. I'm completely speechless with a blank stare on my face so all I do is nod.

"I need your words, Mama. Let me hear that beautiful voice tell me yes."

"Yes," I whisper.

His thumb trails my lower lip and he releases my chin. I'm suddenly cold at the loss of his touch, but that fire is still burning inside me. He stands and nods then leaves the same way he came.

Taking a breath, I realize he made me forget all about the text. Normally I would need to lock myself in the bathroom or excuse myself to leave so I could break down in private. Without even trying, Rio prevented my panic attack.

Alma, sitting at the wheel a few feet from me, snaps me back to the present when she says, "Oh girl. You're in trouble with that one."

As I steady my breathing, all I can think is how absolutely right she is.

I'm in so much trouble.

CHAPTER 6

RIO

*F*uck me. Zane didn't tell me Spencer was hot as hell. I'm going to give him shit for that when I get home later, but the joke is on him. I get to spend one hour a day, two days a week with her for three months.

When I walked in, my eyes went straight to her. As if they could venture anywhere else when she's in the room. Her hair was up in a messy bun with some little pieces framing her face that had escaped. I found myself jealous of those few pieces of fucking hair because they were touching her face while I couldn't, but I rectified that quickly. Coming up with excuses to get my hands on her is going to be my new favorite hobby.

Then she went pale and the energy around her shifted. Before I could stop myself, I reached out and touched her perfectly smooth bronze skin and it was even better than I imagined. When her beautiful honey eyes connected with mine, I felt a tug. She was scared and I knew in that moment I would do anything to erase her fear. I would take down every enemy to see her smile like she had been a few seconds before.

Her laugh captivated me like no other woman's ever has.

I've slept around, but no one compares to her. Absolutely no one. My dick has a new obsession, and her name is Spencer. I'm all for it.

I kept myself composed the whole time. Mostly. I didn't go all caveman, throw her over my shoulder, and beat my chest yelling "mine." I mean, I would have never done that. My instincts are more along the lines of knocking her out, dragging her back home, and keeping her there where no man could ever look at her or even touch her again.

Even though beauty like Spencer's was never meant to be hidden, I'm finding she makes my baser instincts rush to the surface. Fuck. Protect. Fuck some more.

I pull out my phone when I finally get to my car, or rather, Asher's car that I use when he's gone. I don't care that it pisses him off. I tap on the screen a few times and call the fucker who thought these lessons would be the perfect birthday gag gift.

"Hey, man. How did lesson number one go?"

"Shut up, *cabrón*," I greet back then dive right in. "Why didn't you tell me Spencer was a woman?"

"Didn't think it was important." His tone is casual. Too casual.

There's something he's not telling me. That's not like him, we tell each other everything. We've been best friends since college. We were roommates our freshman year and no matter how much he tried to push me away, I wouldn't let him. I could tell he needed a friend and I felt like being that friend. Turns out I was right. He needed me, but I needed him too.

I'm surprised he thinks he can keep whatever he's hiding from me. He knows I see it as a challenge and that I'll figure it out sooner rather than later.

"Is that all it is?" I push back.

"Have you heard from Asher?"

Nice deflection. I'll give it to him.

"Not today. You?" We're men of many words.

"He texted us in our group chat while you were getting in touch with your creative side. By the way, stop changing the name. We're not *The Devil's Army*."

"Aw come on, *amigo*. We need a name." I've been making this argument from day one. If we're going to do the stuff that we do, we need a name.

"No, we don't. Stop it," he barks. Too bad I know he doesn't bite. That's all me.

"Whatever you say. *De todas formas cambiaré el nombre*."

"I know what you're saying when you speak Spanish, idiot. I've been around you and your family enough to know. Don't change the name again." I can practically hear his eyes roll through the phone.

While he continues to nag, I tune him out and pull up the text thread.

> Asher: They found another body in LA. I'm hopping on a flight from Oakland to LAX tonight. He's still on the move. I'll send more details when I get there. Sorry I wasn't there for your birthday, Rio.

Asher travels a lot for his job so he's missed things here and there. We know he feels guilty, but neither Z nor I hold it against him.

"Another body? Damn. How many cities is that for this fucker? Five?"

Asher has been out chasing a serial killer for months. They didn't make the connection between the bodies for years. The bastard has been killing consecutively for the last three years. He leaves a purple hyacinth with each body and the women are always dressed in a white, silk wedding dress. If law enforcement was more willing to work together, they would have caught on to this guy sooner. At first the killings were about six to eight months apart, but this body in LA is only one month after the one in Oakland, which means he's escalating and it's only going to get worse from here.

Sometimes I wish I would have gone to the police academy with Ash and Z, but I chose to stick it out another four years in law school at NYU. I wanted to be part of the final battle making sure fuckers who hurt innocent people are put away for good.

I don't work in the DA's office anymore. Fucking politics and all that shit. It corrupts everyone it touches.

When I caught one of the prosecutors taking bribes to make sure cases were half-assed or dropped altogether from "lack of evidence," let's just say being out of a job wasn't the worst that happened to her. She aided a child rapist, with multiple victims, get off with barely a slap on the wrist by helping the defense attorney fabricate alibis for the ass hat. Now she may or may not be the owner of a set of cement shoes which happened to walk her right into the Atlantic.

Then there was the judge who would give lesser sentences to criminals if they paid the right price. He accepted payment in all forms: drugs, sex, money. Come to find out, the sex wasn't always consensual and was sometimes with girls a fraction of his age. A very small, very young fraction. He was close to retirement and wanted to "enjoy the perks of life." Only predators enjoy young girls and consider their tears a joy, and predators like that don't get to continue in life. They find themselves dismembered and six feet under, which is where he ended up after his boat capsized in a storm. Before the judge died in a mysterious and sudden "boating accident," in which his body was never found, his retirement was distributed to women's shelters across the five boroughs. His offshore accounts filled with bribe money may have been drained overnight and the cash given to the women and children he hurt without a second thought.

I now have my own practice that I run out of our home. I still make sure those who deserve justice are granted it, and when all else fails, that's when Ash, Z and I step in. Just like we did with the so-called prosecutor and judge. Fuck them.

"Yeah, that's five for him. He's clearly not slowing down and thinking about retirement anytime soon."

"Fuck. Okay. We'll wait for word from Ash. I'm on my way to meet with Mrs. Romero."

"Her nephew still giving her shit?"

"Yeah, he broke into her home, but this time stole some valuables. I'm going to make sure no one fucks up her case. She's been reaching out to the police at the 41st for weeks now and they haven't taken her seriously. Even after we filed that restraining order."

"Fucking idiots. Maybe it's time to look into that precinct."

"A Devil's Henchmen's work is never done." I smile at my own joke.

"Oh my God. Stop. Just stop. I'm begging you."

"Not a chance." My smile widens further.

"I'll buy you a meat lovers from Sal's if you stop. Please. I'll throw in his tiramisu too."

"Make it two slices of tiramisu and I'll think about it." We both know I won't stop. It's our thing.

"Only if you promise."

"Sure, sure." I placate him half-heartedly.

"Fuck. Fine. I'll pick it up on my way home tonight."

He hangs up without saying goodbye, but I know he still loves me. That's just how we are.

FRACTURED FEAR

AFTER MY MEETING with Mrs. Romero, I head home to our brownstone in the Bronx. It's shitty, but overall, not bad. It screams bachelor pad. The front door is up six concrete steps and you have to do a little trick to get it open. The key has to be halfway in the lock, then you hit the top right corner of the door to get that unstuck, and finally shove with your shoulder in the center. It's like tackling a linebacker every day.

When you walk in it's a simple layout. Straight ahead are the stairs that lead up to three bedrooms. To the right there is a black leather sectional in front of a TV. Beyond that is the small kitchen we only use when Asher is in town because he's the only one who cooks. Z and I can't cook to save our lives. If takeout wasn't an option, we would starve to death. Which is a fact Ash likes to remind us of often, but we know he loves to cook for us.

Behind the stairs is a door that leads to the "backyard." It's a six-by-six patch of brown grass. It's rickety and quirky, but it's comfortable and houses some of the people I care about most. It's our home.

We all moved in after college. My mom didn't want us too far from her. I grew up just ten minutes from here. My family still lives in my childhood home, a fact I both love and hate. I'm happy to have them nearby. My mom brings Z and I food when Ash is gone and most Sundays our asses are parked at her table, but that home also holds deep heartache. I never want to forget Isabella, but sometimes her memory is too painful. Too close.

I toss my shoes by the front door and drop myself on the couch with a Corona. I get to work typing up documents and keeping track of financials. Being your own boss is great, but that also means you have to be the accountant, customer service rep, and so on.

Just as I finish drafting a contract for a client, I hear someone at the door. I'm not alarmed because clearly they know the secret password, meaning it's Z. Looking up from my screen, I realize the sun has begun to set. I've been sitting here longer than I thought. I stretch my neck side to side and reach my arms above my head to relieve some of the pressure in my back. I need to get to the gym. I'm too old to be sitting like this all day.

When Zane enters, I smell the sweet aroma of marinara.

"You really got Sal's?"

"Of course I did. I said I would."

I get up to take the pizza from him and head to the bar stools. We usually sit in front of the TV for dinner, but we need to talk about what's got him all cagey today.

"Want to watch the Knicks tonight?"

"They're not on for another thirty. Let's sit here and eat." I know he's on to me, but I'm not letting him off the hook.

He grabs two beers from our practically-empty-fridge and sits next to me. We eat in silence for a few minutes, but patience has never been my strong suit.

"Why are you acting so weird?"

He scrunches his eyebrows. "What are you talking about?"

"On the phone earlier, you were weird."

"Uh. Okay." I don't appreciate the sarcasm dripping from his tone.

"Don't deny it." I point my finger at his face.

Zane shakes his head at me. "I didn't deny anything."

"So you admit it?" I narrow my eyes at him. "Don't make me stab you."

"Oh my God. You've gone crazy."

"Call me *loco* one more time," he remains silent. Smart move. "I'll get the truth out of you eventually."

"There's no truth to be told. Drop it." He turns his attention from me and goes back to eating his pizza, but I'm not giving up.

Choosing my next moves carefully, I gracefully get up to stand behind him and nip at his neck. I soothe the sting with a light lick and whisper, "I know how to get you to talk."

Zane's body tenses with anticipation. I know what he likes, and he knows what I like. Occasionally we use that to our advantage. All in good fun.

We've been together for years and although we've never defined what we are, I know we're more than fuck buddies, but not in a relationship. I guess some might call it an open relationship.

When I met Z he was struggling with the shit his foster parents put him through and it pissed me off. They got what they had coming to them in the end, but it didn't erase Zane's scars. Emotional or physical. So, when he came to me and admitted he wanted to experiment, I volunteered as tribute faster than a bullet. He knew I was openly bisexual and knew my family accepted me. I think he was looking for some of that same acceptance, so I gave it. Since then, he's been with other people. Sometimes we're with the same man at the same time, sometimes the same woman, but we never bring people here to our home. We don't share a room or anything, but this is our space. We all need it to stay like that, so no one night stands in the house.

Gliding my hands down his chest, I reach for the bulge tenting his pants. I bite and suck on his ear eliciting a low moan from his throat.

Before I can wrap my hand around his covered cock, Zane jumps from his stool.

"Let's watch Julius and Jalen kick some ass." Then he scurries to the couch and flips on the TV.

Another deflection. All the more intriguing.

CHAPTER 7

RIO

*L*ater that night after Zane and I had both gone to bed, I hear the garage door open. My room is on the second floor, but my hearing has always been sharp. When you have five younger sisters, you need that superhuman ability.

I peek out my window that faces the front and see Zane's car pull out with the lights off and drive away.

Was that his attempt at stealth? Pathetic. He knows better than to think I didn't just see him. And he knows better than to go out on a hunt alone, so this better be something else.

I jump out of bed and rush down the stairs. I'm only in sweats, but I don't care. I slide my feet into my tennis shoes and jog to the garage. Hopping in Asher's Camaro, the engine turns over and lets out a nice purr. Ash hates it when I use his car if it's not necessary. I'm going to consider this an emergency, so I'm sure he won't mind. Always better to ask for forgiveness instead of permission.

Z has a head start, but that's okay. We put trackers in his

and Ash's cars in case of an emergency. I pull the app up on my phone and see that he's disabled the tracker.

Fucking pendejo.

Zane may be extraordinarily talented when it comes to technology, but that genius level brain clearly wasn't smart enough to find the second tracker I put in his car over a month ago.

I follow the dot on my screen until I'm around the corner from his car. I chuckle to myself when I realize where we are. I park Ash's car a block away and jog the remaining distance. It's difficult to sneak up on any of us. We've trained ourselves to always be aware of our surroundings. You kind of have to be when you have a hobby like ours.

That being said, I'm somehow able to get the drop on him. I open the passenger door to his Honda Civic, and he immediately goes for his Glock. I wrap my hand over his before he can get far and slam it down on the center console.

"You're getting soft, *amigo*."

Nostrils flare and his hands clench, ready for a fight. The thought of some action has my blood pumping.

My comment grates on him. He brings his left fist around aiming for my face.

Not the moneymaker. Come on.

I easily block his attempt and goad him further.

"That's it? You can do better." I know he's angry he got caught and I'm trying to not let it get to me that he didn't tell me in the first place, but I'm more upset that I didn't think to do this myself.

He twists my left hand that's still on his and pulls free. Swinging the gun back in my direction, I grab his wrist and aim the barrel towards the ceiling.

Zane would never actually shoot me. I think.

Hand tensed and flat, I aim for his throat but he grabs my wrist and twists my arm at an angle that makes me lean. Without hesitation, Zane pulls his hands towards himself bringing me with them and thrusts his head towards my nose. I turn my face just in time, and his head crashes into my cheekbone.

Not wanting to take it any further, we drop our hands. The only sound in the car is our rapid breathing from the quick spar.

"Where the fuck is your shirt?"

"Didn't have time to put one on when you snuck out like a teenage girl meeting her boyfriend."

He rolls his eyes. "It's not like that. I'm not your sisters."

"You're right, you're nothing like my sisters. You weren't sneaky at all. Solana would have left her window open all day so she could avoid making any sound at night. Elena would be too busy to even attempt sneaking out. Carmen would've just walked out the front door not giving a shit. And Mariela would have snuck the guy inside."

"Point taken." That's basically another way of saying *you're right*, which I fucking am.

He huffs a breath and says, "I'm just making sure she's safe."

"With your perv binoculars?"

"She does yoga at night," he says nonchalantly as if it explains it all. And it kind of does.

Spencer all bendy? I'll take a front row seat please.

"Give me those creeper peepers."

We fight over the binoculars like a pair of toddlers battling for their favorite toy. I finally yank them from his grasp and put them to good use. Can't say I have ever watched a woman through her windows, but there's a first for everything.

I finally spot her through her very large, open window.

We're going to have a little chat about that. A crazy person might see that as an invitation. Or two crazy persons.

Zane was right. She's stretching. No wonder I was able to surprise him. I can't focus on anything but her. She's wearing a sports bra that barely contains her perfectly shaped breasts and matching tiny shorts, if they can even be called that. They're more like a second skin with the way they are molded to her hips and ass. An ass I would love to grip with both hands.

Please fuck me.

I should feel ashamed. I should put the binoculars away and force Zane and myself to go home, but I don't.

"*Mierda...*" I whisper as my dick hardens in my sweats.

It's a good thing I'm wearing sweats. Jeans would be very uncomfortable right now. "Were you here last night too?" My question is met with silence.

"In this exact spot? No. I was a few feet further down," he gives a noncommittal shrug. "She lives alone. I just wanted to make sure she got home okay."

"Yeah, the couple steps from Clay Creations to her apartment door sure are treacherous." I'm giving him a hard time and I know it.

When I look back through the binoculars, Spencer is staring out the window. She looks lost and alone. So very alone. Her eyes are begging, *begging* us to make her feel less empty.

I'm here, Mama.

She shuts her curtains and the lights go out. Then I get it, I get why he didn't tell me.

Z has always had more of a conscience than me. Doctors told my mom I needed to be hospitalized when I was younger. I was "crazy." They said I was a sociopath. I had kicked dumbass Tommy Fowler until three of his ribs broke for reaching his hand down Elena's dress when she was twelve and he was fourteen. I would have kept kicking if a teacher hadn't pulled me off of him. My lack of remorse scared everyone, but I considered it protecting my family. I always will. My mom wasn't scared, she fully accepted the side of me that is darker than the shadows of night. The side that likes the pain I viciously gift to those who deserve it.

Now, after witnessing the shit Z, Ash, and I have all seen—the shit that one human is willing to do to another to make a buck—things like morals go right out the window. Zane still has some, that's why he was hiding this nighttime activity. Ash might have a few left too. But I have none. We don't just dabble in the gray area of life. We paint it red.

I lean the seat back and get comfortable. "Do you have an extra pair?" I'm answered with a punch to the arm and the binoculars are ripped from me. "What the fuck?"

"Those are mine. If you wanted some, should've grabbed them from the house."

He's not wrong.

"Don't hog my new teacher all to yourself. Sharing is caring, *amigo*." I let my double meaning hang in the air.

A growl erupts from his throat. "She's not some piece of ass we'll share for a night, Rio."

"I know that," I punch him back in the arm and he grunts. "Talk to me."

Relief washes over me when he finally gives me what I've been digging for. "She's different. I touched her."

I blink at him a few times in disbelief. Z doesn't let any woman touch him, which is difficult when you live and work in New York, but he's found little ways around it, even in the bedroom. We avoid all the tourist traps like the plague. He drives instead of taking the subway, and he doesn't even shake hands with coworkers. Some people make comments and say shit, but they usually find themselves on the receiving end of mine or Ash's fists.

"I can tell she's different. That's okay. I think she's different too." My words don't bring him comfort. He still won't look me in the eye.

He doesn't speak so I do what I know will bring him comfort. I kiss him. I grab his face with both hands and don't hold back. He opens to me immediately. I pour every ounce of acceptance I have with each swipe of my tongue. He needs to know I'm still here and I always will be. Zane returns the kiss with desperation like he's afraid he'll lose me, but that will never happen.

Our lips part and with my forehead resting against his, I reassure him with my words. "I'm here. We're good. I promise."

I sigh and realize I need sleep. I swipe my fluffy eye mask from my pocket and tell Zane, "I'm tired, wake me when you're ready to switch. Sharing also means we share the load to protect her." I slip on the mask to block out the annoying light from the nearby lamppost.

Before I fall asleep, I say, "And bring some snacks next time. I'm fucking hungry."

What I don't say, is that I also want Spencer.

CHAPTER 8

SPENCER

*T*hursday comes too soon. Way too soon. All my mental preparation to restore the walls around myself prove to be fruitless. Rio flashed one smile my way and I melted on the spot.

The real shock was when Zane showed up with Rio and coffee, no less. My favorite coffee too. I asked him how he knew and his response was to shrug and simply say, "You seemed like a chocolate kind of woman."

Fair enough, plenty of people like chocolate. But he even got the extra whip cream and oat milk substitute correct.

My jaw was on the floor when Zane left and said he would be back later.

Why is he coming back?

Rio read my expression easily and answered my internal question. "He has to pick me up. How do you expect me to get home? Walk all the way to the Bronx?"

"There's a subway for a reason."

"Maybe he just needed an excuse to come back." And then came the wink that incinerated my panties. A wink delivered while he was trying to hint at…what? That his friend wanted to see me? Then why is he flirting with me too?

Right then and there I decided that whatever game they were playing, I would have no part in it. I would not come between two friends. I'm not that kind of woman.

I did another demo for Rio to refresh his memory and now he's ready to go.

"You may want to start off with a piece of clay the size of your fist."

Quirking an eyebrow in my direction Rio looks at me as if I just suggested he streak down Madison Ave. However, something tells me he would do that anyway.

"I think I can handle a bit more than that tiny little thing."

Hayes chuckles behind me but it's Alma who responds. "You should probably listen to the expert, honey. She's not being mean. She's trying to keep your dignity intact."

Rio comically narrows his gaze and adds more clay. After wedging the clay and cleaning up after himself, thank God he's not a slob, he's ready at the wheel. Much as I anticipated, after ten minutes of trying to center his clay, he huffs out a frustrated breath.

"Everything okay?" I ask from the wheel next to him. I'm making soup bowls because I don't know what else to do with my time. My creative brain has left me. At this rate, my exhibit will include paper airplanes and stick figures.

"It's still off." Rio gives the clay a look that promises death if it doesn't fall in line and do what he wants.

I cover my mouth to hide my giggle, but Rio must have super hearing because his focus whips my way with a mock glare. "Is my distress funny, Mama?"

"You're hardly a damsel in distress."

"Are you sure about that?" Rio puts the back of his hand to his forehead in a fainting gesture and raises the pitch of his voice to a level I did not think possible for a man like him. "Oh, Knight Spencer. I have fallen and can't get up."

"Uhhh that's the Life Alert commercial."

Snapping out of character he says, "The sentiment is the same." Then, just as quickly, he returns to his fair maiden persona. "What is a poor pottery student to do? Alone and stranded."

Giving into the silliness, I laugh at his antics. "Fear not, damsel. Brave Knight Spencer is here." The room erupts with applause and laughter from our audience.

"*Ay dios mío.* I was running out of lines."

"I'm sure your creativity would have rescued you there."

I scoot my stool closer to his and hold my finger to the spinning mound of clay. When my finger bumps back and forth, I give Rio a few pointers and encourage him to try again.

He finally gets the clay centered and flashes me a dizzying smile. "I told you I could handle more than a small bit of clay."

"Yeah, yeah. Whatever you say." I motion to move back to my own wheel when I feel a cold finger sweep across my cheek. Raising my hand to my face, I find that Rio has painted my skin with wet clay. "Did you just…"

I'm cut off when he swipes another finger down my nose. Shocked, I sit there with my mouth open. His mischievous smile widens, showing off his perfectly straight teeth and a single dimple on his right cheek.

His smile, just like his laugh, is infectious. I can't stop myself from smiling back and returning his spirited gesture with my own. "You're dead, Casanova."

Dragging my hand against my own clay, I place my palm on the side of his face making a mess of him.

"You asked for it now, Mama." He lunges for me with clay-caked hands, wrapping his arms around me, and pulling me towards him. I let out a squeal and brace my hands against his solid chest as he sits me on his lap with my legs to the side.

"No, no! I take it back! I take it back!"

"Too late." His hands dive into my hair and spread the mess all through my strands and pull my bun from the tie.

"Don't forget that payback's a bitch." I dip both hands in his dirty clay water and run them over his dark chopped hair and over his ears.

After my attack, chaos ensues. We sling wet clay and muddy water at each other until I'm laughing so hard I can't breathe.

Cheers for both of us ring out in the studio. I wouldn't be surprised if they're placing bets. Alma loves a friendly gamble and Paul always appeases her which makes Hayes' FOMO kick in and he ends up participating.

"Show her who's boss!"

"Don't let him beat you!"

Somehow, I end up straddling Rio's lap and he wraps one hand around both of my wrists securing them to his chest. His other hand brings a huge blob of wet clay to the front of my throat and drags it down my chest, slightly pulling my shirt with it. His hand resting right above my cleavage.

My breathing picks up and a flush spreads across my cheeks. His warm skin pressed against mine sends a zap of energy to my clit.

"I think I saw a new painting hanging next door," Alma says.

"Me too," Hayes adds.

"Paul, come look with us." Alma insists not so subtly.

There's a scraping of stools against the concrete floor and I turn just in time to see the door to Abstract Dreams close.

Those traitors. They were supposed to stay and be the cockblock I need right now.

A gentle, yet firm touch guides my face back around and

brings my attention to the tattooed man I'm practically humping. One little rock of my hips and I would be able to feel if he's just as effected as I am.

My palms rest flat over his swiftly beating heart, but his fast heartbeat could be for a number of reasons. He just exerted a lot of energy, or he could also be upset that we're in this situation.

Releasing my wrists, his hands grip my hips, guiding the motion as I glide my pussy over his thick hard length. I tilt my head back as a moan slips free from my lips and an ache builds in my core. One of his hands slides up to cup my breast over my shirt. His thumb finds my nipple easily and swipes back and forth over the peak.

What is this man doing to me? My pussy has been closed for business for the last three years. The only thing that's gone near it is my hand and a few toys.

"*Tan bella.*" His whisper washes over my skin and sends a shiver down my spine. His full lips find a spot free of mud on my neck and softly presses in. The touch is barely there but I feel it all over.

My hands roam from his chest down to his abs. Through his shirt I can feel each ridge and count.

An eight pack? Seriously? I thought those were fake.

Tentatively, I rock my hips on my own and this time Rio lets out a groan. "If you keep doing that, I'm going to have to lay you out on the table right there and strip you bare. My mouth will cover your sweet cunt that I know is dripping for me."

His bold words bring me back to Earth.

What the hell am I doing?

I jump off his lap and put a good six feet between us. "Oh my God." My stomach drops at the realization at what I was about to let him do to me. In public! In *my* shop.

So much for not being that woman.

"Scare that easily, Mama?" He leans back on his seat bringing his hands behind his head and crossing his ankles in front of him.

Ugh. I hate that everything he does is so fucking sexy. He's just relaxing and my slutty pussy is ready to jump his bones.

"I shouldn't have done that. I'm your teacher. I'm a professional. That was anything but professional." Mortified, I cover my face with my hands.

"So? I'm pretty sure I'm older than you."

"That's your rebuttal?" My brows attempt to disappear in my hairline.

"I'm thirty-three."

My jaw goes slack. He's thirty-three? He doesn't look anywhere near thirty-three. But, of course, it's always men who are blessed with perfect skin and his is flawless.

"And you are?"

"Twenty-four."

"See? I'm nine years your senior. You can rest easy now knowing you did not take advantage of me." He gives a satisfied smile as if our age difference makes everything better, but it only makes it worse.

He's definitely had more experienced women. I don't know what I'm doing. I have no business throwing myself at a man like that.

He probably has a girlfriend.

Blood drains from my face at the voice of insecurity in the back of my brain. I'm not the other woman and would never go behind another woman's back. I'm a girl's girl.

"Oh shit. You have a girlfriend, don't you?" Not letting him answer when he sits up I continue, "You definitely have a girlfriend. I mean look at you."

His head tilts down to scan his body as if he doesn't already know how attractive he is.

"With abs and a face like that? You're taken for sure. What woman wouldn't want you? And here I am grinding on you like a bitch in heat. This is so embarrassing. Tell your girlfriend I am so sorry. I broke the girl code. My sister's club membership is going to get revoked. I'm going to have to move to Maine and change my name. I—"

Rio's hands on my shoulders interrupt me. "I don't have a girlfriend. If I did, none of that would have happened. Also, you can grind on me like a bitch in heat anytime." His smirk makes my panties flood. Again.

Refusing to let his charm get to me, I step back. "Good to know. Regardless, that should not have happened. I promise it won't happen again."

"I really hope it does though."

Letting out a sigh I crane my neck to look at the ceiling. "You're impossible."

"Impossibly sexy?"

"Impossibly delusional." I snap back.

Instead of responding, his gaze wanders up and down my body and I feel it as if he's touching me everywhere he looks. His attention locks on the apex of my thighs and I realize I'm rubbing them together.

I need to pump the brakes before I tackle him to the ground and let him do what he promised.

"Anyways, I'm going to go wash the clay off."

Before I can get to the door his hand tugs on my elbow. "I don't think so. If I have to stay in this mess, so do you."

I glance down at my dirty clothes and realize there's dried clay all over my shirt on top of my breasts. "Are you serious?" My question comes out as a screech.

His eyes dip to my breasts and back up to my face. "Oh yeah, Mama. Deadly serious." His smile this time is slightly feral as if he's proud of his hand prints on my boobs.

"You're on my shit list, Casanova." I point my finger at his chest as I look up at him and hope it's as threatening as I mean it to be.

"Casanova, huh?"

"If I have to explain it, then I'll downgrade you to himbo." Rio's laugh follows me as I stalk off to my wheel to continue with the soup bowls.

I can survive eight more weeks without asking Rio to glaze my donut hole. I can survive eight more weeks without asking Rio to glaze my donut hole.

You keep telling yourself that.

CHAPTER 9

SPENCER

After thirty minutes of everyone hanging out in the gallery, I dragged them all back. Their protests did nothing to deter me. I need my cockblocks right next to me, where they belong, so I don't do stupid things.

Hayes gave me a knowing look and gestured to my chest where I momentarily forgot Rio's handprint was still visible. I immediately turned and sprinted for the bathroom. Rio can keep me from going upstairs for a shower, but I can at least rinse off my shirt.

Rio ended up staying longer than his lesson time, saying he wanted to flex his creative brain. He ended up with two small bowls and a vase. A little thick, but they're thin enough to fire in the kiln.

I ended with eight soup bowls. Not that I need them. I'll probably add some pretty decals on them and give them to Alma once they're done.

While Rio and I clean up our work stations, my stomach lets out a sound that could be compared to a bear roar.

"Uh oh," Hayes says from his spot at one of the worktables. "Boss needs food."

I cross my arms tightly over my chest. "I'm not that bad."

"Sure you aren't."

Rio's focus bounces between Hayes and me. "What's going on?"

"Spencer isn't all that kind when she gets hangry," Alma pipes up.

"I'm. Not. That. Bad." I emphasize each word as I repeat them.

Alma gives me a disbelieving look. "What about the time you just about bit Hayes' head off because he sneezed?"

"That sneeze was at a volume so loud I'm sure New Jersey could hear it. Scientists would study him if they knew."

Hayes scoffs and adds to Alma's argument. "There was also the time you cried because Paul dropped his teapot."

"He worked so hard on that! I felt bad!" I don't like the points they're making, no matter how right everyone is.

"You know good and well it was a shit teapot," Paul says.

"Agree to disagree."

Paul makes a face that says he isn't convinced. "Okay then. What about when you said you would eat anchovies?"

"We agreed we would never talk about that." I will eat anything. Except anchovies. Who wants to eat little bits of fish from a jar? But that day, I was on the verge of starvation.

"No, you agreed," Hayes points his finger in my direction then gestures to everyone else. "None of us did."

Zane interrupts "embarrass Spencer time" by walking in the door with a large brown paper bag.

"Hello there, handsome," Alma greets Zane with a flirtatious tone.

"Uh. Hi?"

Rio hops up from his front row seat where he was enjoying

73

my embarrassment show. "Just in time, Z. Turns out our girl gets grumpy when she's hungry," Rio unloads the bag from Zane's hands. "Zane, this is Alma, Hayes, and Paul. Everyone, this is Zane, the friend who signed me up here."

"Oh," Alma smirks in my direction. "So this is the man who came the other day."

I groan and give Hayes my best evil eye. He just shrugs a single shoulder. We both know he told everyone how I embarrassed myself and he doesn't feel the least bit guilty.

Zane smirks my way and I swear there are literal butterflies inside my body. What two people came together and made this man who is too gorgeous to be real? "You ready for lunch, Angel?"

Glancing at Zane out of the corner of my eye, I try to look uninterested even though I really am a hungry hippo. I didn't realize it until Hayes pointed it out, but now all I can think about is food and the lack of it in my belly. God, I'm close to tears.

"Maybe." My nonchalance is argued with another bear roar from my stomach.

Zane gives me a mocking snort. "I brought egg rolls."

If he's trying to entice me, it's working. With the temptation of egg rolls in front of me, I do my best to keep my pride intact.

"Anything else in your bag of wonders?"

My attitude is rewarded with another small curve of his lips. "Kung pao chicken, fried rice, and wonton soup."

I feel bad about taking food he now won't get to eat, but hunger wins out, and I know I won't be able to come back from crying in front of everyone when I'm hungry. It will just give Hayes, Alma, and Paul another example to use against me in the future.

"You twisted my arm," I say, knowing full well that I

became this food's bitch the moment egg rolls were mentioned. Rio and I finish cleaning up our mess then the two follow me.

Walking into the gallery I immediately realize my mistake. A throat clears and I mentally kick myself in the ass. I should have thought ahead.

Iris stands there shooting a look my way that begs me to explain what's going on. I subtly shake my head in return and send her the signal all females know. *Not now.*

Ignoring my cue, Iris does what she does best. Pushing me out of my comfort zone. "What's up, Spencer? Where did you get the two pieces of eye candy?"

My face flushes as I point to each man, knowing she won't give up until I give in. "Rio and Zane. Guys, this is my good friend, Iris. She works here at the gallery." They each give Iris a kind smile and wave.

I want to bury my face in the sand and hide for the next century when Iris gives them both a once over. She's trying to suss out who the story she heard from Hayes is about. She notes Rio's clay covered clothing and then zeroes in on my chest. A quick glance downward and I see that everyone can still see the outline of a handprint over the top of my breasts.

Shit.

I know her perfectly shaped brow being raised the way it is isn't to judge me, but because she wants clarification, and there is no way I'm giving that to her right now. I give her the same look from earlier, but thankfully this time she heeds my sign.

Moving on to another subject, she asks, "What is that deliciousness I smell?"

"Zane brought Chinese."

"Oh did he?" The sudden change of expression on her face lets me know the devil on her shoulder has taken over. "Zane, do you want some dessert with your lunch?"

Zane slides his hands into his pockets and squints. "Sure."

"I'm sure Spencer could spread—"

"Okay!" I shout. "And on that note, we're going to go." I grasp each of their arms and pull them into the breakroom with me.

"This is cozy," Rio comments.

"Um, thanks." I tuck a wayward lock of hair behind my ear.

Rio immediately makes himself at home by spreading out the food on the table for us to share. Zane places a guiding hand on the small of my back that makes my skin heat. That same spark from the other day is still there.

Nice to know I didn't imagine it.

Zane pulls out my chair and tucks it in behind me while Rio plops the container of yummy poultry in front of me.

"How did you..."

"You practically salivated when Zane said 'Kung Pao chicken.'"

"You okay with just eating out of the containers?" Zane asks courteously.

"Yeah. Less dishes." I hate dishes just as much as I hate cooking.

Rio scoots his chair right next to mine so we're touching shoulder to hip. It takes every bit of focus to ignore him and concentrate on eating.

We all fall into an easy rhythm of taking a few bites and passing the white boxes. I practically leap into a food coma as the hangry beast inside is satisfied.

Rio eats like he'll never see food again. How can he eat like he eats, but still look how he looks?

"I'm going to go. I have work to get to." Standing from his chair, he gives me a kiss on my cheek and I swear my face turns into a tomato.

Physically, my heart can only handle so much from this

man. He needs to slow down before his forward nature puts me in an early grave. Right now, my heart is working overtime especially since Zane is looking right at us as Rio plants his lips on my cheek. "I'll see you next week, Mama. Thanks for lunch, Z."

When the door closes behind Rio with a snick, the discomfort surrounding my body intensifies. Zane didn't do anything wrong, but I feel like I did. He didn't look upset by the simple kiss, but he still saw it.

Is he secretly pissed about it? Is he mad at Rio? Does he regret coming back? Rio implied earlier that Zane just wanted an excuse to see me. Are they fighting over me?

Why do I even care? I shouldn't. I'm a grown ass woman and can do what I want. I don't want to be the source of contention between the two, but I can't control what they do.

While I stew in my spiraling anxiety, Zane takes Rio's seat next to me. Now it's Zane's hip and shoulder against mine and I cannot shift my attention to anything else. Not my to-do list, not my upcoming exhibit. Nothing.

My body tingles from his touch. I'm sure he just doesn't want any conversation between us to become awkward because of how far apart we were sitting, and he can't move the chair because then that would acknowledge he knew Rio was right against me the whole time. I know mine and Rio's touching shoulders were visible, but denial is my current home, and I'll die here if I have to.

The silence that continues doesn't dull my inner panic, but I keep eating as if nothing is amiss.

A huge swirl of Chow Mein tries to escape my fork as I attempt to get it in my mouth. That's the moment Zane chooses to finally speak.

"Tell me about your grandmother."

With my mouth open and noodles falling, I choke.

Coughing a few times, Zane pats my back and looks like he's ready to perform the Heimlich which will only bring to light the fact that I'm not choking on food, just my own fucking spit.

"My Abuela? Uh. Sure. What do you want to know?"

"You two must have been pretty close for her to have left this place to you."

Happy memories flood my consciousness. The moment must have reflected on my face because Zane's eyes turn soft. "We were. My mom is a single parent, so Abuela would take me during summer break every year. My love of art came from her. One time we were in San Francisco at a figure drawing open studio—"

"Figure drawing?"

"Yeah, drawing the human body. There's a model in the middle of the room and everyone sits around with sketchbooks and draws what they see."

Zane angles his body so he's facing me with his arm resting along the back of my chair. "Like, nude models?"

"Yes." I smile to myself. Nudity usually makes people uncomfortable, but in the art world a penis is just a penis. Just another part of the human body.

Zane doesn't respond so I continue, "Anyway, this other artist kept critiquing my sketch and telling me that my proportions of the model's body were off, that I was making his torso too long."

"His?"

Snorting is not my norm, but nevertheless I snort at Zane's disbelief. "Yes. *His.*" I chuckle softly and continue, "I was embarrassed and tried ignoring her, but she wouldn't let up. Finally, Abuela snapped at the woman and told her to leave me alone and that I could draw however my sixteen-year-old mind chose to. Abuela was protective and encouraged me to create all the time no matter how shitty it turned out."

"You were sixteen and drawing naked men?" Zane strikes me as the quiet type, but I think I have just shocked the quiet out of him.

"Pablo Picasso was drawing nude models at age nine." I cross my arms and lean back.

"I don't know if that makes it any better."

"Nudity is part of being an artist. Plenty of artists started young."

He tilts his head to the side and narrows his gaze, studying my face as if it has the answer that will end world hunger. "It's not that. I don't think I like the idea of you seeing another man naked."

Is he…jealous?

No, that can't be it. He probably just doesn't like the idea of a sixteen-year-old girl drawing an adult nude man. But I was mature for my age, I didn't laugh uncomfortably or anything. I was just studying the human body and admiring its beauty just like any other artist would.

His attention strays from my face and glides down my body snagging on my chest. The heat behind his eyes could light the building on fire.

Shit. The handprint.

I lean forward and bring my elbow to the table blocking his view of my shirt.

"So. Tell me about yourself, Zane. I think I should probably get to know the man who paid for my lunch."

Mimicking my position, Zane indulges my subject change. "What do you want to know?"

His green eyes connect with mine and it's as if all the oxygen is sucked out of the room. My brain drains of all thought and all I can focus on are his green irises with little gold flecks in them. When we met the other day I didn't notice the hint of gold, but with his close proximity I can't help but take it in.

The stubble along his jaw looks like it would slightly scrape against my skin, but I would welcome the rough texture. The sharpness of his cheekbones makes me swoon, and I imagine how I would cup his face in the palm of my hand before we…

Nope! Not going there. Can't go there. Won't go there.

What were we talking about?

Oh yeah. Him.

"Where did you grow up?"

What an original question. You hit that one out of the park.

"New Jersey." His answer is straight to the point, and he doesn't expound on it.

Crickets could be heard chirping. How do I get this man to actually talk to me? It's like pulling teeth.

"Okay. What do you do for a living?"

"I'm a detective."

"That's so cool. Can you make some parking tickets disappear?"

"Not really."

"That's okay. I don't even have a car."

A deep booming laugh echoes in the space and a warmth fills my chest. I like making this man laugh. I like knowing I cracked his composed exterior.

Maybe he doesn't need to spill his life's story to me. I'm fine with being the one who makes him smile.

After we finish eating, we clean up and I walk Zane to the front of the gallery. The goodbye isn't uncomfortable, and I get the feeling it isn't a "goodbye forever," it's a "goodbye for now."

My feeling is proven correct when Zane shows up the next day with gyros. The conversation is light and easy and filled with laughter.

Over the next week Zane brings me lunch almost every day.

I learned that Zane grew up in foster care, is an only child like me, and knew he wanted to be a cop from a young age.

We exchanged phone numbers because he felt bad that he couldn't make it a few times and had no way of letting me know. I reassured him that I'm a big girl who can get her own food, but he wasn't having it.

Rio kisses me on the cheek after each lesson and Zane hugs me goodbye each time we part. They're simple acts that friends do, so why does it feel like more?

CHAPTER 10

SPENCER

*D*ressed in my boss bitch getup—black heels and an ivory, silk, button up blouse tucked into fall green, wide-leg dress pants—I look over paperwork for Abstract Dreams. I applied a little more makeup than usual. When Iris saw my red lipstick, she gave me a big whistle in appreciation and hasn't stopped dropping comments since, making me regret my decision.

I did it because I felt like it. Not at all because I had a man or two in mind while getting ready. And they definitely weren't on my mind because I had a steamy dream about the two of them.

In the dream, one of them definitely did not say to me "wrap those pretty lips around my dick and swallow like a good girl" after which I woke up and had to finish myself off before going to the gym. That's not my motivation at all.

I haven't seen Zane in a few days, so lunch has been boring. Ever since he came into the studio the first time I swear I see him out of the corner of my eye sometimes, but when I look no one is there.

I'm going crazy.

"So"—Iris smacks her gum while parking her ass on the front desk right next to the papers I'm reviewing—"since you're already all dressed up, want to go to Moonlit tonight?"

I immediately use one of my ready-made excuses. "I can't. I have to do inventory."

"Nice try, Hayes did that this morning. I would know. I sat and watched him," she stares over my head dreamily, not actually looking at anything. "The muscles on that man. Ooo. Just thinking about them gets me going." She does a little shimmy as if I don't know what she means.

"What?!" I shout. "When did you two finally get together? I've been pushing for a while, and when y'all finally decide to date, you don't even tell me? Not cool, babe." My scolding has a little fire behind it.

"We were keeping things on the down low, but when you get good dick, you can't keep your mouth shut."

I slap my hands over my ears. "Ew. Ew. Ew. Never talk about Hayes like that to me again. The guy is like my little brother. I don't want to know what my brother is like in bed."

"Point made. But it does sound like you have a difficult decision in front of you, I can keep talking about Hayes and his *appetite* or you can agree to go to Moonlit with me and Alma tonight. It's been over a month since we last went. Please"—she puts her hands together under her chin—"Please, please, please."

"Ugh. Fine. As long as there is no more talk of the bedroom escapades going on between you and Hayes for the rest of the night. Promise me."

"Oh, it's not always in the bedroom. Sometimes it's—"

I cut her off with a scowl.

"Got it. No talking about Hayes and his monster dick," she

hops off the desk with too much pep in her high heeled step. "I'll go tell Alma."

I make a point of rolling my eyes so she notices.

She just laughs at my distress and continues on her merry way.

With Iris gone I'm under the impression I can work in peace, but that illusion is shattered when the bane of my existence walks in. Lance Fucking Richards. He used to make me feel uncomfortable with his sly touches and subtle innuendos. The only person that thought he was slick, was himself.

Now he just pisses me off.

He's wearing a designer, light gray suit with an unbuttoned, pastel pink dress shirt, a matching pocket square, and shiny black loafers. His pale tuscan hair is parted on the side and styled to give the impression of volume with what I'm sure is copious amounts of expensive hair gel. He tries to come off cool with his high-end sunglasses that he doesn't actually need since it's overcast outside. Don't get me started on what he's obviously compensating for with his cherry-red Ferrari parked out front.

It's true what they say, you can't buy taste.

"Spencer, my dear." Just the way he says my name makes me want to buy a lifetime supply of earplugs. His eyes sweep over me in a way that makes me feel like I need a shower. His gaze sticks to my mouth and the red lipstick. Damn Morning Spencer for thinking that was a good idea.

"How are you? How is business?" He asks, as if we both don't know how this is going to go. It's what he always does. He asks about business, I tell him it's going great, he asks if he can take me out, I tell him no, and he tries to convince me I'm missing out on an extravagant date. Sometimes he buys a couple paintings hanging on the wall for more than the asking price.

I don't know why he thinks that would impress me. I don't even paint. Not that he knows, he's never fucking asked.

"What do you want, Lance?" I ask, trying to sound bored. I need to stay professional, but my patience is absent when it comes to him.

I stand on my three-inch heels and cross my arms. My new height puts me at eye level with him so he can't look down at me and use his stature to make me feel small. Other men have done it and I refuse to let this douchebag do the same and succeed.

He smiles at me in a way I'm sure he thinks comes off as charming, but it just adds to my annoyance. He flashes a smile at me so full it makes the corner of his eyes crease. He probably thinks it's charming but his Cheshire smile creeps me out and just adds to my annoyance.

Fuck him for invading my happy Saturday.

"I have an extra ticket to a gala tonight at The Plaza. I need someone on my arm at the event and I figured since you're a single woman, you'd be perfect."

Is he fucking kidding right now? He wants me to be his arm candy at some ritzy event where I'll be bored and miserable as hell. Of course, that doesn't matter to him, as long as he looks good in the process.

And he just assumed since I'm single that I would be available at the last minute? Wow.

Thank God I can actually say I'm busy. I'll always be too busy to spend time with this gnat of a man.

"I can't. I have plans." He doesn't need more detail than that.

He condescends in his airy voice that grates on my nerves. "Surely you can reschedule." He inches closer as if I welcomed him into my space.

Oh. My. God. This is how I lose my mind, isn't it? I'm finally going to snap.

"No, actually. I can't reschedule," I state with a firm voice, bordering on brash.

"Oh God. Lance? Seriously? What is it you want this time?" Iris chides as she saunters up next to me. Her stance mirrors my own. I mentally pull out the popcorn because on the occasion that Iris is here when Lance stops by, she rips him apart like a lion eating its prey.

"Not that it's any of your business, but I was just extending an invitation to Spencer to attend a gala at The Plaza with me tonight."

"She can't. She has plans."

"Plans she can reschedule."

"That's quite the assumption, Mr. Small Dick Energy," Iris gives him her best inconvenienced look then waves her hand to shoo him away. "Run along and find someone else to take to your boring event. Better yet, don't. The female population does not deserve your whiny voice screeching in their ears. As a parting gift, here's some free advice: you need to stop shopping for yourself. That outfit is not doing you any favors. Have you tried not shopping with your eyes closed? It makes a difference, I promise."

"That's no way to talk to a customer." He tries to sound like he's asserting authority, but it comes off as querulous.

"You're not a real customer. You just want to get into Spencer's pants. I feel bad for you, so I'll let you in on a little secret"—she leans towards him and stage whispers—"it's never gonna happen."

I burst out laughing, unable to hold it in anymore.

"Need me to go get Paul or Hayes?" Iris directs her question at me.

I eventually stop laughing and answer, "No, it's okay. I'm

sure Lance here has a lot to do before his big gala tonight; he'll be on his way now."

Finally taking the hint, Lance walks to the door, but before he leaves he turns back to me. "You really should consider hiring more professional staff. I'll see you next time, Spencer."

"God. He's like a fly in the summer. You open the door for half a second and he comes in like he has a right then refuses to leave."

"You're not wrong there."

We stare out the window and watch as Lance struggles to reverse out of his parking spot and peel away.

Once he's finally gone, Iris grabs my arm and turns me to her.

"So, I talked to Alma and she's good to meet up at eight which means I'll be by at six to get you all dolled up and—"

"Dolled up for what?" A voice questions from behind me.

Not registering the voice and figuring the douchebag came back for seconds, I roll my eyes so hard I'm sure they'll never come back to the front of my head.

"Not now, Lance. I told you I'm not…" I trail off when I finally turn towards the door.

It's none other than one of the two men currently occupying all of my thoughts.

Zane. Fucking. Kingston.

CHAPTER 11

ZANE

*W*ho the fuck is Lance? Just the name sounds punchable. Spencer's greeting is a dead giveaway that he's bothering her, and now I have the urge to go find the guy and make sure he stays away. I'm willing to ask every man on the street if his name is Lance to find the fucker. No one bothers my Angel.

"Oh my God. I'm so sorry. I thought you were someone else."

"Lance?"

"Yeah." Spencer's head tilts down and she shifts her weight back and forth.

Interesting.

"Who is he?"

"Oh he's no one. Don't worry—"

Spencer doesn't get to finish because she's interrupted by Iris. She's short but looks like she could hold her own in any verbal sparring match. Sassy women have that energy.

"He's this annoying guy who thinks he's God's gift to women, and always comes by to ask Spencer out. Not that she's ever given any indication that she'd go out with him. He thinks every woman is dying to spread their legs for him."

He better fucking not or else he'll find himself with a few broken bones to make sure he can't utter another word to Spencer, let alone ask her out. Then when it heals, I'll break it again. This time for pure pleasure.

"Iris!"

"What? Am I wrong?" Iris doesn't look remorseful.

Little does she know, I already know almost everything there is to know about her: where she was born, how often she drinks coffee, what her most watched show on Netflix is.

"Well, no, but you don't have to say it like that," Spencer's attention comes back to me. "What's up? It's a little early for lunch."

"I wanted to check out the gallery." More like I just wanted to see her again and not at 10x magnification from my car.

"Oh. Do you want to just browse or would you like a tour?"

A smile sneaks across my face at the thought of spending time with her. Just her. The lunches have been fun and all that, but I need more. I need more of her words, more of her time, more of her.

"A tour would be great."

"Follow me."

I'll follow you anywhere, Angel.

She shows me a few landscape paintings that I would not normally be interested in, but when it comes to Spencer, her interests are my interests. Her passions are my passions, and her desires are my desires. I nod along and drink in everything she says. She explains the stippling technique in one painting and the use of light and shadow in another. She could be reading me an instruction manual on plumbing, and I would hang on her every word.

I love seeing her in her element. She's confident and

comfortable. As she continues to speak, her voice soothes me. Being in her presence makes all the shit I've seen and done drift away. She makes my world brighter just by existing. When she exists in my space, my world isn't the dark, depressing place I've known my whole life. There's color and joy.

As we drift through the showroom, I allow myself little touches here and there. A simple hand on her lower back, a brush of my hand against hers. Every time it happens a blush takes over her cheeks. A blush I bet spreads down her neck to her chest and across her perfect tits.

I stop at a sculpture of a woman that piques my interest. Her eyes are closed, and she has hollowed cheeks as if she's underweight and starved. Her hair is in a messy updo and her brows are slightly pinched giving off the impression she's in pain. I move to look at the other side of her face only to see it's not there. It's as if someone dropped the bust and it broke, but this looks more deliberate. The artist purposefully broke off the side of the face. Destroyed it.

As if the artist was destroying their pain. The agony they have lived. They want it gone. Obliterated.

I look at the tag and see the words "Moving On by Unknown."

Glancing up, I see Spencer worrying her bottom lip between her teeth waiting for my opinion and it clicks—she made it.

"What do you think?" She's nervous.

Does she want me to understand? Does she want me to know it was her?

Everyone wants to be seen. All their ugly, broken pieces. We're all just wandering this Earth waiting for someone to reassure us that we're not as broken as we think. That our scars aren't that hideous.

I don't need that validation. I know my scars are hideous. I know my broken pieces are ugly. I accepted that truth years ago.

Spencer is different. Her scars and broken pieces draw me to her. They have a tight fist clenched around my heart and pull me towards her every minute of the day.

I see her alright and not just through her window at night.

I tilt my head to the side and ask, "Are you the artist?"

She glances to the side, wanting to hide the truth, but I already know the answer. The sculpture may not be an exact depiction of her face, but it's clear this is how she sees herself. Weak and starved. Starved of safety, protection, love.

Beautiful, I will give you all of that and so much more.

"Who hurt you?"

She looks shocked at my question and scrambles to deflect. "I don't know what you're talking about."

I go to her and gently grasp her upper arms. Pulling her close and leaning in I whisper, "I see you. You don't have to hide."

Spencer looks up at me through her lashes and my cock stirs. Unable to resist, I slowly lower my face to hers.

"Tell me to stop, Angel." My lips brush hers in a tender caress. I wrap my arms around her lower back and align my body with hers. I want her to feel all of me. To feel what she does to me.

She gasps when she feels how hard I am. Her whispers tease across my mouth. "Please don't stop."

My heart comes alive in my chest. Looking into Spencer's eyes, I feel like I'm whole again. Her perfect hands are molding to my chest, and as our lips connect, I hear a door swing open.

"Hey Spencer? The clay supplier is on the phone in the studio wanting to double check the order." Hayes' voice is loud and oblivious to what's going on in front of him.

Spencer jumps from my arms and bumps into the wall. She

leans to the side so she can see around me. I'm not a big guy, but I'm not a twig either.

"Would you mind taking care of that, Hayes?"

When I glance over my shoulder I see the kid with horrible timing. He has his brow raised, checking to see if Spencer is okay. I look back and she gives him a subtle nod with wide eyes as if to tell him to clear out.

"Yeah, I got it."

"Thanks."

Hayes leaves and I turn back to Spencer who is clearly flustered.

"So. Umm. Thank you for coming by. Feel free to keep looking. I need to get back to some paperwork."

She goes to leave but I grab her hand to halt her hasty exit. "Thank you."

"For what?"

"For letting me see you."

That adorable blush returns and I allow the back of my hand to trace lightly down her heated cheek.

"I need to get going anyways, so I'll walk you to the front."

"That's alright. I should head over to Clay Creations. Thank you again for coming, Zane." She practically sprints to the connecting door.

The door's resistance to let her through causes a blush to rise up the back of her neck. She kicks the door for good measure but eventually gets it open and leaves.

I make a mental note to fix that for her.

Her departure cuts off the light I have become addicted to. The light I can't live without.

As I pass the front desk, I give a small goodbye nod to Iris.

"You should meet us at Moonlit tonight at eight. Jerry usually hooks us up with a few free drinks." Iris' invitation stops me in my tracks.

Another guy? What the fuck?

"Who's Jerry?"

"Jerry is an old man, but his bar is pretty cool. We go out every so often for a little Ladies Night with Alma."

Oh.

I smile at Iris but don't give her an answer.

Looks like I'm crashing Ladies' Night.

CHAPTER 12

SPENCER

I sit at the sticky bar top sipping on my rosemary vodka tonic, wondering why I let Iris talk me into tonight. She invited some of her friends so at least all the attention isn't on me and my lack of donut glazing. Alma had to cancel because her sitter is sick and her husband is out of town on a work trip. I pushed Iris and her friends to let loose on the small dance floor so I could sit by myself for a bit and decompress.

I don't particularly like drinking. I don't like it when my head gets fuzzy or I forget what I do or say. I like always being aware. When I'm not aware I'm vulnerable, so while I enjoy spending time with Iris and Alma, I have a one drink limit.

Shifting in my seat, I adjust my dress for the millionth time tonight. It's a simple, spaghetti strap, ruched bodycon in deep blue. At least that's what the online description said. It's more like a boa constrictor trying to squeeze the life out of me. I bought it so Iris couldn't talk me into wearing one of her dresses. I curled my hair so it would fall into natural looking waves, and Iris applied a smokey eye that makes me look alluring. Too bad I can't talk to a man without short-circuiting. That has been proven multiple times recently.

Or maybe it's just two men in particular.

Every time I see an attractive guy, I don't get those flutters in my stomach. Not like I did when I met *them*.

Instead, I see a hand itching to leave bruises on my body or words perfectly sharpened and aimed to hit where it'll hurt for years to come.

How does one even date in today's world? I'm not downloading Tinder on my phone so I can get harassed by men asking if I'm "DTF." As if the catcalls in the street aren't enough? No thanks.

Iris slings her arm around my neck and says too loud, "Come dance with us!" She's not drunk but well on her way.

"I'm good. I'll just sit here."

"Aww. Come on! What if I request your favorite song?"

"Nope. Still good."

"Please! Consider it team bonding."

Knowing she won't give up until I give in, I cave. "Fine, but just one song. Okay?"

"Yeah sure. Whatever you say, Boss."

By her tone I know she won't let me sit down until my feet feel like they're going to fall off. Damn Earlier Spencer for thinking these heels were a good idea. I should have just worn tennis shoes.

When we first get out to the dance floor, I feel awkward and uncomfortable. I'm self-conscious, thinking people are watching and judging. Worried that the wrong man will get a dumb idea, and we'll have a repeat of what happened the first time I went out.

Slowly, I allow myself to feel the beat and get lost in the moment. It's difficult for me to let go, but I remind myself that Iris' friends are nice. They're the kind of women who build each other up. The kind we need more of in the world. They have my back simply because of my XX chromosomes.

Swaying my hips, I allow myself to feel free even if it's just for a moment.

Everything I do in my life is to keep myself safe. The running, the workouts, the meticulous perimeter checks, making sure no one is going to jump out at me. But right now, I can simply be. Just like when I'm creating with clay.

Next thing I know, there's a pair of hands on my hips and they're definitely a man's hands. I go to step out of his hold but he pulls me back, so my ass is flush with his unimpressive dick. My fear takes over in the moment and I struggle. Suddenly I'm not in Moonlit anymore, I'm in a cold house with unfeeling rooms and a monster who doesn't care when I beg and plead with him.

"Spencer, Spencer. What am I going to do with you now?"

"P-please don't hurt me. I'm sorry. I'm so sorry."

"Let me go!" I ram my elbow back into the guy's stomach at the same time I throw my head back, hoping I hit something, which I do. I don't hear a crunch over the loud music, but I hear an "oof" and he lets go.

"What the hell, bitch!"

I turn and see a man I don't recognize. Shame and panic wash over me in an unbearable wave.

Oh my God. I just did that.

I turn to leave but an inked arm wraps around me. "You're okay, Mama. I got you."

"Did you just put your hands on her?" I peek over my shoulder to see Zane in the stranger's face.

"I was just having some fun, man. It's not like there's a ring on her finger."

"I don't give a *fuck* if there's a ring or not. You touched her." Zane leans in and says something in the man's ear. His skin turns ashen, and he scurries away.

What did Zane say to him?

Rio's soothing words fade as I breathe.

One. Two. Three. Four—breathe in. Breathe in the shame. Breathe in the fear.

One. Two. Three. Four—hold. Feel the memories.

One. Two. Three. Four—breathe out. Breathe out the past. Breathe out the regret.

Feeling my panic subside, I open my eyes and find myself back at the bar. Rio on one side and Zane on the other, boxing me in. Not in a way that feels claustrophobic, but a way that feels comforting.

He's just a man. He can't hurt me.

I sit down and Jerry gets me another drink. Staring at it, I wonder if I just give in then maybe the pain will go away. The worry, the exhaustion. I could so easily just slip into a state of numbness, but I know that won't change anything. I'll still be here, wondering if *he* will ever show up.

"You okay, Angel?" Zane's hand lifts my chin tilting my head to meet his assessing gaze.

"Oh my God!" Iris squeals in my ears behind me and spins my stool to face her.

My face pinches. "Too high-pitched. Please come back to normal human volumes."

I look at Iris and see her staring at the men on either side of me and then it hits me. Zane and Rio are here. *Here.* At Moonlit.

Did they know I was going to be here? Or are they just out to blow off some steam on a Saturday night? Are they planning on taking someone home?

A green haze coats my body, and I'm assaulted with violent

images of what I would do to the women they took home tonight.

The jealousy leaves as swiftly as it came, and shock mars my face. It may appear as shock due to Rio and Zane's attendance, but it's actually due to how dark my brain went. For a second, I actually thought I could do those things to someone.

I remind myself that they're not mine and I'm not theirs. I will admit here and now—but never again—that I'm attracted to both of them. I've even had hot dreams about both of them, but I have no claim over them…and I never will.

I need to take my feelings I have towards them, shove it in a box, and lock it behind a thick steel door.

"They came! I told Zane, but wow. I can't believe he brought the other one too." She talks as if they can't hear every word she's saying.

"You told them?"

"Only Zane. But hey, now there's two. Double the glaze."

My eyes widen in alarm. I can't believe she just said that in front of them. She must be more drunk than I thought. "For the love of femininity! I do not need to get laid."

"You absolutely do. When you do, you'll thank me, especially if it's one of them. Or both," she says with a wink then sashays away leaving me gaping after her.

Hiding my face, I pray that when I turn back around Zane and Rio will have disappeared. If they were smart, they would book it, lose my number, and never talk to me again. I would even give Zane a full refund for Rio's pottery lessons.

But when I turn, they're not gone. They're still here, asses happily planted in their seats.

Two sets of heated eyes lock on my face and trail down my body.

What the fuck am I doing?

CHAPTER 13

SPENCER

Rio's focus doesn't stray from the attire that I'm regretting all over again. "Nice dress."

My insides drop and do a little dance at the same time while I stare into my drink. My lungs don't have air and I'm not angry about it.

Zane has done nothing but purchase lessons for his friend and walk around my gallery.

He also brought you lunch almost every day.

Shut up.

And Rio has been to the studio only a handful of times. So why am I breathless at the sight of them?

They have that effortless hot guy look. Zane with his faded jeans, plain black shirt, and classically beautiful face; Rio with his black jeans, heathered red tee, and bad boy countenance. They're polar opposites in appearance, but they both make me feel alive and wanted.

That doesn't mean I should feel secure around them, right? And why do they both have to have muscles like that? My lady bits cannot handle this much sex appeal in one room.

"You look beautiful tonight," Zane says.

I can't believe Iris invited them. This is going to be a disaster, I just know it. I'm going to do something dumb, or worse, watch them flirt their way through the bar. Not that I would blame another woman for noticing. I mean really, I've already clocked three women checking them out.

The green monster that reared its head a second ago needs to stay away.

"Hey, guys. Sorry if Iris made you feel like you had to come out here. You really didn't."

"We wanted to," Zane says that as if it's a given.

The fuck it is.

"Can we get you something to drink?" Rio asks.

"No, I'm good. I normally have a one drink limit. Tonight might be the exception with this extra one here, and after what happened over there I think I need this." I knock back a large gulp and allow the burn to calm my nerves.

"You're safe now." Zane emphasizes his statement by rubbing his hand in calming circles on my bare upper back. Unfortunately, his touch has the opposite effect and my body heats at his touch.

"Really, it was nothing. My fault entirely. He touched me and I freaked out. I shouldn't have reacted like that."

"Where exactly did he touch you?" Rio asks through gritted teeth.

"I'm fine. He's the one who walked away with a bloody nose."

"Don't make me ask again, Mama. Where did he touch you?" That authority from the first day makes a reappearance with his demand. Firm but not scary.

"Just my hips. Honestly, it's okay."

Zane leans back but doesn't remove his hand and watches as Rio leans in close.

"He never should've touched what isn't his." Rio's fingertips trail down my arm. His tone is menacing, but it's not me he's threatening. Instead of retreating back to his space, he continues to invade mine. His large hand fits perfectly over my thigh and moves with me as I squirm in place.

Zane leans in next and says, "Don't make excuses for that sad specimen of a man. He doesn't deserve your kindness. No other man should ever touch you." He tucks my hair behind my ear and then settles back in his seat.

Did I just get a pep talk in consent? And why did he say, "other man?"

Jerry approaches and asks for the guys' drink orders. They each order a Corona and silence settles in. I cannot handle this pregnant silence. They're sitting here as if we hang out every Saturday doing just this, but I need words. So, of course, in classic Spencer fashion, I make it awkward.

"How is work going, Zane? Not that you have to tell me. Or we can talk about something else? This isn't an interview. Not that I'm interviewing you to be my boyfriend or anything," my eyes go wide and I try to backpedal as fast as possible. "Oh my God. I'm not holding boyfriend interviews. I don't want you to be my boyfriend. Not that you wouldn't make a great boyfriend if you wanted to be one. I'm sure you're amazing," heat washes over my face and I snap my attention forward, avoiding all eye contact. "Y'all can go sit somewhere else now and pretend not to know me."

I dare myself to peek at Rio. He's holding a perfectly tattooed hand over his mouth trying not to laugh.

"She's cute when she's nervous." Zane volleys over my head to Rio.

"I'm going to die of embarrassment," I whisper to myself and rest my head in my hands.

"I love how she blushes at everything." Rio tosses back.

Covering my eyes, I plan my escape. I can say I'm not

feeling well and call an Uber. I can claim I have work to catch up on.

Before I can get a word out, Zane answers my incredibly humiliating question. "Work is good. Same old, same old."

If they can ignore my word vomit, I can too. I can be normal for one night.

Forcing myself to engage in small talk; I intentionally become oblivious to the fact that the two men on either side of me look like they just walked off a movie set. It doesn't help that my insides are fluttering with each word oozing from their mouths.

They tell me how they met at NYU. Rio said Zane was grumpy and hated him, which isn't all that hard to imagine.

They tell me about their other roommate, Asher, who works for the FBI and is currently traveling for work. They said I'll meet him soon, but I don't know if I can. If he's anything like these two—drop dead gorgeous and charming in his own right—I won't survive it.

As we talk, I finish my drink and decide to switch to water. I don't need to embarrass myself further by being intoxicated in front of them. Thankfully, the scales begin to balance as they dive into embarrassing college stories of one another.

"Remember that one time you got drunk and thought the tree in Central Park was a bear and you decided you wanted to befriend it?" Rio teases Zane.

Zane turns to me. "It was my first time drinking and I accidentally got hammered"—he shoots back at Rio—"but you got nothing on me. What about the time you said the weed was safe, but it was actually laced with acid? Then during your trip, you decided it would be a great idea to get a tattoo."

I let out an obnoxious laugh. "Which tattoo is your drunk tattoo?"

Rio winks at me and answers, "You'll have to at least buy me a drink first if you want to see it."

Trying to deflect the heat in his gaze I turn to Zane. "What about you? Any drunk tattoos?"

"You don't need to buy me anything to get my shirt off, Angel." He reaches for the hem of his shirt and I gasp at the sliver of smooth skin.

Snatching his hands with my own, I stop his stripping. "I didn't mean you had to show me now."

"Would you like to take me home first?"

"You're a shameless flirt, Zane Kingston."

"There's no shame in flirting with a beautiful woman."

I go to pull my hands away but he grabs my left hand and traces an invisible pattern across my skin.

"I'd like to change my answer. You don't need to buy me a drink. I'll take my pants off for you for free." Rio's humor breaks the moment, and we all laugh. I turn towards Rio and he places his hand back on my thigh, at the same time a warm arm is laid across my shoulders.

After a few minutes I realize I'm not bothered by their touch. There are no memories of pain, no panic about knowing a potential escape route, just intoxicating pleasure.

These men are different, and if I'm not careful I'll get too comfortable. Being comfortable means letting my guard down, which means they can get close. Close enough to cause real damage. I can't become complacent.

Excusing myself, I dart to the bathroom. I think I hide my emotions well but these two read me like an open book. As much as they scare me, I want them to stick around. I don't want to scare them off with the constant back and forth in my mind. It's giving me whiplash, so I'm sure they'll grow tired of it too.

Thankfully the bathroom is clear so I'm able to do my business in peace. As I'm washing my hands, I hear the door open and close with a click. When I look up into the mirror, Rio is standing there with his arms crossed and his back resting on the door.

"What's going on in that pretty head of yours, little Mama?"

Keeping eye contact with his reflection I answer, "Nothing I'm fine."

He approaches with measured steps and an energy that makes my heart pick up speed. He grabs my hips and steps up so his front is flush with my back.

"Is this how he touched you?"

Unable to speak, I frantically nod and my heart continues to race. But this time with a man's hands on my hips, it's not fear I'm feeling, it's excitement. Anticipation. I allow myself to give in a little and lean back into his firm chest.

"What about like this?" Rio moves my hair to my right shoulder and leisurely runs his lips up the length of my neck. I gasp when he finds that spot right below my ear and sucks.

"Answer me, Spencer."

"No," I breathe out.

"Good girl."

I'm not going to live through this. He's going to kill me from praise alone. I never thought I'd be into that kind of thing, but apparently, I am. I guess I wouldn't know if I was into certain things, having never felt the urge to explore. That, and if I had felt an urge to explore, it would have been shut down in my previous relationship. I knew only what *he* liked, what *he* wanted to do.

"Now tell me what's going on."

"Huh?" Rio has single handedly emptied my brain.

His right arm bands around my middle securing me to him while his left hand measuredly travels up to cup my breast. His thumb begins to swipe back and forth over my peaked nipple. This dress didn't have room for a bra so the only thing between his thumb and my chest is a thin piece of fabric.

"Why did you run off?"

Pushing myself to think through the jolts of electricity he's sending straight to my clit, I answer. "I just needed to pee." I shut my eyes thinking he won't be able to see the lie.

"Be honest."

I'm torn between anxiety and pleasure. I roll my lips inward to keep the truth inside. I don't want him and Zane to know how fucked up in the head I am and bolt. No one else has ever made me feel safe. No one else has ever tried. I can't lose that.

"You can tell me."

"I'm waiting for you and Zane to realize how much of a mess I am and give up on me. But I don't want to lose our friendship."

"You won't lose us, Spencer. Neither of us are going anywhere." Zane's voice snaps my eyes open. I didn't even hear him come in, but he's right here next to us. His firm body crowds Rio and me from the side.

Tears gather and I will them to stay put. I don't want to ruin my makeup and have everyone know I was in here crying when I leave, but one slips free and runs down to my neck. Rio licks up my tear without thought then begins placing open mouth kisses up and down my neck.

Zane's mouth descends on the other side and traces my neck with his tongue. His hand squeezes my other breast and I get lost in the sensation of their hands on me for a moment. My panties are soaking. My body melting under their touch.

Oh my God. What am I doing?

I jump away and start backing up to my exit. Now instead of just one predator tracking my movements, there's two.

"Seems the party moved in here and no one invited me. Figured I'd join in on the fun." Zane grins at us.

Why is he smiling right now?

"It's not what it looked like. I—and Rio—"

"It's exactly what it looked like," Rio interjects.

"This isn't happening," I say to myself as I turn my attention to the graffitied wall. Then a set of calloused hands pull my attention back to them.

"Don't hide your eyes from me, Angel. I can't take it."

Why does he have to say such sweet things?

"You must think I'm a slut."

"Why would I think that?" His head tilts in a way that I have come to know is uniquely Zane.

"Because!"

He quirks a brow in response.

"You're going to make me say it, aren't you?"

Still nothing. Damn him.

"Because we…you know…earlier today. And then me and Rio just now and you," I throw my hands at my sides. "God! I'm one woman. You're friends. I don't want to get in between that, and there's no way I can choose. You both make me feel comfortable and I just…I can't—"

I feel heat at my back and a set of arms wrap around me offering comfort.

"We would never make you choose, Spencer." Rio's statement doesn't soothe me as he intended. Instead, my confusion reaches a new height.

"You're kidding, right? This is some practical joke. No man would be okay with something like that."

"Who hurt you, Mama?"

"What?"

"Someone must have messed with your beautiful brain real good to give you such a narrow-minded view."

Rio's question jars me. What am I doing? If *he* ever found me he would be furious. Doesn't matter that I made it clear we were over. *He* would hurt them just to teach me a lesson.

That's the type of man I know. The type of man who would never be okay sharing.

Just another reminder that his level of possessiveness was toxic and destructive. I can't bring that kind of destruction here to rain down on Rio and Zane, that's not fair to them. I need to redraw the lines in the sand so they understand. We're friends. No almost-kisses, no nipple rubs, no delicious lips running up and down my neck…Nope. None of that.

I sidestep both of them again and continue my path to the door. "No one, don't worry about it. I should get going anyways. I have paperwork to catch up on tomorrow, suppliers to pay, payroll to do, and all that, so I'm just going to catch a cab and head home. This was fun, but we shouldn't. We're all just friends, right? Friends don't kiss and…" I hesitate to find the appropriate words for what I've done with them. "Stuff. So let's pretend it never happened, okay? Start over." I finally bump into the door and grasp the handle like a lifeline.

They stalk towards me as if they know I'm about to run.

Rio responds first. "I'm not forgetting shit, Spencer."

"Me either." Zane adds.

"This isn't over. We'll give you space if you need it, but be prepared because we're talking all of this out. We're not quitting. We know you're scared, but you're safe with us."

They're getting too close. If they touch me again, I'll cave and give in to whatever wild fantasy my mind can conjure and it's conjured quite a bit in the last ten seconds.

"Awesome. Talk later. Bye!" Before I know it I'm sprinting out of the bathroom and through the bar. I spot Iris and signal that I'm heading home. She gives me a pout seeing that I'm leaving alone but then smiles. Suspiciously so. I peer over my shoulder and see two men pursuing me. The same two men I left in the bathroom, or thought I left.

No way am I letting them follow me home.

I dart out of the bar and thank the man upstairs that there's someone getting out of a cab at that same moment. I dive right in and spout off my address.

As the car drives away, I peek behind me through the window and see them standing there in the street. Rio with his arms folded and Zane with his hand in his pockets; both have a determined look on their faces.

I have a feeling that determination isn't targeted at trailing me home. It's directed at me in general, and I'm not so sure Safe Spencer will survive their plans.

CHAPTER 14

SPENCER

The cabbie drops me off in front of Clay Creations and speeds away as if I smell like a dumpster and he can't get away fast enough. I probably do smell. That's what happens when you're in a crowded space, dancing, and get worked up by two sexy men.

The air is still and the street oddly empty. Shadows from the warm streetlamps creep towards me. I sigh and ignore it as I make my way to the clear door separating the sidewalk from the stairs to my apartment, digging for my keys in my purse.

I'm not paying attention to the lamppost a few feet away that's suddenly out or the fact that the street is empty.

That's mistake number one.

Before I get to the door, I'm hit with the earthy scent of cigars and a set of arms immediately encircle my upper body and the asshole attached to the arms lifts me off my feet.

I hesitate.

Mistake number two.

He carries me a few steps to the side when I finally get with the program and fight back. I try dropping my weight to throw him off balance, but he's too big. He easily corrects himself and keeps carrying me backwards to God knows what.

I scream and scream, but not a soul responds. My heart begins to sink when no one comes running to my rescue. I'm alone. Just like I was the day Abuela died. Just like I was the day I left Houston. No one to lean on. I only have me. No one else gives a damn enough in this moment to save me.

I only have me.

Fear isn't going to win. I have to rely on what I've been taught. Fight dirty. This guy engaged me in an unfair fight by picking a smaller opponent and coming at me from behind. Not today, asshole.

My pumps fall off and I begin bringing the heels of my feet down on his shins repeatedly. I reach for whatever I can and start scratching. I keep my nails short for the studio, but I find a way to make my short nails hurt. I hear him hiss when my nails score his skin which gives me satisfaction, but not the freedom I need.

I slip a little in his arms and he effortlessly swings me to the side so my head hits the side of a car, meaning he's dragged me into the street. Pain radiates from my temple and my vision blurs. He grits out in my ear, "You're not getting away from me that easily. Quit fighting, Flower."

I freeze, stuck in the terror of the moment. Did he just? *No.* There's no way he found me. I never told Mom where I am. I got new credit cards, new bank accounts, new everything when I moved here. I even sold my car. I made sure my information wasn't available online and I don't have any social media accounts.

It's not him. It can't be him. I won't get away if he's found me.

But he said it. *Flower.* No one else has ever called me that. I can't let him take me back.

My energy is waning, but I refuse to go quietly. Never again will I comply.

I thrash about more.

"Stop. Fighting. Me." He grunts out as I throw my body around every which way.

He sets me on my feet and spins me to face him. Before I can even try to get a look at his face, his hand meets my right cheek with a loud slap. The force of the strike has my body flipping back around and dropping to the rough sidewalk. My head bounces. I feel the ragged concrete cut into my legs and arms.

I can't let the pain take over. I've survived worse.

Realizing I'm no longer confined in his arms, I know this is my chance. I may be tired, but he's not desperate like I am.

Coming up with a plan, I pretend to pass out when he tries to pick me back up. I must have worn him out because I hear him breathing heavily.

When he grabs my shoulders to haul me up, I flip onto my back and kick him in the balls as hard as possible. He immediately doubles over and yells out, "YOU BITCH!"

I stand and grab his head on either side and bring my knee up to his face. Hard.

"I fight dirty too, asshole!"

Then I run for the stairs and find my keys on the ground. I look over my shoulder and see him hobbling away to a parked sedan. I can't see his face. I can't even see the color of his hair in the dim moonlight. He's hunched over, no doubt from the kick to his balls, so I can't tell how tall he is, and I'm not sticking around to find out.

But I'm positive. It's *him*. He found me.

There's a throbbing in my head, but I ignore it. I sprint up the stairs taking them two at a time, not caring that my skintight dress is riding up. I don't care if I flash someone as long as I get to my apartment safely.

I fumble with my keys while I hurriedly unlock my door. When I get inside, I slam it behind me and secure the deadbolt. Thank you to whoever invented crossbody purses because it's still on me with my phone inside.

I rip out my cell and dial the first number I can think of.

"Hello, Angel."

"Zane?" I get out on a sob.

"Spencer? What's wrong?" I hear the alarm in his tone and swear I hear someone in the background say, "What's going on?" Followed by a few grunts and moans from a third person.

"He found me. I got away, but—" The tears are flowing now.

"Are you safe?"

"I don't know. I'm in my apartment, but…I feel weird."

"Babe. Stay on the phone with me. We're coming."

"I think I'm just going to lay down for a minute." I fumble over to my couch.

"What's happening? Spencer, talk to me."

I think he says more, but I don't hear him. I'm drifting off and can't fight the pull of unconsciousness anymore.

CHAPTER 15

ASHER

I hate planes. I hate flying. Men my size were not meant to be packed like a sardine in a metal machine that flies through the sky and occasionally shakes.

Mother Nature does not want me here and she's making it clear.

Message received.

I'm six foot five and weigh three hundred pounds. I take up more space than the engineers planned for one passenger, but driving from Los Angeles to New York wasn't an option.

I haven't been back here in months. Not that I'm home much anyways. I travel a lot for work.

My job has made seeing my brothers and being there for important things—like Rio's birthday—difficult.

When the plane lands, the wheels skip a few times on the runway.

Not cool, pilot.

Thankfully, I was able to get a seat towards the front of the plane and get off this death trap as fast as possible.

As I make my way to the exit, the flight attendant doesn't hide her perusal of my body.

"Welcome to La Guardia Airport! Enjoy your trip. Let me know if there's anything I can do to make it more enjoyable." She bats her thick fake lashes and slides a folded up piece of paper in my pocket. She may be discreet about slipping me her number, but she's not discreet about how she reaches for my dick.

Before she knows what's happening, I grab her wrist and shove it away from me.

Leaning in close, I narrow my eyes and growl, "Keep your hands to yourself." Then I turn and smile at the other flight attendant who watched the whole thing from the open door and continue off the plane.

I don't care that handsy flight attendant is a woman or that she's smaller than me. Women can still inflict pain, I see it every day.

Besides, she didn't ask before trying to touch the family jewels. I'm thirty-five, not twenty-five.

My mother showed me the antithesis of how a woman should be treated. I always tell whoever I'm going home with, that it's just for the night. I don't give them my number, and I don't make any promises other than a good time. So, no. The flight attendant will not be getting a call from me. All I want is to see my friends and sleep in a real bed. Not another notch in a cheap motel bed.

After grabbing my suitcase at baggage claim, I make my way to passenger pickup and spot Rio smiling proudly with a neon pink poster that reads "The Wolf."

That motherfucker. He knows I hate that nickname. If I didn't love my mother so much, I would blame her for naming me Asher Wolfgang Dawson.

"The Wolf is back!" he shouts across the crowds of people and proceeds to howl which turns some heads.

I scowl at him as I make my way over to where he's standing. I know he's just doing it to get a rise out of me. That's Rio. Good to know that the only thing that has changed about him is the addition of a few tattoos. I'm surprised he still has skin to cover.

"Shut the fuck up, dickhead. You're scaring the little grandmas."

"Nah. The cougars love me." He winks at the white haired woman leaning on her cane standing next to us.

"You're an idiot," I say and punch his arm before I pull him into a hug.

"Where's Z?"

"He's at the hospital with Spencer."

Ah, yes. The victim.

Zane and Rio swear it's the same group we've been trying to dismantle for over a year now. If she hadn't been scrappy, she would have been sold to some sick fuck who would have taken her against her will over and over, or she would've ended up in a hell hole where it would have been more than one sick fuck.

Rio called me last night and told me to get my ass back to New York ASAP. The case in LA was stagnant anyways. It was clear my guy wasn't even in the state anymore. He's yet to kill in the same place twice, so I figured now was a good time to head home for some R&R. And by R&R I mean busting some assholes who think it's okay to sell people.

"But he said he'd pick up a couple pizzas from Sal's on his way home to make up for not being here," Rio adds.

"Meat lovers?"

"Wolf, you know he's got you." Rio smirks, knowing he's ruffling my feathers.

"Stop calling me that." I say with a growl.

"But everyone calls you that."

"Absolutely no one calls me that."

"To your face."

"Whatever you say, dipshit. Can we get out of here now? I'd like a shower, pizza, cold beer, and a good night's sleep. In that order."

"On it, *hombre*. ¡*Vamanos*!"

As we walk away, I spot the grabby flight attendant getting onto a hotel shuttle. We make eye contact and she grimaces. Her ego is probably shot, but that's not my problem. I smile wide and show her the crazy in my eyes. The crazy that comes out when I'm close to catching a perp who enjoys hurting someone smaller than them. The kind of perp who takes what isn't theirs to take.

Her eyes widen, and she quickly looks away.

That's right. Next time keep your hands to yourself, lady. You might avoid going home with a serial killer.

Rio rushes me through the parking lot, and we make our way to where he parked my car. With my bag loaded up in the back, we hop in.

Once the doors are closed, his demeanor instantly shifts. Yep, still the same Rio. Hot to cold in a flash.

"So, are you going to fill me in on what's happening with your killer?"

I mean, one could classify me as such. But people usually call me Asher, shit face, "The Wolf," apparently, or Special Agent Asher Dawson.

And fucking hell. Rio doesn't know how to ease into a conversation, not that I expected him to change in the last few months since I'd last seen him.

"We'll talk about it when we're with Z," Rio huffs a frustrated breath so I continue, "Look, I'm sorry I didn't call, but I couldn't talk about it on the phone." That's probably what he's truly upset about. That I didn't call and check in.

"That's what we have the burners for, *puto*."

"You can push all you want, but we're not talking about it without Z. So drop it."

"Whatever. I'll drop you off at the house then head back to the hospital."

Twenty minutes into the drive and Rio still isn't talking to me. He has perfected the silent treatment. I would know. Once when we were roommates in college, he didn't talk to me for a week because I ate the rest of the arroz con pollo his sister made.

"Rio, I'm serious. I'm not going to talk about it without Z."

He gives me a side-eye and keeps driving. This is going to be a long drive.

Welcome home to me.

CHAPTER 16

SPENCER

*I*s my alarm going off? Did I change the sound by accident? Either way, it's annoying as hell.

I reach to turn it off, but my arm is caught on something. What the fuck? Peeling my eyes open is a chore, but when I manage to crack them open, I'm met with harsh overhead lights that send a sharp ache through my skull. I hiss at the pain.

"Go back to sleep, Angel. I'll still be here when you wake up."

Why is Zane in my apartment? My mind is fuzzy, and sleep sounds good. It's Sunday anyways so I might as well take advantage and sleep in.

※ ※ ※

WHEN I WAKE LATER my eyes still feel heavy. The annoying as fuck lights are still glaring overhead and that incessant beeping is still going strong.

Why didn't Zane turn off my alarm?

I groan and try to roll over but am stopped by a tug on my arm and everything clicks.

The bar. Running away from Zane and Rio. Being pulled into the street, getting away, collapsing on my couch after I called...Oh shit. Zane.

Slowly sitting up, I realize where I am. The overwhelming stench of antiseptic, the rhythmic beep of the heart monitor, the indistinct chatter of nurses outside my door.

I'm in the hospital.

Zane is asleep in what must be the most uncomfortable chair known to humankind. It's short, much too short for his tall frame. He's slumped down with his head resting on the back. How is it possible that he looks just as beautiful sleeping as he does awake? I normally wake up with a dry mouth and drool crusted on my cheek, but not Zane. Of course, not Zane. He's captivating even while unconscious.

"You're staring."

Startled, I snap my attention to a man in the doorway. I didn't even hear him come in. He's standing there leaning against the doorframe with a coffee in each hand looking perfectly rumpled in his slightly wrinkled, heather-gray T-shirt and straight leg jeans. Did he sleep here too?

"Rio. Umm. I wasn't staring. Merely wondering how he looks so peaceful in that chair."

"It's okay, Spencer. Your secret is safe with me." His smug grin causes my face to heat.

Rio chuckles as the heart monitor beeps quicken. Oh my hell. That machine has got to go.

"I like knowing how we affect you," he confesses.

"Well I don't like you knowing, so maybe I can just unhook myself and we can get going." I go to remove the heart monitor but an inked hand settles over mine, halting my progress.

"Don't you dare, Mama. We're staying here until the doc gives us the green light."

"Please, Rio. I don't want to be here."

"Hey. Babygirl, look at me," Rio's hand lands gently on my cheek and guides my gaze to his. Searching my gaze, he finds whatever it is he's looking for. "I'll go find the doctor and see about putting a rush on your discharge, okay?"

"Okay," I nod. "Thank you."

He turns to grab the coffees from the chair where he must have set them down. He places one on the floor next to Zane and makes a swift exit.

The door slams shut, jolting Zane awake.

"Hey, sleepyhead. Got some good rest?"

Yawning, he reaches high, stretching his muscles. I can't help but notice how his shirt rises displaying a strip of hair that disappears into his pants. "I should be saying that to you. You've been asleep for over twelve hours."

"What?" How did I not notice the time? I reach for my phone on the side table, but the forest of wires makes the action impossible. "A little help, please?"

Taking a sip of the hospital coffee, he saunters over without a care in the world. Thank God. Relief floods my system at his relaxed state. If he's calm, it must not be that bad.

"Checking to see if your boyfriend called?"

"You know I don't have a boyfriend." With a roll of my eyes, I grab my phone.

"Oh really?"

"Yes. You saw me with Rio last night and we…you know…yesterday. Not to mention no one wants to deal with my mess," I say as I gesture to the entirety of my being.

If I were to have a boyfriend, it'd be you or Rio…or both.

Lost in that thought, I'm reminded of what they said last

night about not making me choose. They couldn't have meant that…right?

"Rio and I would have no problem being your boyfriends." Zane doesn't realize that when he says stuff like that, it's like dropping a bomb in my lap. What the hell am I supposed to do with it? I'm not a bomb tech.

Wait.

Oh my God, I said that out loud, didn't I?

How hard did I hit my head?

"Pretty hard. You have some scrapes and bruises, and you have a pretty big lump on your temple," as I reach up to assess and feel the damage, Zane chimes, "You don't want to do that."

I stop mid reach and retort, "I need to know how bad it is."

Zane's light touch traces over the side of my face as if willing my injuries to heal. "It's nothing that won't heal."

The pace of my heart monitor shoots off like a bullet.

With a groan, I cover my face. "Please just leave and let me die of embarrassment in peace."

"Never. You're not allowed to die on me, Angel."

His words pull at my heart strings, and his face radiates sincerity. If I died, would he feel like I abandoned him? Not that I blame him. When Abuela died, I felt truly alone for the first time in my life.

Abuela couldn't magic the cancer away, but I know if she could, she would have in a heartbeat. She left me. She passed on and went wherever we go when we die. Whether it be Heaven, Hell, or just an abyss of nothing, she left.

I should be nothing to Zane. My existence shouldn't matter. I should be able to be plucked out of his life, and there should be no trace of a Spencer-shaped hole. He and Rio should go on as normal. He and Rio *should* go on as normal.

"Whatever you're thinking right now, Spencer. Stop it."

"How do you do that?"

"Do what?"

"Know exactly what I'm thinking or feeling in the moment."

"It's easy. Your eyes say it all."

Zane kisses the top of my head, and I feel it radiate throughout my body. I didn't know a simple kiss could be so sweet, and my heart fills at the action.

A familiar buzz calls my attention to the flood of texts from everyone asking what happened. Alma sounds like she's cooking for an army with all the meals she's promising to drop off, Iris is ready to hunt down my attacker, and Hayes is losing his mind.

Before I can ask, Zane answers my question with a sympathetic grin. "I called Hayes."

"What? Why?" My heart rate starts up again.

"I didn't know how long you'd be in the hospital. I figured you would want him to know so he didn't freak out when you were a no show at work on Monday."

My head leans back against the pillows and my shoulders droop ever so slightly. Dealing with everyone is going to be such a bitch.

Zane's demeanor shifts from calm to serious. "Spencer, I need to ask you some questions."

My head nod is all he needs to continue.

"Do you remember what happened?"

"Yes." My answer is barely audible.

"Do you think you could tell me about it?"

"…Why?"

"I've been assigned to your case."

"Oh," the news settles in. "Wouldn't that be a conflict of interest?"

"That's not something you need to worry about."

"I don't want you to get in trouble, Zane."

"I won't. Now about last night…"

"I'm not so sure I'm ready to answer those questions."

"Okay. We can do this another time, Angel," Zane leans forward and places another gentle kiss on the crown of my head. "Crime scene techs came by. There was no viable evidence at the scene, but you had DNA under your fingernails, so they took samples. We'll run it through CODIS and get a hit soon. Don't worry. We'll catch this guy."

No, they won't.

When Rio re-enters the room, he has a dowdy, gray-haired woman with glasses in tow.

"Spencer Gray. I'm Dr. Cody. It's good to see you awake," her welcoming smile puts me at ease. "How are you feeling?"

"Pretty good," I lie. "Can I go home?"

"Your tests came back. Everything looks good," she explains as she flips through my boring beige file. "No serious brain injuries. You do have a small concussion though. I'd like to keep you here another night to observe you. Make sure nothing else comes up."

Nope. Not gonna happen.

"I'm good. I'd like to leave. I promise I'll rest at home." My composed tone must be what begins to sway her.

"Do you have anyone who can stay with you tonight?"

Defeat crushes my chest. Do I have someone? No. I couldn't ask that favor of anyone I know. Sneaking out of the hospital might be my only option.

"Yes, she does. I'll be with her," Zane speaks up.

"Me too," Rio adds.

My head snaps back and forth between the two of them. Is this a joke?

"And you are?"

"We're her boyfriends," Zane answers plainly, giving his million dollar smile.

Unphased, Dr. Cody continues, "There are a few things you'll need to look out for." Her voice fades as I sneak a glance at Rio. A ghost of a smile rests on his lips.

I'm still trying to formulate whether or not they said that to get a reaction out of her. That must be it. I'm not girlfriend material, not even close to relationship ready.

The next thing I know the t's are crossed, the i's are dotted, and I'm in the back seat of Zane's cramped car headed home.

There's no way they're actually staying. No fucking way. My apartment isn't small, but the walls cannot contain the big dick energy that is Zane and Rio. Their mere presence will blow the place sky high.

I have to think of a way to get rid of them, but that's assuming they intend on staying, which I'm not sure they plan on doing, so it's okay. There's no need to get myself worked up because it's not happening.

Not. Fucking. Happening.

At this moment, I'm grateful that I'm no longer connected to anything monitoring my heart rate.

CHAPTER 17

SPENCER

We're only a few minutes from my apartment and I can't handle it anymore. Working up the courage to bring up the *sleepover* is proving to be an epic failure. Plus, every time I was ready to speak up, Rio and Zane would start arguing over the music. Rio is a big Latin pop and rap fan, but Zane is a rock groupie.

The argument was a bit hard to follow because half of what Rio said was in Spanish and I'm pretty sure most of it was just insults. *Tus gustos musicales son una mierda* definitely doesn't mean "You're my best friend." My conclusion was that Rio and Zane bicker like an old married couple.

Abuela didn't speak Spanish in front of me often, but she was fluent. Mom is too, but she never taught me. Now I wish she had.

When I was discharged, Rio and Zane already had a new set of clothes for me to wear. I don't even want to acknowledge that they rummaged through my drawers…especially my underwear drawer.

I don't need or want anyone else in my space. Rio and Zane

sleeping in my apartment freaks me out. Not because they're creepy. Quite the opposite. I feel comfortable with them, too comfortable, and that's what is making me freak out. My lack of panic has me panicking. It makes perfect sense.

About as much sense as a ten thousand piece jigsaw puzzle.

If I could bitch slap Inner Spencer into next week, I would.

"So, guys, thanks for driving me home—"

"What do you want for dinner?" Rio interrupts.

"What?"

"Dinner, babe? We're getting hungry," Zane explains as if I don't know what the last meal of the day is called.

"Do I have to cook it?"

"What? No. Of course not. We'd never expect that. Besides, you have a concussion. The doctor said you need rest." Rio's bewildered face peeks at me via the rear view mirror.

"Then I don't care what I eat. If I don't have to make it, I'll eat it."

"Noted," Zane replies.

"After we order dinner, what are we doing first? Pillow fight, gossip, braid each other's hair?"

I can't tell if Rio is joking or not.

"Braiding hair? Do you even know how to do that?"

"I do," Zane answers. Another bomb in my lap. "My foster sister Sarah loved her hair in two pigtail braids and my foster mom couldn't be bothered. So I learned how and would do her hair every day."

Wow. So much to unpack there. "Umm y'all aren't spending the night."

"Of course we are," Rio's indignation causes a seed of guilt to take root. "We told the doc we would. I'm not a liar and please don't make us sleep in Zane's fun-sized car. That would make getting into your apartment very difficult if anything happens."

He has a point.

"I have my gym bag in the back so it's perfect. I was going to workout later but clearly the universe was preparing me for an impromptu sleepover," Rio adds.

Is this what delusion looks like?

"Well the universe and I haven't gotten along lately, so I don't think that 'sign' means what you think it means."

"Nonsense. Everything happens for a reason. The reason for today, a sleepover." They're acting as if this is normal. This is anything but normal.

"Do this a lot, do you? Sleep at a random woman's house?"

"Can't say I've done this before. You'd be my first," Rio quips.

"Me too," Zane says.

"Thanks for popping that cherry. I've been meaning to get that out of the way for a while." Rio wipes sweat from his forehead that isn't there.

"Glad to be of service," I reply sarcastically.

"I have some cherries you can pop too, Spencer," Zane declares.

What! Did he just say what I think he said?

"All jokes aside…Do you like Spencer or Spence? Beautiful? Gorgeous?" Rio asks.

"Spence or Spencer is fine."

He flashes his signature smile at me and it's official. All he has to do is smile and I'd do whatever he wants. I bet he gets a lot done with that smile.

"Spence, I know you know this, but I think you're forgetting. You were attacked. Attempted kidnapping. Everything points to your attacker knowing your routine and knowing things about your life," another bomb dropped and he's still not done throwing truths my way. "This wasn't a crime of opportunity. This was planned. He was waiting for you. I don't think it's smart for you to be alone tonight, maybe a few nights. We can either sleep on the couch or in Zane's clown car—"

"Lay off my car, man."

"But, like I said, it'd be easier if I didn't have to break down your door if you need help."

Shit. I don't want to think about it. I just want to get back to my life. I need normal, but I have a feeling I'm not going to know normal for a while.

We finish the drive to my apartment in silence minus the Latin music blaring from the speakers.

How did *he* find me? I guess it wouldn't be too hard considering I'm in Abuela's old apartment, but he never knew where Abuela lived. He never asked.

And why is *he* still looking for me? I figured he'd be married to some blonde haired leggy woman and have a kid or two by now. Why come after me?

Once we're parked, I realize where I am. Sweat forms on the back of my neck, my chest tightens, and my stomach churns. I was grabbed right there.

I could have been taken to God knows where. Anything could have happened once he got me in his car. I was lucky. I wasn't prepared. I wasn't ready. No one would have noticed I was gone until it was too late.

"Spencer? Spencer! Angel, look at me."

Zane's face swims into view after I blink the tears away. He's kneeling outside the car on the pavement and my door is open. His strong, callused hands hold mine. His unblinking green eyes echo his concern. Why do his eyes have to be so perfect?

"They're not perfect, I promise. But if it helps, you can look all you want. I don't mind."

Oh shit.

I need to calm it with these thoughts. If I keep saying what

I'm thinking, I'm going to end up doing something I may regret. Something like kissing both of these men.

"Come on. Let's get you inside," Zane prompts gently.

My hands grip his, and my skin crawls at the thought of going by that spot. I know I'll have to suck it up one day, but I'm not ready.

"Please. No. I can't," I whine quietly.

Warm hands frame my face and Zane leans in close. His lips almost touch mine.

"Can I carry you?"

A slight nod is all I give, and before I know it I'm up in his arms with my face in his neck.

"You don't have to look. Hand me your keys and I'll get you inside."

I blindly dig through my purse wrapped around my body then pass my keys to him. When all three of us are over the threshold to my apartment, I don't attempt to leave the comfort his body gives me.

"Spencer? Is that you?"

Hayes? *Shit. What is he doing here?* I breathe deeply, readying myself to handle the situation. But I can't, all I smell is Zane. My brain is instantly scrambled. That's all it takes for me to forget my current situation. Cedar with hints of citrus. His scent will be forever associated with safety and comfort.

Hayes makes eye contact with Rio and Zane. "What the fuck are you two doing here?"

"Hayes!" I scold. What crawled up his ass?

I move to extract myself from Zane's arms, but he doesn't budge.

"And what are you doing out of the hospital, Spencer? You shouldn't be out yet." Hayes presses. "I said, what the fuck are you two doing here?"

"Hayes, lay off." What is his problem? I've never seen him so angry before.

"They shouldn't be here. Do you even know who attacked you? It could have been one of them," he accuses.

Rio steps forward. "You think we'd do that?"

"I don't know you all that well to begin with." I have never seen this side of Hayes. He's like a protective little brother.

My head tips forward and I take a deep breath. "It wasn't them, Hayes. That much I know for sure. You can relax."

"You still shouldn't be out of the hospital."

"He's right, Angel."

I'm getting a little tired of all the mother-henning going on here. I don't need anyone to take care of me. I've been doing just fine these last few years on my own.

Until last night.

I push that last thought away.

"How many times do I have to tell everyone that I'm fine? I really am fine."

Hayes rolls his eyes. "Sure you are."

"Hayes? Where are you? I brought lunch!" I hear Iris call from behind us.

Oh God. Please don't let this be real.

"Oh! Spencer!" She scans the room. "What are you doing out of the hospital? Shouldn't you be resting? At least you have your knights in shining armor with you."

"What makes you think they're my knights?" I snap.

"Well, he's holding you…like that and Rio is standing there like he's ready to slit anyone's throat who gets too close."

"*Ella no está equivocada,*" Rio mumbles.

"Did they end up helping you glaze your donut last night? Or *donuts.*" Iris pretend whispers with a gleam of mischief in her eyes. Hayes frowns at her.

Regret fills my features. I realize I shouldn't have snapped. They're just concerned. They care.

"There was no *glazing*, so get that out of your head, and I'm fine. Zane and Rio were just giving me a ride home."

"And spending the night," Zane chimes in.

Hayes and Iris' eyes go wide. "Oh. Ohhhhh," Iris answers. "We'll just leave you to it then. Come on, Hayes. Let's go have lunch at my place and do some glazing of our own." Iris waggles her eyebrows at me teasingly before grabbing Hayes' hand and marching them out.

"Wait! That's not what he meant," I try to explain, but they're no longer listening. I huff and glare at Zane. "You can put me down now."

"No can do, Spence. Your knights in shining armor need to deliver their fair maiden to her chambers."

I sigh and give up. Getting rid of these men isn't going to be that easy.

But then again, do I even want to?

CHAPTER 18

SPENCER

"How do we feel about pizza?"

Zane and Rio have been in my apartment for all of five minutes and have already made themselves comfortable. I don't know what that says about me or about them.

Did I really let them into my apartment? Am I actually going to let them stay?

I'm insane. My attacker must have hit my head harder than I thought because this isn't me. This isn't staying safe. No matter how they make me feel.

The fact that Zane and Rio are in a stranger's apartment and are pushing to spend the night shows they must be crazy too. At least our crazies match each other's.

Let's not even touch the fact that they have stirred something inside me I thought was long dead. Zane looks at me with those emerald eyes and I'm done for. My body fills with lust and I would give anything to know his touch again. All Rio has to do is smile and I would volunteer to be his slave for a week. A ravenous beast comes out that is only satisfied with orgasms. The self-induced kind won't cut it. Trust me, I know.

"Spence? Pizza?" Zane asks from the kitchen.

I snap back to reality. "Do I have to make it?"

"No." He scrunches his face.

"Then I'm game. If I don't have to make it, I'll eat it," I say emphasizing my earlier statement.

I don't care how much money I have to spend on frozen meals and takeout, my budget will happily take the hit if it means I never have to cook another meal.

"A woman after my own heart," Zane says with a smirk.

"You say that because you also suck at cooking. You can't even microwave popcorn." Rio teases Zane as he returns from the bathroom.

"At least I've never burned a bowl of cereal."

"That was one time!"

"Burned a bowl of cereal?" I question with a head tilt. "How do you manage that? You don't warm up cold cereal."

"To be fair, I was high." Rio says it so factually like it's not a big deal, but I burst out laughing. When I come down from my hysterics, they're both staring at me. Mouths open ready to catch flies and everything.

"*Eres la criatura más bella. Por favor, ten mis hijos,*" Rio whispers.

"What he said," Zane agrees.

"Did you say something about kids?" I ask, breaking them from their spell. Instead of responding, they just look at each other and smile as if they know something I don't. Which they do and only serves to irritate me. "Fine. Don't tell me. But one of these days I'm whipping out Google Translate."

"Good luck with that, Mama." Rio laughs.

To prove a point, I pull out my phone and type in his earlier statement. The results range from "You sexy beast, please have babies" to "Kids are beasts. Please have them."

That's the last time I try that. I'll just have to secretly record him and ask Alma for her help.

But the sentiment was clear. He thinks I'm pretty, but for how long?

I know I'm not interesting. I'm not a party girl. I don't put myself out there or wear clothes that show off my natural curves. I actively avoid male attention. I hide and I have been hiding for the last three years, and I thought I'd been successful at it.

Until last night.

Besides, Zane is a man who looks like he'd be with a model, an actress, or some kind of superstar. She'd be sensual and confident. She'd know how to do a proper cat eye; know how to seduce him and make him go wild. The kind of woman that would make him want her every minute of the day.

Rio would be with a sexy bad bitch. She would dominate a room and have just as many tattoos and piercings as him, whereas I only have a single ear piercing. She wouldn't need him to protect her, and she wouldn't need anyone to hold her hand.

That's definitely not me.

I choose D. None of the above.

I can't even send my food back at a restaurant when they make it wrong. My preference is to silently eat my steak well done when I actually enjoy it medium rare.

He didn't like it when I used my voice. *He* never wanted my opinions. *He* never would have asked what I wanted for dinner. *He* always just told me, and I had to go with it. Every time I think about it I get angry with myself.

Why did I stay so long? Why did I let him do that to me? Why did I go along with everything he said?

Because I'm weak. That's why.

Quiet has always been safe. Keeping things to myself is safe.

However, Rio and Zane aren't the type of men who would shut down my ideas and feelings. They ask a question and I answer. Simple as that. I don't hold back even when I feel like I should.

Comparing is a dangerous game, and I shouldn't participate. But how can I not? They're night and day and it's throwing me off. I mean, it's a good thing Zane and Rio aren't like *him*. That would mean that I'm currently allowing abusers in my home.

The likelihood of me entering another abusive relationship is actually statistically probable. Not that I'm in a relationship with Zane or Rio. They're just friends who wanted to make sure I got home safe…and am going to stay safe…all night long.

"What do you like on your pizza?" Rio shouts.

"Order whatever you want. I can pick off anything I don't like. Except anchovies. Those leave behind a distinct anchovy taste." With a press of a button, I turn on the TV and find my favorite show.

"Spencer." Rio startles me. I didn't hear him move.

I jump and look over my shoulder. I really need to be more aware of my surroundings. Or maybe Rio is just light on his feet.

He rests his hands on the back of the couch and leans down so his face is only inches from mine.

"What do you like on your pizza?"

His breath fans over my skin. Of course, his breath smells good. Like mint. The kind I'd like to taste with my tongue, but I can't go there. I won't go there. I'm not reckless. I plan, and I did not plan for Navarro Flores. So he has got to go asap.

Asap may not be until tomorrow morning.

His face is so close. Everything about him puts me into a trance, making me forget. I forget the pounding headache I've had since I woke up in the hospital, that I was attacked just last night and very likely by my ex, that I have a super long to-do list I'll never be able to finish in one lifetime, that I'm technically in hiding.

His eyes drop to my lips causing my chest to rise and fall faster. I lick my lips and his eyes track the movement.

Shit. This can't keep happening.

I clear my throat and answer, "Vegetables."

He draws his eyebrows together. "What?"

"I like vegetables on my pizza."

"Vegetables aren't real toppings," Zane teases from next to Rio.

I hunch my shoulders slightly and say, "Yeah, you're right. Y'all can get whatever and I can pick off anything I don't want."

"Yes, they are. Don't pizza shame her." Rio swats Zane on the arm.

"Pizza shame?" he asks amused.

Rio gives Zane a signal I don't understand and says, "Yeah, pizza shame."

Zane looks to me, and I chime in quickly. "No, really. It's okay. Get what you want." My attempt to placate them doesn't seem to have the intended effect. I don't want to cause extra fuss.

Zane and Rio give each other a look and round the couch together, bracketing me on either side as they sit with me.

"Angel, you can get what you want," Zane says as he grabs my hand.

"Tell us what you want, Mama." Rio's innuendo causes a chill to rattle my spine.

I refuse to look at them and answer, "Vegetables."

Rio shoulders me playfully and states, "Okay I'll order one rabbit food pizza and—"

"Let me guess, meat lovers," I interrupt. Sassy Spencer has been unleashed.

"Hey! Don't hate. We like meat. All kinds," Zane says in a smug tone and winks.

"I'm not hating. Just pizza shaming the pizza shamer."

Zane and Rio break out in laughter together, a beautiful sound.

As much as I've liked an empty apartment, having them here is nice. Comforting. It feels like a home.

Still laughing, Zane pulls his phone out of his back pocket and places our order, including my rabbit food pizza.

Damn these perfect men.

※ ※ ※

As we sit side by side at my breakfast bar, Zane polishes off his pizza and I stare with my mouth open as I watch him chew. Zane poured my can of Coke he had ordered into a glass and added ice while he and Rio just drank out of the cans. Rio finished his a few minutes before, and I know that because when he was done, he shouted, "I win!"

Where does all that food go? Are they still "growing boys?"

Ha! Yeah, there's nothing "boy" about them. They're definitely all man.

We had a nice, light conversation while eating. I avoided all topics that could circle to discussing my attack.

As we talked, I felt myself gravitating towards them. Literally. My knees rested against Zane's as we angled towards each other, and Rio inched closer and closer behind me. With each word out of their mouths, no matter how mundane, my muscles relaxed one by one. I couldn't look away from Zane's lips as they formed each word. The lilt of Rio's voice soothed the stirring in my chest. I wanted to know what it would feel like to have each of their mouths on me.

I would never be able to choose between the two. One day I'm sure they'd make me. They already mean so much to me, and their presence makes me feel less alone.

Oh my God. I need space from these men. I can't keep going down this trail. I internally shake my head at the constant back and forth.

I face forward so I don't have to see the expression on their faces when I say what I'm about to. "Zane. Rio. I really appreciate you bringing me home and buying me dinner—"

"But?" Zane interjects.

"But, I'm not okay with either of you staying the night. I need to be alone, I need time." I hold my breath waiting for their response.

Not so subtly, I sneak a glance at Zane. Zane looks me up and down, assessing me. He's cataloging everything. Every bruise, every scratch. No one has ever cared to look so close like that. Only Abuela, but never a man like Zane.

On my right Rio sits back quietly, remaining closer than what is considered acceptable for friends.

"Look. I promise if anything happens, I'll call 911, okay?"

"No, Angel. You need someone, you call me or Rio. We'll leave Asher's number too," he stands and crowds my space from the side, forcing me to lean backwards into Rio's warm, solid chest. "Promise me."

My focus wanders from his sinewy sculpted arms to his face, then I look up at him from under my lashes.

"I promise," I whisper breathlessly.

"Good girl," Rio praises in my ear.

"Let me check your head, then we'll go and let you get some sleep," Zane says.

"Okay," I acquiesce.

He makes quick work of poking and prodding gently while asking some medical questions. Have I gotten dizzy lately, how's my headache, etc. I answer each one correctly to get them to leave. All the while Rio is behind me playing with my hair, brushing the rough pads off his fingertips over my neck and shoulders. His actions wreak havoc on my concentration. More than once I stumble over my answers.

When Zane is done with his assessment, I realize he's leaning close while he studies the bump on the side of my head. Perfectly close.

I turn my face to him, and he goes from analyzing my injury to zeroing in on my lips. Anxious to see what he'll do, I hold my breath. Rio's hands find my waist and he gives me a whisper of touch to the underside of my breasts. Discreetly, I squirm and squeeze my thighs together. Zane's gaze drops and his eyes shine with an impish glimmer.

Shit. Caught red handed. More like caught wet pantied.

He leans closer so our lips touch as he says, "Call me if you need me. For anything."

A whimper escapes my lips and Rio places a soft kiss on my neck in that sweet spot, but then they draw back and head out. On shaky legs I follow them to the door to say goodnight.

Zane lingers over the threshold. "Tomorrow we're going to have to talk about what happened."

A hesitant nod is all I can give as a wave of acid wells up in my stomach.

"Lock the door behind us," Zane instructs.

"Have a good night," Rio says.

My legs almost give out when they're gone.

What are these men doing to me? In less than a few weeks

they have managed to break down my walls and set up camp. I never let men get close. Let alone close enough to touch. Each caress from them sends the best chills down my spine, and more than that, it's always a kind touch. There's no malice behind it. I would know. *He* touched me with anger. His grip was like a vice when he got in my face and yelled with a rage I had never seen before—or since.

Zane and Rio may be safe, but I can't go there with them. No matter how much my body and heart ache for the security they give me.

CHAPTER 19

ZANE

She thinks we're leaving, and we are.
    Sort of.
We're leaving her apartment, but we're not leaving the street. Another night in my car is going to suck ass, but sacrifices are made for angels all the time.

Sliding into my car, I answer my phone when it rings and put it on speaker.

"Where the hell are you?" Asher's greeting is filled with a special kind of love. I haven't seen him since he got in, which isn't like me.

"Where the hell are we? Where the hell are you?" Rio answers.

"I'm at the Black Horse."

"Why?" Rio and I ask in unison.

"What do you mean why? I'm waiting for my welcome home drinks that we get every time I come home," Asher responds outraged.

When all three of us met, I had stopped searching for where I belonged. I had given up, thinking that was my lot in life. My parents didn't want me. My foster parents had thoroughly fucked me up. I figured no one else needed to deal with my shitshow of a life, but Rio wouldn't take no for an answer. It helped that he was my roommate and was around twenty-four-seven. He helped me embrace my desires and accepted me for *me*. Then we met Asher and he fit right in. We were all forged in the fires of Hell, but we fought our way out and found each other.

"Something came up," I explain oh-so-thoroughly.

Asher perks up. "And you didn't call? Was it Cain? The fuck man," he whisper shouts.

"Calm the fuck down. We've been with Spencer all day. She needed a ride home from the hospital. We're sitting outside her place in case the guy comes back. You know how these people operate," Rio says.

There's a pause on the line and I know what he's thinking. I don't actively seek out women. They come to me and if I feel like it, we fuck. That's it. But I took care of Spencer, bought her dinner and am now going to sleep in my car to keep watch. Fortunately, he doesn't know about our lunch dates.

"You should've called," he grumbles. "It would've been nice to know so I didn't get stood up. No excuses, dickbags."

"I'm sorry. I'll buy you a pie from Sal's to make up for it." My attempt to make up for our no-show is weak since we get our pies for free, but it's still an olive branch.

Sal's makes the best pies in New York. I don't care what anyone says. He has the perfect sauce to cheese ratio. After what happened with his daughter Emilia, the scales of justice needed balance. We brought that balance. We never told Sal specifically what we did, but he knows. Sometimes a father just knows. Now he gives us free pizza whenever we want.

"You fucking better. Place the order and meet me at home then you can tell me about her interview."

"No can do, man. We already ate and we're camping outside her apartment tonight."

"Are you shitting me? Wait. Did you eat Sal's without me tonight?"

"Shut up. You know we'd never cheat on you by eating Sal's with someone else." Rio's argument is valid however false.

"I can smell the lies and marinara from here, assholes."

"She needed the cheesy goodness to cheer her up! You know Sal's cures any ailment." Rio tries to reason with him.

Asher's sigh crackles through the phone. "Fine. I'll see you guys tomorrow."

He hangs up and I settle in for the night. Eyes on the building, I let my mind wander to the woman inside.

She kicked me out in a kind way. Can't say that's ever happened before. When I go to a woman or man's house, I leave before they wake. Which makes Spencer asking me to leave, a first. I could tell she was battling herself. She couldn't hide the way her luscious thighs clenched, seeking relief. Relief I would gladly provide.

She's not ready for that yet, and that's okay. I'll wait. I'm a patient devil.

Twenty minutes after her lights flick off, Rio unfolds himself from the car.

I follow suit and question, "We really doing this?"

"You're the one who slipped her the sleeping pills," Rio states plainly.

"I know, but—"

"I'm not leaving her alone with her nightmares. We've heard her scream in her sleep almost every night since we started *Operation Spy Through the Pottery Teacher's Windows*."

"I was just making sure you were okay with breaking and entering."

"Do you really have to ask?"

I roll my eyes at his sass and we proceed up the stairs under the cover of night. The broken lamp post must be how the trafficking asshole was able to get the drop on Spencer. I nod to the diffused light and Rio grunts. Sometimes we don't need words to communicate. We both know what the absent light means. Premeditation.

I'm positive it's the same group. This matches their MO. Single, attractive woman, who lives alone, with no health problems. People think traffickers just take anyone and everyone, but that's not necessarily true. People are products to them, not living beings with feelings and dreams. Traffickers usually inspect their "product" first, which means they must have been watching Spencer for a while before trying to take her.

But how long were they stalking her? A week? Two weeks?

I go down on one knee at Spencer's shitty front door and pull out my lock pick set. A twelve-year-old could break into this place. The locked pantry at my foster home made me learn how to unlock doors from the outside by the time I was seven. I had to learn young. If I didn't learn, then I didn't eat. My foster parents often forgot about Sarah and me until their *friends* came by.

Leaving that particular darkness behind, I get Spencer's door open just like I did last night. Thankfully, she never asked how we got in to take her to the hospital. I wouldn't have lied, but I don't think it's an answer she's ready for.

Our empty pizza boxes remain on her kitchen counter where we left them. Rio reaches for the cardboard and places them by the front so we can take them to the trash when we leave. We're men, but that doesn't mean we have to be slobs. No woman should have to clean after a man's mess.

On light feet we enter her room and I'm overcome with the sweet scent of jasmine. Spencer's perfume. My cock hardens as

I take in a deep breath inhaling more of her. Needing to will my semi away, I think of anything to handle the situation.

Sharks. Old grandmas. Driving in traffic. Vegetarian pizza. That did it. Vegetarian pizza. Huh. Good to know

Rio strips off his shirt and slides under the fluffy white comforter behind Spencer. When he lifts the blanket, Spencer's perfectly round ass comes into view and I groan. She's wearing a simple black thong and an oversized tee. That's it. With that, blood rushes south again.

"*Métete a la cama, idiota.*"

"I have a bit of an issue." My hands gesture to my hard dick.

"I do too, but you don't see me complaining about it. Especially not with her ass so close."

Now I wish I would've climbed in first. I round to the other side and silently lay beside a sleeping Spencer. Her bed is only a queen so we're short on space, but that just means we both get to be closer to her.

On my side I'm able to take her in. Her face is pinched, and sweat has formed on her brow. I smooth the stress lines away with my touch. My hand moves away, but she reaches out in her sleep and brings my hand close, right against her perfect breasts. She inhales deep and when she lets it out, she relaxes all over. Her body leans into Rio more and drags me closer. I happily follow her lead and tangle my legs with hers.

"Sweet dreams, Angel," I whisper in her ear and allow myself to give in to a blissful sleep next to the person who has quickly come to mean more to me than any other woman.

CHAPTER 20

SPENCER

"*Flowerrrrrr,*" another round of chills zips up and down my back at his call for me. "*Floooooower.*" His voice echoes from upstairs. I compel myself to move again even though my mind is screaming for me to go back to the safety under the bed.

At the end of the hallway, I pause and open my ears for any noise.

A clank rings out from the second floor.

Desperate to believe they're both back in the office, I creep through the living room. Every step brings another wave of terror. Terror at the thought of being spotted. Terror at the possibility of making a noise.

I jump and a scream almost escapes me when a crash of thunder shakes the windows along the back of the house. Allowing my gaze to wander above me, I check for any signs that they heard my almost shriek.

A flash of lightning casts light on the second floor and I see a reflection in the window of a figure outlined on the balcony right above me.

The face of my fiancé smiles wide as he says, "Gotcha."

I wake with a scream. Sweat dripping down my spine. There are hands on me. I try to jerk away, but they pull me back to my pillow.

"Shhh. You're safe, Spencer."

"No one will get you while we're here."

I'm encompassed by the faint smell of mint and cedar. I'm safe. It wasn't real.

He didn't find me tonight.

※ ※ ※

THE BELLOW of my alarm wakes me, and I consider turning it off and falling back to sleep. I was attacked so I deserve to sleep in, right?

Wrong. He got the drop on me. A day without training is not something I can afford.

With one eye open, because I'm still in denial, I stumble to my phone and turn off the alarm.

I can't believe I fell back asleep after my nightmare. That's not usual for me, but I won't look the gift horse in the mouth. Sleep is something I normally lack.

The temptation to inhale the scent on my pillows is strong. They smell like *them*. I don't know how it's possible, but I'm positive it's why I was able to fall back asleep.

Maybe I'm going crazy.

I prepare for my run to the gym and I remember I'm going to have to go by that spot. Avoidance isn't an option. It's literally impossible. I'm not moving apartments, so I might as well get it over with.

Normal. That's what I'm going for.

I exit my building alert, and my gaze connects with the dynamic duo who are effortlessly carving out a permanent place in my life.

Fuck. What are they doing here? Did they actually sleep in that toddler car?

They take in my appearance and jog over to me.

"Good morning, Spencer. Going for a run?" Zane is a little too chipper for the early hour. His hair is slightly rumpled in a sexy way that has me melting on the spot.

"Uh, yes?" Why does that come out as a question?

"You don't seem so sure," Rio teases.

My voice goes more firm. "I mean, yes. I run every morning to the gym."

"Of course you do," he huffs out.

"Uhh. Yeah. So I better get going." My statement trails off and I aim to move around them, but Zane hooks an arm around my waist and pulls me close.

"You really think we'd let you go anywhere alone after the other night?"

Rio uses his hand to turn my attention to him and runs his thumb along my lower lip. "We let you go and something bad happened. Worse could've happened. Never again, Mama."

"I guess y'all can drive alongside me as I run."

"No need. We're ready. Let's go." Zane's words have me taking in their attire. Gym shorts, T-shirts, and running shoes. How could they possibly have changed in that cramped car? Did someone see? A rush of jealousy overtakes me. The thought of another woman seeing them would cause a rage I don't appreciate. It's like being possessed by a green demon. If they continue to elicit this kind of reaction from me, I won't be responsible for my actions.

The reality of the situation hits me. They slept in that mini car to protect me and now they want to go running with me. Is this still a joke? If it is, I'm not seeing the punchline.

"Are you sure? You know you're not my bodyguards, right?"

"I mean I can run behind you if you want," Rio says as he waggles his eyebrows.

"I missed my workout yesterday, so I need to make up for

it." Zane stretches his muscular arms over his head. I'm distracted by his rigid abs as his shirt rises slightly.

Nope. Horny Spencer is not welcome.

Shouldn't she be though? This internal back and forth is giving me whiplash.

When I think about it, they stayed with me in the hospital, watched over me while I slept, made me laugh and feel safe. I'm starting to think this isn't a joke. They actually care. They want to be here. But can I handle two men? I barely remember to do my laundry.

"No, no. With me is fine, but it's a long run. Don't you want to go home and rest? Sleeping in that toy Honda couldn't have been comfortable."

"Are you trying to get rid of us, Spence?" Zane crowds my space and trails a finger down the side of my arm. I'm so happy I'm wearing long sleeves to hide the chills that erupt all over.

"Of course not." Panting out my words is a dead giveaway, letting him know that his touch riles me.

"Then lead the way, Spencer," he says as he takes a step back and releases me.

My headphones go in and I wince, feeling guilty that I'm tuning them out, but I need this. I need to reset. They're disrupting my routine, and I have a feeling if I told them they couldn't run with me, they'd still follow.

Brain Stew by Green Day blasts through my ears, effectively shutting out the buzz of the city around me. After a few light stretches, I'm ready. Starting off at an easy pace warms up my body. I peek to my left and sure enough, Zane is right there, and to my right is Rio. I don't know how they feel about cardio, but they clearly don't hate it enough to skip the run and drive alongside me.

Or maybe they like you that *much.*

My stride picks up speed, leaving my intrusive thoughts behind on the sidewalk. Rio and Zane adjust with me without breaking a sweat. I may not be competitive, but their natural athleticism feels like a slight. I run alone. It's quieter that way and I'm able to focus on me, but here is Rio with his panty-dropping smile and Zane with his hands that make me wet at the sight of them.

Horny Spencer needs to take a backseat.

Attempting to leave my hormones in the dust, I increase to an all out sprint. They stay with me, but now this feels like a race. A race I cannot let them win.

That numbing burn spreads through my legs as I push myself faster. I have reached that point when the brain isn't sure you can keep up with the speed you're going, but I will not let myself faceplant on the asphalt in front of two drop-dead gorgeous men. Talk about embarrassing. I've done enough of that in front of them. The tally doesn't need an additional mark.

We're all struggling for air when we stop at the entrance to the gym. Zane brings his hands to his head while Rio bends over, rests his hands on his knees, and wheezes out, "You're trying to kill us, aren't you?"

"What gave you that idea?" I pant with a self-satisfied smile.

"No one likes cardio, but you practically begged us to come with you and then you run like your pants are on fire the whole way here. I don't want to die young. I still have many good years ahead of me," Rio rasps.

"What?" I blurt out. "I didn't beg—" When I look at Rio's face, I realize he's teasing me and I roll my eyes. "Hilarious. Okay, well I'm going inside. I'll see y'all later I guess."

With reflexes I should have expected, Zane snags my hand, preventing me from walking away. "You think we're just going to leave you here?"

"Well, yeah. Don't you have to go to work?"

I really need them to go. My workout needs to be distraction free, and I need to feel the sting of my fists connecting with the bag to chase my demons away.

"Not at six in the morning. My captain may run the station like a drill sergeant, but he's not unfeeling. We adhere to normal work hours."

Rio raises his hand. "I'm self-employed, so you're stuck with us for now."

"Oh…That's good…" I fumble over my words trying to come up with more excuses for them to leave, but before I can put together an argument, Zane holds the door open and gestures for me to go ahead of him.

With my defeat accepted, I go inside.

Joey is right where he always is and greets me as he does every day. "You look like shit."

Finally, something normal.

"And you look like a shriveled up dick."

Joey does a double take and drops the paperwork he was sifting through at the front desk. Storming over to me he shouts, "What the fuck happened!"

Taken aback by his outburst, it takes me a moment to realize he's talking about my banged up face. Not wanting to draw more attention to my bruises, I play it down. "I'm fine. It looks worse than it is."

"Don't lie to me, kid. You're a shit liar. Now what happened?"

"It's no big deal. I swear I'm okay."

Joey's eyes snap over my shoulder to Zane and Rio who have been standing back and observing the exchange.

"Who the fuck are you two?"

Zane steps forward. "Detective Zane Kingston."

"Rio Flores."

"Why are you hanging out with a detective and a tattooed bad boy? What's going on?"

Zane snickers at Joey's observation of Rio.

I sigh and surrender to the fact that Joey won't stop until I give him the truth. "There was an incident when I got home from the bar the other night. But I'm fine. I fought him off."

Joey looks me up and down, assessing my injuries. He still looks pissed as hell but says, "Good. Does he look worse than you?"

"I'm not sure. He grabbed me from behind, but I scratched him pretty good, took my knee to his face, and kicked him where the sun don't shine."

"Attagirl," his brief smile warms my heart. "I'm proud of you, but you need to go back home and rest."

"What? No. I need to be here. Please don't make me leave." Tears well up in my eyes.

I've only come to tears a few times in front of Joey. I know it makes him uncomfortable. Hell. It makes me uncomfortable.

Joey deflates. "Calm down, calm down. I won't make you leave, but if I sense that you're wavering in the slightest, you're going home. I'll drive you myself if I have to."

My shoulders drop and I let out the breath I didn't know I was holding. "Thank you."

On the mats, I stretch as usual. Hopefully Zane and Rio will get the hint and leave. I can't fight the darkness with them watching. No one needs to see inside my head and I'm too tired to school my face with every wave of emotion.

By the time I'm done, Zane is next to me stretching as well.

"I'm pretty sure you need to be a member to be over here."

"Good thing I'm the newest member of Joey's Gym."

My jaw drops. "What?"

"Me too," Rio says from my other side, making me jump.

Fuck. I can't keep letting them breeze by my defenses.

"I figure if we're going to do this every day, I'd save money with a membership instead of getting a day pass every time." Zane's reasoning has merit, but this is still blowing my mind.

"I'm sorry, what?"

"I don't know what's so confusing about it," Rio slows his speech as if I'm not understanding what they're saying—which I'm not. "We. Got. Memberships."

I breathe in deep and let it out. Lord, I'm not going to survive these men if they stick around like this.

Normal. I'm getting back to normal. Review what I know. *He* tried to take me, but I'm okay. I'm not dead. I'm here getting back to my routine.

But I'm going to have to leave to keep the people I care about safe.

Now review what I feel: Scared that someone got to me so easily. Terrified that the 'someone' is my ex-fiancé. Confused as to why Zane and Rio insist on hanging around. They say they're interested, but this feels…different.

This hot detective and sexy lawyer have disrupted everything. A few weeks ago, I never would have allowed two men in my apartment for pizza. I never would have entertained the idea of spending the night, and I can't ignore them. My body reacts to everything they say and do, betraying my own thoughts in the process. My eyes are constantly drawn to them, it makes me feel like a creep. The number of times I have caught myself staring is embarrassing, and more than half the time they're staring right back, unapologetically.

My feet follow Joey to the bag hanging along the wall. I wrap my hands and lose myself in the motions.

Right foot slightly in front of my left, feet apart, knees slightly bent. I tighten my core with each swing while Joey stands on the other side holding the bag and watching without judgment. He never would. Instead of judgment, I see concern.

Please not here. I can't cry here, but I can't stop the tears from falling. I can't stop the flashes of memory.

Punch. Jab. One. Two.

Running as he calls out that haunting nickname.

One. Two.

Hiding under the bed as he walks by.

One. Two.

His laughs while I lay broken on the checkered tile.

"Spencer."

One. Two. One. Two.

"Spencer."

Waking up on the cold floor used and beaten.

"Spencer. Baby, please." Someone grabs my shoulders and on instinct I turn with my fists ready.

I won't go down so easily this time. I'm not fractured by my fear like I was that night. He left me unconscious and bleeding, and I got up stronger than ever.

I swing at the man behind me, but he easily blocks my hit with his arm. I bring my left into action and aim for his gut. He dodges the blow and follows up with a swing of his own. I duck, go to the floor, and attempt to sweep his legs out from under him. He gracefully jumps, avoiding my foot.

We fall into a rhythm. Me swinging and battling through the deep red haze of anger. Anger at *him*. Anger at myself for not being stronger. My opponent dodges and blocks every one of my hits, only throwing a few himself. I land a few punches, but not many. I'm lost in a mess of my own making. Too lost to be present and understand what's right in front of me.

When I go to land another punch, he grabs both of my wrists and pulls me in close. I begin to thrash like a chained wild animal.

"Angel, come back to me. I'm here. You're safe."

Angel. *He* never called me Angel.

Blinking, I find that it's not *him* in front of me. I'm not in that dreaded house that was my prison. The prison where I was suffocating. Dying day by day and didn't even realize it.

Instead there's a set of tender emerald eyes gazing back at me, begging me.

"Oh my God! I'm so sorry. Did I hurt you? Are you okay?"

Zane ignores my concern. "Where did you go, Spencer?"

"Nowhere. I'm fine. I got lost in the moment is all."

"Spencer, that wasn't lost in the moment. That was lost in the dark." Rio says from behind me, concern lacing his every word. His hands land delicately on my hips. Warming the chill that made its way down my spine.

The inside of my cheek gets the brunt of my stubbornness as I gnaw on it to keep the words inside. This truth can never see the light of day. No one can ever know. I can't tell them how I was given everything, showered with expensive gifts, while the monster I lived with thrived. What would they think? Would they still see me the same way?

All I can do is shake my head. If I open my mouth now I'll give in to the yearning to tell them and let them wipe my slate clean.

Zane studies me, his gaze a little too perceptive, as always. I allow him to see my vulnerability, to see how much my secret would kill me, maybe even kill him and Rio.

"Okay, fine. But this conversation isn't over." Zane concedes.

"Let's get you home, Mama." Rio brushes his lips tenderly across my cheek.

I turn to Joey who has been watching our whole exchange. He's too observant like Zane. But again, there's no judgment.

"Go home, kid. Get some rest. I don't want to see you here

tomorrow, got it? You need rest. In fact, don't come back for the rest of the week."

"What? Joey, please. I'm fine."

"Get a run in if you need to," he interrupts. "But you need to heal." He approaches me slowly as if he's walking up to a predator, which is odd. I may have fought off an attacker, but I'm not close to his level of skill.

He tentatively pulls me away from Rio and Zane. "You need to heal this"—he points to the scrapes and bruises on my face—"and this," he adds and points to my heart. "It's time, Spencer. Get your head on straight. The gym can only get you so far. You need to forgive yourself and let go of whatever you're blaming yourself for."

"I'm not blam—"

"I'm old. Not blind." Joey doesn't let me get another word in as he gives me his back and strolls away.

Defeated, I allow Rio and Zane to guide me out of the gym. As we pass the front desk where Joey relocated, he calls out, "Don't let her back here tomorrow, ya hear?"

They both give a slight chin lift at Joey. His look back is one of respect with a hint of fear.

Seriously? They're not my keepers. My guys don't get to dictate how I spend my time.

No. Not *my* guys. Not my anything. They're just two men who came with me to the gym, who I almost kissed, and who I can't stop thinking about…that's all.

On our run back to my apartment, Rio and Zane won't let me go faster than a jog. Every time I try to speed up, Zane snags my elbow and Rio grabs the other. Even though their simple touch is a precautionary one, I can't help but be annoyed at the overprotective gesture.

When we get to the sidewalk in front of the studio, I halt

ready to give them my "you need to back off speech," but Rio beats me to the punch.

"Asher will be by later. We both have to go to work, but he has the next few days off, so he'll be with you in the studio and gallery while you work."

"Umm. I think the fuck not," my well-thought-out speech has completely gone out the window and landed right in the middle of a pile of rat shit that has caught fire because how dare they. "I appreciate the safety instincts guys, but I can protect myself. I more than proved that the other night."

"He won't be in the way, Spence. I promise." Zane attempts to reassure me.

"It's not that. I don't even know him and he's just going to hang around all day? Fuck that. And again, I don't need a bodyguard."

"You got a mouth on you, Mama. I like that," Rio says, swiping his thumb across my lower lip.

"No you don't, sir. You're not going to distract me right now. I don't want a bodyguard nor do I need one."

"Sir? I could get used to that. Want to try that kind of name calling upstairs in your bed?" Rio waggles his eyebrows.

"Ugh. You two are impossible. Let me say this plain and simple," I place my hands on my hips and emphasize my next words. "No. No bodyguard."

"It's happening. Might as well get on board now so it's not awkward when Ash gets here." Yet again, Zane's reasoning leaves me baffled.

"It's going to be awkward no matter what! Have you met me?"

"If I had the time, I'd spank you for being a brat," Zane invades my space. He lowers his head so it's even with my ear. "So we'll have to save that for later. Go upstairs, baby, and get

157

ready for work." He nips my lobe and my traitorous pussy floods.

"Go on," Zane urges as he spins me around and smacks my ass. I jolt and scurry upstairs.

I'm not ready to meet the final member of this bizarre, yet hot as fuck, trio.

Please let Asher be a wrinkly seventy-year-old man.

CHAPTER 21

SPENCER

Be cool. Be cool. Don't act like an idiot. Yes, a complete stranger is coming to hang around in the shadows like you work, but it's no big deal. If Rio and Zane trust him then you can trust him too.

My inner pep talk is shit. I fully intend on hiding in the storage room pretending to take inventory or camping out in the breakroom.

After the guys left, I ran upstairs and got ready for the day. My morning is going to be spent at the gallery so I wrestled my ass into a pencil skirt, realizing there was a glimmer of excitement that Rio and Zane might notice how it accentuates my curves. I did my best to cover my bruises with makeup, but my attempts were futile. The black and blue marring my skin isn't easy to conceal.

I'm adjusting an oil landscape painting on the wall when I hear the front door open. My clomp echoes behind me as I make my way to the breakroom. Safe to say I can take "expert in stealth" off my resume. The people in The Mudhouse next door could hear me.

My workspace for the day consists of a simple kitchenette with a table, a few chairs, and a cushy couch I found online. The patrons from Clay Creations use the breakroom to eat lunch if they don't want to ingest a pound of clay dust with their food. It's a simple setup, but cozy.

The door bangs open and I just about jump out of my skin. A squeak may or may not escape my lips at the noise.

"What are you doing back here?" Iris questions.

"Working?" Note to self: work on my confidence when lying.

"Without your laptop or paperwork of any kind?" Iris lets out a laugh.

"Shut up. What do you need?"

Iris grins at me. "There's a Viking here to see you."

"A what?"

"That's what I'm calling him. It's either Viking Hottie or Thor."

"Girl, stop with the nicknames." I pull a face to emphasize my point.

"Why would I do that when I'm so good at them?" Iris replies with her signature cheeky grin.

Even though Iris makes me uncomfortable by pushing me outside my comfort zone, she makes me laugh just as often and I desperately need that.

"Could you tell *the Viking* I'm not here?"

Iris frowns. "Now why would I do that?"

"Because you're my friend and you love me?" The desperation in my eyes leaves Iris unconvinced.

"Try again, babe."

I scoff. "Oh my God! How is being friends not enough to lie for me?"

"Because one"—Iris holds up a finger—"that man is hot as

fuck. The harem you're gathering could use a third to round out the group. Not to mention he looks like he has abs that any woman would die to lick"—another finger goes up—"and two, that God out there is not the kind of man you lie to. He looks like he could snap me in half with his pinky, and I'd thank him afterwards because *that's* how fuckable he is."

"You can't talk like that about customers. What if they hear you?"

Iris offers me a bemused smile. "I'm sure he'd be flattered. Besides, I'm in a happy relationship."

My eyes roll at her antics. Again, I needed the laugh.

Timidly, I make my way to the front of the gallery. Each step bringing me closer to whom I'm praying is not my babysitter for the day.

When I round the partition dividing the showroom and the front desk, my jaw drops. Iris was right. Standing in front of me is a rugged man that I would indeed thank for breaking me with his pinky—or his dick.

He has honey hair tied in a bun at the top of his head. Man buns were never my thing before, but now they are. His thick muscular thighs are encased in denim, and a simple white tee leaves his colorfully inked arms exposed. He really does give Viking energy. I notice his ocean blue eyes are staring at me with indifference, possibly annoyance.

"Hi, I'm Spencer Gray. What can I do for you?"

"I'm your shadow for the day," he retorts in a curt tone. Definitely annoyed. Not that I blame him. I'm just as annoyed, but his shitty attitude isn't helping anything.

"Oh. Asher. Nice to meet you."

"It's Asher Dawson."

"Yes. Well, thank you for coming by. I'm sure you'd rather be at home right now—"

"You're not getting rid of me that easily, Princess."

I lift my chin. "Excuse me?"

"Let's cut the bullshit. I know you don't want me here and you know I don't want to be here. I've been traveling for work for the last few months. So yes, I'd rather be home, but here I am. I don't know what you did to make Rio and Zane follow you around like lost puppies, but they're important to me. They're my family, so when they ask for a favor, I jump to it."

"Are you serious right now?" I can feel my scowl conveying everything my words aren't.

His slow, steady gait brings him right to me. "I don't like wasting time," he whispers.

"Neither do I, but I'm not a dick about it," I whisper back.

"I'm not here to make friends, Princess. I'm just here to make sure no one else tries to snatch you up."

His words make me flinch, but the hurt quickly turns. My mouth flattens. "Stop calling me Princess."

"Whatever you say," he quips back.

I steady a heavy frown in his direction. I cannot believe this asshole.

"Princess."

My stubborn side refuses to dignify his adolescence with a response. So instead, I turn on my heel and head back to the breakroom, stomping the entire way.

The gall of that man!

When I turn to slam the door, he's right there, causing me to jump back and ball my fists at my sides.

"You don't need to follow me everywhere, Asshole Dawson." When I say his new name, I spit it out like rotten food. I know I'm throwing a temper tantrum, but I'm way beyond giving a shit. Hell hath no fury.

Asher steps into me. With him this close I can see the outline of his pectoral muscles; wafts of eucalyptus and sandalwood invade my senses. I have an overwhelming impulse to unwind his hair and run my fingers through his silky strands. His lips are a sultry soft pink that is drawing me closer. He's taller than Rio and Zane, and his height only adds to the Viking persona.

"I think I do, Spencer Gray." My name on his lips sends a jolt of lust straight to my core. My body once again betraying me.

A huff of air leaves my lungs and causes the tips of my breasts to graze his upper abs. The move was supposed to calm my reactive hormones, instead my breathing increases and a heat rises in my cheeks.

He leans in close, leveling his face with mine, lips drawing closer, but not close enough. I lean in ever so slightly anticipating his mouth on mine, but he halts his movement.

"Get used to me being in your space. You're stuck with me for the next few days." Then he pulls away, leaving me feeling hot and cold.

What was I thinking? I'm not a fan of Asher Dawson.

Then why was I desperate for his kiss?

※ ※ ※

AFTER AN HOUR OF VIKING HOTTIE—WHICH Iris had decided on—hovering like a damn helicopter mom, I'm ready to rip my hair out. I should be grateful to Rio and Zane, they asked their overworked friend to protect me even if that friend is an overbearing boulder.

A sexy boulder.

Rocks aren't sexy, dammit. It doesn't matter, I would lick Asher's rock hard abs if he asked.

He's distracting everyone, myself included, and it's frustrating as hell.

Alma was more than happy to welcome Asher. She said that it was time we had some more eye candy in the studio, as if she doesn't get enough from Rio and Zane. Even Paul struck up a conversation with the man. I didn't stick around to listen, but apparently, they made plans to go to a shooting range. I didn't even know Paul was interested in that kind of thing.

The real kick to the gut was when Asher won over Hayes without even trying. Hayes took one look at Asher's tattoos and they were instant bffs.

Traitors. All of them.

Don't get me started on Inner Spencer. I constantly find myself watching him and more than half the time he's watching me back. I don't like how that causes flutters in my stomach and heat rushes to my center. He's annoying and rude.

Noticing he's occupied with Hayes, as they discuss where Hayes should go for his first tattoo, I discreetly slink out the front door and take in deep breaths of fresh air. I know the guys mean well, but I like my space.

The heavenly scent of rich espresso draws me to The Mudhouse. Deciding caffeine is the perfect cure, I peruse the menu at the coffee shop. I do this every time, even though I know I'm going to get my usual: a venti mocha with extra whip cream and oat milk.

As I order my coffee, I feel guilty for sneaking away and decide to order one for Asher. He doesn't seem like a fellow chocoholic, so I go with classic black coffee. He can always get creamer or sugar from the break room if he has a secret sweet tooth. Maybe some good old bean juice will put him in a better mood. Plus, you can't hate the person who brings you coffee, it's the law.

With a to-go cup in each hand, I stroll back to Clay

Creations. When I walk through the door I feel better. I needed that little reset, but that contentment disappears as soon as I spot Asher. To describe him as furious would be an understatement, he looks ready to explode.

Nostrils flaring, he barrels towards me. "Where the fuck did you go?" he barks.

I hold up his cup as if it's obvious. "Coffee." I muster half a smile.

He crosses his arms and stands in front of me with a lethal stillness that seems to come to him naturally. "Did you forget you're not supposed to go anywhere without me?"

Refusing to be intimidated I widen my stance. "I needed to get out of the studio for a second. It's not like I went far. I was right next door. No need to get your panties in a twist."

"If my eyes aren't on you, it's too far. Got it? You do not go anywhere without me."

I cock my head to the side. "Whatever you say, big guy."

"Big guy?"

I gesture to his formidable size. "Do I really need to explain it? You can't be that oblivious," before he can respond I continue, "Look, there's no need for us to argue the point further. Next time I get the urge for a hit of bean fuel, you can tag along."

His only response is to glower. I guess the giant has gone silent. Can't say I'm bothered by it, but his silence is deafening.

Unsure of how to make the situation better, I give him my peace offering. "Here, it's just black." I thrust the white cup forward urging him to take it. Instead, he narrows his gaze at the drink as if it kicked his puppy.

After what feels like an abnormal amount of time, he reluctantly grabs the cup. His fingers brush mine as he takes it from me. When we touch, I let out a small gasp and those flutters make another appearance, but they go into overdrive. I notice his eyes flare with heat. He's just as affected as I am, but neither of us say a word.

Expressionless, he takes his coffee back to his comically short stool. I go back to working on a chunk of clay but steal a glance in Asher's direction out of the corner of my eye. I watch him sip his coffee and his shoulders relax.

One point for Spencer.

CHAPTER 22

ASHER

*R*io and Zane are going to owe me Sal's for a fucking year. I had to sit and watch this vixen in her tight ass pencil skirt and fuck me heels walk back and forth throughout her gallery all day. The fabric of her skirt perfectly hugged her waist and ass, an ass I'd be more than happy to sink my teeth into.

Then she went upstairs and just as I thought I'd get relief from the tightness in my pants, she changed into a pair of leggings. *Fucking leggings!* I was so engrossed with her body that I missed three people approaching the studio because she was bent over with her delectable ass in the air.

I've never been so hard just watching a woman. If I'm not careful, watching her is going to become my favorite pastime. A pastime I can't afford.

She offered me water a couple times, but I refused. Water means needing to relieve myself which means having to take my eyes off of her. I don't know if she has a golden pussy or what, but she has Rio and Zane wrapped around her perfect fingers…fingers I'd like to see wrapped around my cock.

I don't like the distraction she's been today. I need to focus on my case, on Cain. There's no space for anyone else. There's no space for anyone extra, and I can tell she's more than extra. She's a pain in my ass with sass effortlessly that pours out of her mouth. I've imagined, more than once, shutting her up by shoving my dick down her throat.

She can't mouth off when with my cock in her throat.

At one point she disappeared without a word and came back with coffee. One for me and one for her. The brat had snuck out and gone to the coffee shop next door. Rookie mistake on my part, and I hate that she got my order right, black coffee.

Now I'm waiting for her to finish up with Paul so we can go upstairs. I pull out my phone to review my case notes to occupy my time.

Five murdered women. All of them fitting the exact same description: early to mid-twenties, tan skin, brown hair, brown eyes, with Latina background. They were all low-risk victims abducted from various places—one from a restaurant, two from their homes, and two from parking garages.

This guy is all over the place. He's mobile, each woman was killed in a different city.

The only consistency between each woman is how he kills and displays them. He rapes them then strangles them to death. After, he cleans and dresses them in a silk wedding dress and lays them on the ground. They're posed with a purple hyacinth clutched in their cold hands, resting on their chest.

I'm counting myself lucky the media hasn't put it all together yet. If more bodies pile up, it'll be my ass on the line. My supervisor isn't happy that this psycho is still on the loose. Add in bad press and I'll be getting reamed out by my boss at the office, and it'll suck. A lot.

I tuck my phone in my pocket and run my hands through my hair.

A grunt pulls my attention away from my pity party. Spencer is struggling to get a bag of clay down from the top shelf of her stuffed storage closet.

"Let me help you," I say as I step up behind her.

"No need. Go back to your perch, big guy. I got this."

I rub my eyes, warding off a Spencer size headache. "You don't need to be stubborn. I'm here. I'm tall. Let me help."

"No. I don't need you." Each word is difficult for her to get out as she struggles to leverage the heavy block of clay.

Done with watching her battle and fail at what she can't achieve, I reach over her and snag the clay from her hands. She turns in place and rests her hands on her curvy hips

"I had it handled."

"Sure you did," I say, humoring her, but she can read my sarcasm. "Where do you want this?"

She answers with a flat tone, "That table right there is fine."

When I turn back around, Spencer is gathering her things preparing to leave.

"Don't leave without me, Princess." Her nostrils flare at the nickname.

Doesn't she know the more she reacts, the more I'll say it?

"How can I forget you? You take up so much fucking space it's hard to miss you're here."

I raise my eyebrows at her in response.

"I can't with you. It's been a long day," Spencer says as she massages her temples.

She turns to leave and I snatch her elbow, drawing her back to my front. I leave a little space so she can't feel how her closeness affects me.

My jaw clenches. "I meant what I said. Don't leave without me."

169

"It's not like I'm going far."

"There you go with that mouth again."

She throws her arms out to her sides. "You're impossible."

"Maybe."

I pull her back so she's behind me. "I go out doors first to check the area. When we go upstairs—"

"You're not coming upstairs with me."

"Don't argue. You're not going to win."

She rolls her eyes and I think about bending her over my knee to teach her a lesson.

"Keep pushing and see what happens." Her eyes widen at my threat.

Turning away from her, I open the glass door and scan the street. I clock a couple of guys in hoodies and sweats two hundred yards away, huddled together. With the way their heads are bent together glancing up and down the street, I'm betting drug deal.

I also note a few women dressed like they are heading to the club, walking the direction away from us. Gender doesn't matter, age doesn't even matter. Evil is evil and evil wears many faces.

Deeming the street temporarily clear, I reach back for Spencer and lead her up to her apartment. On her doorstep is a large box that reads "Flor's Arrangements."

"Seems like you got an admirer."

"If you say so." Spencer shoulders past me to open the door.

I grab the box for her and haul it inside. It's lighter than I thought it would be.

When I set the box down on the counter, Spencer is already walking back out of her bedroom in a baggy shirt and a sad excuse for shorts with how tiny they are. My gaze zeroes in on her exposed legs.

Talk about legs for days.

I clear my throat. "You going to open it?"

"I guess?" She shrugs a shoulder and grabs a black kitchen knife. She twirls it in her hand and approaches the box.

I never thought seeing a sexy woman wield a knife would be what gets me hard, but here we are and I'm not ashamed in the slightest.

"Know your way around knives?"

"What? Oh. Not really. Just a little skill I picked up visiting my Abuela one summer."

"Grandma liked to entertain herself with knives?"

My comment causes a laugh to break free from her mouth and just like that, I'm entranced.

I can't go down this path. I've already been wrapped up in her orbit all day and she hasn't given me more than a few sentences here and there. Rio and Z are already skirting the line of obsession. One of us needs to keep their head on straight.

"No," she chuckles again. "Just some boy I met that summer."

Boy? You've got to be fucking kidding me. No boy needs to be showing her any *skills*.

Spencer gracefully slices the brown tape concealing the gift inside. As she reaches down with her delicate hands to remove the flowers, she jumps back and drops the vase. The clear glass shatters into a million tiny pieces across her pristine white tile.

I rush to her side and shove her behind me, alert and ready to take on the threat.

When I look down at the broken glass, I'm stunned into silence.

Purple hyacinths are spread amongst the spilled water and splintered vase.

CHAPTER 23

ZANE

I am done with today. Fuck these trafficking assholes. Fuck Cain. I can't prove it's him as of right now. I can't even officially prove he exists. All I have on record are whispers of his name and Hank's account of Cain's tattoo.

How are we supposed to nail this guy when we can't even get a description? Let alone someone who has seen him and lived to tell about it. Cain isn't the fucking boogeyman. He can't be who people dread will appear in their nightmares. Cain should be dreaming of us slicing his throat. He has to know we're coming for him.

"Quite the day, partner." Liam comments as we finish up paperwork.

"If you say so." I'm being an ass, but Liam needs to get used to it. I need to get back to my touchstone. My Angel. She calms me in a way no one else has or does. Rio lights me on fire, but Spencer soothes the crawling beneath my skin, the buzzing in my ears.

When I get frustrated like this, very few things calm me.

One in particular, hunting those who shouldn't be

breathing anymore, watching their blood drain from their lifeless bodies. Unfortunately, that's not an option right now. I have no leads, so I need to make my way back to her. Just a glimpse is enough.

For now at least.

My phone begins to buzz in my pocket. I answer as soon as I see Asher's name on the screen. He's kept us updated throughout the day, but his updates are one word answers. Rio asked for pictures, and Asher refused, said it'd make him feel like a creep. Too bad Rio and I are already there.

"What's up, Ash?"

"Get here now." I push to my feet and grab my keys. Heading toward the door I leave without saying goodbye to Liam. The ringing in my ears was already at an annoyance, now it's out of control.

"What happened?"

"Just get here." Ash ends the calls abruptly.

I wanted to ask more questions, asshole.

If there's even a scratch on her, a single hair out of place, I will bathe the streets with blood. No one touches Spencer.

Speeding through the streets without a care isn't smart, but I'll do whatever it takes to get to her. She could tell me to jump and I really would answer with "how high?"

Rio says we're obsessed, but obsessed doesn't accurately describe how I feel. I'd consume her. I want her every thought, her every breath. They're mine. She's mine. I don't care what I have to do to make her see it.

⚜ ⚜ ⚜

W*HEN* I *ARRIVE*, I double park and don't give a shit. I normally don't use the "I'm a cop" excuse, but now seems like the perfect time to use my privilege.

I take the stairs two at a time and don't bother knocking. Asher is there at the front sitting on a stool with his Glock in hand.

"What the hell happened?" I scan the room and notice the box and a jumble of flowers on the counter. Spencer is on the couch staring out the window. She's upright in the fetal position. The fear in her eyes makes me pause. I'm choking on the anxiety radiating from her. Her terror causes a fracture across my cold heart.

Ash gestures to the counter behind him. "It's the flowers. I have to call it in."

"What are you talking about?" The tension in my voice fills the space between us.

"When we came up here, there was a box in front of the door. After we got inside, she opened it and dropped the flowers. They're purple hyacinths, Z."

I know there's a significance here, but I can't remember why. Ash must read the confusion on my face because he answers my question before I can ask it.

"The killer I've been hunting. He leaves a purple hyacinth with the bodies."

"Okay I see your concern, but like you said. *Hyacinth*. Singular. There's a whole bouquet of them here. Serials don't stray so far from their MO."

"This guy is a preferential killer, and Spencer fits his victim profile. Brunette, low-risk, lives alone, mid twenties," Ash whispers not wanting Spencer to overhear.

"You just described a good portion of the women in Manhattan," I retort.

Ash crosses his arms and leans back in his seat. "I'm not

wrong about this. My gut is screaming at me, she's next on this fucker's list."

Ash is notorious for being stubborn. When he was still a beat cop he camped outside of a suspect's house even when he wasn't on the clock to prove the guy was guilty. The guy was accused of raping eleven boys. He'd drug them on their walk home from school and bring them back to his house where he'd spend all night with them in his basement and then drop them off on a random curb the next day; the boys were all too drugged to remember much. Ash was right, he had the right guy. Trusting his gut is what moved him up the ranks so fast in law enforcement. He went from cop to detective to the FBI academy in the span of five years.

He's been wrong only a few times, but Rio and I don't like to remind him. I'm betting this is one of those times.

"Has she said anything?" I know I'm not going to change his mind so I might as well let it play out.

"She's mumbled some things here and there, but I can't make out what she's saying."

Right then Rio obnoxiously bursts in. "I brought pizza!"

I cut him a glare and approach Spencer cautiously. Ash fills Rio in, and I tune them out. My Angel deserves all of me—needs all of me—so she'll get all of me.

"Spencer? Are you okay?" She doesn't respond to my voice. Another fracture. I sweep my finger over her arm and she flinches away from me. That's the last time I'll allow that to happen. I'll do anything to take away her pain.

"Spencer, look at me." Her eyes grip me in a vice, and I can't breathe. The trepidation pouring from her soul drowns me. She should never have to experience this kind of debilitating fear.

Not my Angel. Never her.

"You shouldn't be here," her voice is hollow. "None of you should be here. You have to go."

"What are you talking about?" Rio asks from behind me. He and Ash join us on the couch.

Spencer jumps to her feet. "You can't be here! He's going to find you! He can't find you!" She's close to being lost in her hysteria.

"Of course we're going to be here. We'll be here for you every time." My voice is gentle.

"You can't make promises like that. You don't know," she whimpers and tears begin to roll down her soft cheeks.

Unable to bear anymore of her pain, I clasp her hands in mine, willing her agony to flow into me. "I promise you, Angel. I swear it. We will always be here for you, and we will always come for you."

Her face is ashen as she whispers, "I can't let him find you."

"Who?" Rio urges.

"My fiancé."

Her *what*?

CHAPTER 24

SPENCER

"You're engaged?" Asher asks in indignation.

Asher is just trying to protect his friends, but his tone still stings. It reminds me I can't let the guys get too close. They're already breaking down my walls without even trying. And now there's Asher. It's too much.

In shame, I pull my hands away from Zane's comforting touch, but he won't let go.

"Technically, no, but it's likely that Anthony didn't take our break up well."

"You need to fill us in, Mama. You're not making any sense." Rio takes a seat next to me. Right next to me. There's zero space between his hip and mine.

"Please don't make me talk about it. I can't."

"It's time for that interview, Angel."

My heart leaps. "Please, Zane. Please don't make me."

"We should wait until the FBI gets here," Asher interjects.

"You called them?" Zane bites at him.

"I told you I thought it was the same guy," Asher says

without remorse as if inviting more people into my safe space was okay.

It was *your safe space. Was.*

For once I agree with my inner annoying self. I need to go. As much as it'll kill me, I have to go.

I have letters already written for Hayes, Iris, Alma, and Paul. I can leave them on the Abstract Creations front desk for Iris to find. It's best if it's her. She'll be able to break the news to everyone for me.

This dose of guilt is nothing to the mass amount that would suffocate me if anything were to happen to them because of me.

"She's not going to be interviewed by a ton of strangers. Not happening. We'll do this now," Zane argues.

"We need—" Asher begins to protest.

"Get her some water, asshole." Zane demands Asher.

When Asher returns with a glass of water, I take a generous sip and set it on my coffee table. I didn't realize how parched I was until now.

"You can do this another time, Spencer. No need to push yourself," Rio whispers in my ear.

"This is going to be difficult, but I wouldn't ask if it wasn't necessary," Asher interjects.

"I know. I can do it," I insist.

"Tell us what happened."

I take a deep breath and prepare to disconnect. Rio senses my mood shift because he wraps an arm around me and gives me a light squeeze.

"Let's try this," Asher says. "Close your eyes and walk us through it. Imagine yourself back there."

"I guess I can do that," I agree shakily.

My eyes close and my head leans against Rio's shoulder.

"From what I gathered from Rio and Z, you were just

getting home from the bar," Asher says but his voice is softer. A tone he has never used with me.

I try to focus on that night and not the sexy voice speaking to me.

"Yes. I was dropped off by a cab. He sped away quickly. I was tired and had a lot on my mind, so I wasn't paying attention to anything around me."

"What time was it?"

"A little after eleven p.m. I think?"

"What did you do after you exited the cab?"

"I was digging through my purse for my keys and walking to the door."

The scene plays out in my mind. I wish I could be a bird in the sky and watch it unfold from above, completely detached from the moment. I wish I was able to warn my past self that he was going to sneak up behind me, but that's not how this goes. The horror movie in my head continues, and I give Asher as much detail as I can.

"I like to have my keys in hand before I get to my front door, but my brain was all fuddled."

"That's very smart, Spencer," Zane says proudly.

"The streetlamps are on, but the one closest to me is out. I'm about to grab the door handle, that's when he grabs me."

His arms constrict around my upper body, and I hyperventilate.

Not again. Please not again.

Rio gives my arm another squeeze. "You're okay. You're here with us. You're safe, Mama."

My breaths slow, but are still too fast to be considered calm.

"He pulls me to the street. I was shocked at first but he didn't cover my mouth, so I scream. But no one is coming." My voice cracks on the last few words and I can feel tears stream down my face.

"I try to catch him off balance, but he's too big. I try throwing my weight around, and scratch at his hands, he's not wearing gloves, but that only makes him angry. He swings my body to the side and hits my head against a parked car. My vision blurs, but I fight to stay awake. Then he whispers something in my ear. I don't remember exactly what, but he called me 'flower.' He...Anthony is the *only* one who has ever called me that..."

"What does he do next?" Asher asks.

"He carries me backwards again. I don't stop trying to get away and he gets angry. He stands me on my feet and slaps me so hard I fall to the ground," I allow a deep breath and continue forward. "I pretend to pass out, and when he tries to pick me up I kick him between the legs and knee his face."

"Then what?"

"He calls me a bitch and I run. I look back to see if he's following me, but he's not. His hands are covering his face."

"Do you see anything else in the street?"

The vision in my mind turns hazy. I don't want to be there anymore. I have to get away. My breathing picks up again and my heart kicks into high gear. "I need to leave. I can't stay here. He'll get me again."

"You're safe. You're always safe with us. Please tell us what you see." I'm not sure who gives the reassurance.

"I see...I see a silver sedan. New Jersey license plate...D5."

"That's enough," Zane snaps. His voice is angrier than before. "We got more than needed. She's done."

"One more question," Rio edges in. "Is that who texted you the day we met?"

I gulp, but it does nothing to abate my shame. "Yes."

"How long have the texts been going on?"

"Years." I can't give more than one word answers.

"Did you ever tell anyone?"

"Yes."

"Mama. I need more. You're not in trouble here."

Another deep breath. "I told the police. I've filed multiple reports, but I was always told there was nothing they could do because the texts never contained 'real' threats."

"What do you mean?" Rio sneers.

"The police I talked to said Anthony never threatened to kill me so they couldn't do more than file a report."

"*Pendejos!*" Rio turns to Zane. "I'll pull the case files and check it out."

"Who were the officers you talked to?" Zane asks.

"Officers Dustin Cox and Troy Dick."

Zane tilts his head. "You don't need to double check that?"

"No. I'll never forget them. They told me to let it go and not to worry about Anthony," a shiver runs down my spine. "They said the texts weren't a priority."

"They said that?" The veins in Zane's neck strain. "I'll talk to them. I know them. Annoying fucks."

The way he says "talk" sounds like there may not be much talking. This version of Zane is kind of terrifying, but that doesn't stop me from leaning towards him and cupping his face.

"It's okay, Zane. I'll be okay." I flip a switch and project a calm demeanor. They can't suspect anything is amiss. I can't let them know my plans. If they know then they'll stop me.

"It's not okay, Spencer, but it will be," he reaches for my glass and hands it to me. "Here. Drink your water."

But, of course, I don't grab the cup right. My hands are still shaking, and it slips from my grasp.

"Oh my God! I'm so sorry!" I jump up to grab napkins or anything to stop the water, but all three men are frozen and staring at me.

What the hell? It's just some water.

That's when I notice their eyes aren't on my face. They're a little lower.

Oh for fuck's sake.

I look down and yep. My white T-shirt is now see through, and you can clearly see my hunter green lacy bra. Fuck laundry day for making me pair a dark bra and a white top in the first place.

I hurry to cover up by crossing my arms and can feel the heat in my face as I burn with embarrassment.

Covering up gets them all to spring into action. Rio rips off his jacket and throws it over my shoulders while Zane jumps up from the ground and rushes to the kitchen grabbing some napkins, but Asher still stares gobsmacked.

Rio guides me back onto the couch with his arm around me and I refuse to make eye contact. I can answer any other questions they have staring at my lap. It'll be awkward, but there's no way in hell I'll ever be able to look these men in the face ever again. They're all about to get well acquainted with the top of my head.

"Spencer," Rio says, trying to get my attention.

"Mama," Rio tries again. This time he uses his other hand to lift my chin forcing me to look at him. The action makes my insides melt and my panties dampen.

There's humor in his eyes. I can tell he's trying not to laugh, but there's also something else. Desire?

He smiles at me and I do my best not to smile back, but it's difficult. His smile is contagious just like his laugh. When I'm finally smiling back, he says to the room, "Now can we finish this without anyone trying to look at my client's bra?"

"Client?" My voice is high-pitched with surprise.

"You're officially mine, Mama."

"Your client, you mean."

"Sure," he says with a wink.

CHAPTER 25

ASHER

After Berkowitz and Kowalski leave Spencer's, the palpable tension dissipates. Rio ushered Spencer to her room to change as soon as they arrived. Kowalski bagged and tagged the evidence while Berkowitz took the photos.

Z tried to get Spencer to eat the pizza Rio brought from Sal's, but she refused, which goes against one of the basic commandments. Thou shalt not refuse Sal's pies. Rio had no problem demolishing a pie on his own though.

Rio and Z helped dispose of the rest of the mess from those fucking flowers. I cleaned up the broken glass and spilled water earlier. Spencer didn't need to deal with that. I've never cleaned up for a victim, but she shouldn't have to. She wouldn't tell us about her time with Anthony, but it's clear it wasn't good.

Spencer thinks the flowers are from her ex-fiancé. Zane and Rio don't know what to make of it all, yet. I think they're still focused on keeping Spencer safe.

As for me? I know it's him. The fucker I've tracked from coast to coast. He's kept me on my toes, and I refuse to give him a fucking name. Assholes like him don't deserve anything other than a bullet between the eyes.

If the media gets hold of this, they'll give him the attention he seeks. The praise. It makes me sick to my stomach just thinking about it.

"Thank you, guys, for everything. I think I'm going to head to bed so—" Spencer starts.

"Are you kicking us out, Mama?" Rio asks with a head tilt.

"Umm. Well. I need sleep and I'm sure you do too. I have work tomorrow and I still want to run in the morning. So in a way, I guess I am, but it's not because I'm not appreciative of what you did for me tonight. I'm beyond grateful. Really. Thank you. I don't know what I would've done if you hadn't been here. Y'all were amazing. Not that you're not usually amazing every day," she takes a moment to close her eyes and breathe. I didn't know the Princess could get so nervous. "That's not how I meant it."

Rio and Zane are holding in their laughter. No wonder they're smitten little kittens. Spencer is adorable as fuck. Add in her curves, independence, and strength, I'd be just as haunted by her. But I'm not, so it's not an issue.

"Hey, I know you can't keep your hands off me, so if me leaving helps you get some sleep, fine by me," Rio jests and Zane just nods his head.

It's lighthearted, but something is off. They're giving in too easily. If this were my woman, nothing could make me walk out her door tonight, but she's not mine so it doesn't matter.

Her jasmine perfume still invades my senses, but I can ignore it. I can ignore the instinctual pull. The need to wrap her in my arms, kiss her, and make her scream until she forgets every name but one.

Mine.

"Come on. Leave the woman be. She says she wants us

gone, we're gone." I grab both of the clowns by the back of their shirts and haul them out like a sack of potatoes. Again, they don't put up much fight.

"Asher, wait," Spencer calls. I shove the two idiots to move down the stairs and turn in her doorway. "Thank you. For being here. I know you don't like being my bodyguard but thank you. I don't know how I would have handled it earlier on my own."

I nod my head. "Anytime, Princess."

Exhaustion sweeps over her, but a small smile still tugs at her lips. "Stop calling me that."

"As you wish, Princess." I can't help the grin that beams her way.

She playfully swats my chest and chuckles. I'd do anything to hear that sound, but I don't have time to lose my head. Whatever is stirring in this pot of uncertainty has to go.

Without any more words, I shut down my inclinations that are screaming at me, and leave behind the siren who calls to my baser self. I can't let those propensities take over now. Not when her life, and very likely the lives of the two people who mean the most to me, are in danger.

※ ※ ※

IT'S BEEN over an hour and a half and the guys still aren't home. I was too tired to cook and Rio ate all the damn pizza, so I stopped at Sal's for food. I've been hanging out in the living room watching trash TV to numb my brain, expecting Z and Rio to show up any minute, but they don't.

Me: Where the fuck are you two?

> Z:....

> Rio: Don't wait up, Wolf baby.

Wolf baby? He needs to cut that shit out.

> Me: Seriously. Stop calling me that.

> Rio: If you insist...puppy.

> Z: We're just out. We'll be back sometime later.

> Me: Where are you?

> Z: Don't worry about it.

> Me: Tell me you're not at Spencer's apartment.

> Z:....

> Rio: We're not at Spencer's apartment.

> Me: Now tell me the truth.

> Rio: We're at Spencer's apartment.

Motherfuckers. With a big sigh I heave myself off the couch, and ignore the snaps and cracks of my joints.

I've already dressed down into shorts and a T-shirt so all I have to do is slide on some shoes and I'm out the door.

They better have a damn good reason for this.

CHAPTER 26

ASHER

When I park my Camaro next to Zane's travel-size car, they don't even notice me. Idiots. They're usually more aware.

I walk over to the passenger window and bang on it, surprising them both. Zane looks chastised without me saying a word. Rio looks ready to kill me for interrupting their Peeping Tom session.

Rio rolls down his window and greets me with, "Get in, *hijo de puta.*"

"I'm not cramming myself into the clown car. Let's go home."

"No can do, Wolf."

"Fine," I huff out. Opening the back door I shove myself in the pint-size backseat. "Okay, I'm fucking here. Let's talk—" I'm cut off when Rio bursts out laughing. Zane's laugh isn't audible, but I know he's laughing by the way his shoulders are shaking.

"Got enough room back there?" Rio asks through his sniggering.

"Ha. Ha," I deadpan. "Focus, shitheads. We need to get on the same page." They don't need me to clarify.

They sober their expressions, and Zane says, "I want to believe it's Cain and his men, but I don't think this one is them."

"Same. The fact that it was one guy instead of two or three and the car was completely different," Rio explains.

"She's convinced it's her ex, but I'm not so sure," I add.

"I'll dig into him real quick and see what I can find." Before Zane is even finished with his sentence, he has his laptop out and is pounding away on the keys.

"The guy was strong enough to lift her off her feet and carry her almost the whole way to his car. So he's fit," Rio mutters.

"He had no problem hitting her. He cares enough that he wants her, but doesn't care enough what state she's in when he has her. I would venture to assume he intended on hurting her," I say. Rio nods his head as I continue. "If Anthony wants her back and is in love with her, then he would want her safe and unharmed."

"You're assuming he's a good guy. The way she shivers and panics at the mere thought of him tells me he wasn't much of a gentleman. He probably hurt her," Zane grits out, a vein in his forehead pulses more and more with each inference.

"But he had confidence. There was no hesitation. I think he's done this before," I argue.

"Maybe. Or are you using this situation to fit your narrative?" Rio tosses back.

I clench my jaw. "I'm not. I'm analyzing the facts. She fits the killer's preferred victim profile, her attacker has done this before, and he sent her purple hyacinths."

"We don't know for sure who the flowers came from," Zane says and stops typing. "I got him. Anthony Cole. Age thirty-four, six foot two, hundred seventy-four pounds, born in Austin, Texas. His parents were old money. They died right after his eighteenth birthday, and he inherited everything. After that, he attended UT and graduated with a degree in accounting, and later a masters in finance and data analytics. He finished all his schooling by age twenty-four."

"So he's smart. Good for him," I spit sarcastically.

"He currently resides in Katy, Texas. Looks like he bought that home eight years ago and he has a summer home in LA," a few more keystrokes. "He's big. Not huge. Could be strong enough to carry Spencer." Zane turns his screen so Rio and I can see him.

"He's an okay looking guy I guess. I'm hotter though," Rio criticizes.

"This isn't a dick measuring contest," I bark. I scrutinize the photo and commit it to memory. "He's good looking and he's probably charismatic. He has to be to have landed someone like Spencer."

"You got something else you want to share with the class?" Rio asks with a raised brow.

"No."

"Do you find the sexy artist hot?" Rio pushes.

"That's not what I said." I bare my teeth at him.

"You're not denying it either," Zane chimes in.

Changing the subject I say, "We've been here long enough. Let's go."

Instead of agreeing, they exit the car. Rio stretches his arms above his head. "No thanks. Time for some B&E."

I somehow get out of the backseat and a deep furrow forms between my brows. Rio smirks, and the fucking lightbulb goes off in my head. "Please tell me you haven't been breaking into her apartment every night," I say, pinching the bridge of my nose.

I will never admit it out loud, but I'd be doing the same thing for the woman if I was just as infatuated. I've never had a serious girlfriend, only fuck buddies and I use that term loosely.

"We haven't been breaking into her apartment every night."

I'm done with their fucking antics. "Z?"

Rio cuts Zane off before he can start. "Who do you think I caught with the creeper peepers in the first place?"

I level a glare at Zane, but he looks unrelenting with his arms folded and his own glare speared my way.

"She has nightmares, Ash," Zane explains as if that's a good enough reason to be camped outside his little crush's home.

"Whoop dee doo. Who doesn't? That doesn't make her special."

Zane's scowl turns lethal. "Fuck you, man. If you don't like it then go home. Call the cops. I don't give a fuck, but you're not stopping me from going up there and comforting her when the screaming starts."

I refuse to let the shock of the moment show on my face. Zane never willingly touches anyone. We've hugged maybe five times since I've known him. The only exception to his rule is Rio. They've been that way since I met them, but no one else.

"Fuck, fine. I'm in."

"You weren't invited, *gruñón*."

"I'm still coming."

"Good luck fitting in her bed," Rio says with a wink.

Her bed? Fuck. I'd probably do that too.

After Zane gets Spencer's door open, they both stop in their tracks in front of me.

"Seriously?" I whisper-shout.

"Shhhhh," they both return.

I'm only a few inches taller than them, so I go up on my toes to see what has them stuck.

Spencer is on the couch, sitting up, but passed out. She keeps jerking and nodding as if she's still not fully asleep.

"Let's just go," I order, but they ignore me and stalk towards her. I sigh and follow suit.

"How many pills did you give her?" Rio whispers.

"Enough. She should be knocked out cold," Zane answers.

"You idiots did *what*?" My eyes almost pop out of my head. I'm surprised but at the same time, I'm not.

"Don't judge us. You would have done the same," Rio retorts.

Yet another thing I won't admit to.

My brows try to disappear in my hairline when I notice the handgun on the cushion next to Spencer.

Where the hell did she get that?

Zane and Rio act unaffected by the Glock and move it to the coffee table. Zane sits to her right while Rio gets comfortable on her left. They work in tandem laying her down on Zane's lap and situating her feet in Rio's. Zane strokes her hair with care and Rio massages her lean legs. Eventually, the tension in Spencer's body fades away and she falls into a deeper sleep.

I reach for the gun and notice the serial number is filed off. The little Princess and I are going to have a talk about that later.

Lightly dropping myself on the other side of Zane, I lean back into the couch, and settle in for the night. My eyes close and I'm ready to slip off into a light sleep. When you have a job like mine, you can fall asleep just about anywhere and Spencer's couch feels like a fucking cloud.

After a few minutes of peace, Spencer whimpers. I pop one eye open and see the strain in her face. Her eyebrows are pinched and her mouth in a frown. Seeing her like this is unsettling. She's already working her way under my skin. I don't need to see her vulnerable like this.

A small cry falls from her lips and before I know it, I'm kneeling at her side with her hand clasped in mine. I rub circles on the back with my thumb hoping it'll ease her.

"No. Don't touch me. Get off me!" She begins to thrash and sob harder. Zane continues stroking her hair and Rio does his best to dodge a foot to the face.

"It's okay, Princess," I gently whisper in her ear. "We're here. You're safe. No one will get to you with us around."

Her breathing is as erratic as her heartbeat, but she stops fighting. Z eyes me skeptically while Rio smiles wide.

"Not a fucking word," I threaten them both. Zane huffs like a fucking dog while Rio mimes zipping his lips and throwing away the key even though he doesn't actually keep his damn mouth shut.

"Welcome to the Spencer Gray fan club. We meet every night outside, and end up here tucked in with her sexy body."

"Dude. Stop," I interrupt, but he just keeps on going as if I haven't spoken at all.

"Our meetings end at four thirty a.m. before she wakes up. Oh and it's BYOB."

"BYOB? Bring your own beer? Where's the beer?"

"Bring your own binoculars," he answers with a smirk.

"I can't believe I'm complicit in this bullshit." Little do they know—and I'll forever deny it—I probably would have found myself here in a week or so. There's no way in hell I'm leaving her alone while there's a serial killer out there. He's already made one attempt and I doubt he'll stop there.

We fall into a comfortable silence. Each of us staring down at the woman who's captivated us all, but I can't allow her to detract me from what's important; catching a killer, stopping the skin trade in New York, and keeping my family safe.

CHAPTER 27

SPENCER

Staying isn't an option anymore. Especially after the attack then the flowers. Anthony found me. If he gets ahold of me again, I know he'll lock me up and throw away the key. I'd rather die before I go back with him.

My bag is packed with the cash and clothes, the letters for Iris rest on top. I've added three more letters to the pile. They're going to be upset when I'm gone, but hopefully by leaving a piece of me in these letters, my guys won't hurt as badly. It tore me up inside to have to write them, but I can't leave without saying some kind of goodbye.

I grab Abuela from below the TV and add her to my duffle. I couldn't leave her in Texas and I can't leave her here either.

With my bag hidden in my room, I crawl to the couch, and prop myself up facing the door. My handgun rests next to me. I took some classes at a shooting range and while that doesn't make me an expert marksman, I know the basics of how to use it.

My phone buzzes with an incoming text and I'm reluctant to look at it, but I have to know.

Unknown: Don't you dare run from me again, Flower. See you soon.

I open my laptop and search for bus tickets. There's one leaving Port Authority tomorrow afternoon and arriving in LA two days after that. Quickly purchasing the ticket before I chicken out, I set my laptop on the coffee table.

My head falls against the back of the couch and eventually I drift to sleep. When I wake in the morning, I'm on my side and there's dried drool on my cheek. How I fell into such a deep sleep is a mystery, but beggars can't be choosers.

With a yawn, I force myself from the couch. I suspect I'll find Rio and Zane downstairs again, so I need to cover up the prominent dark circles under my eyes, but when I look in the mirror I notice the circles are gone and set the makeup aside.

After applying concealer and dressing in leggings and a cropped tank, I head downstairs ready for my run. The sight before me pulls me up short. Not only are Rio and Zane here, but so is Asher. All three looking seductively disheveled in their workout gear. I wonder if they slept out here again?

My gaze connects with Asher's and I'm trapped, locked in his orbit. I never know where I stand with him. One minute he's teasing me, purposely pushing my buttons, and the next he's giving me the cold shoulder. But now? His beautiful ocean blues roam up and down my body repeatedly, and I sense his hunger, a craving for my flesh.

Rio's eyes trail over my plain frame, but he looks at me as if I'm a cover model for a fashion magazine. He makes me feel beautiful. Desired. He catalogs every aspect of my body with his gaze. He always sees more than I want him to. Keeping my plans a secret from him is going to be especially difficult.

Zane's assessment makes me feel cared for and treasured. Protected. His eyes linger on my hips. My leggings are like a second skin and have always been my go-to choice for pants, but under Zane's inspection, I feel bare and exposed.

"Seriously guys?" I ask, masking my guilt.

Zane just shrugs unbothered, and Asher rolls his eyes as if he wasn't on board with the car sleeping plan. Rio ignores my question and asks one of his own, "Care for some company?"

"Are we starting a running club or something?"

"Apparently," Asher mumbles, barely loud enough to hear.

"You don't have to come, big guy. Wouldn't want to injure your old bones," I snap at Asher.

"Not a chance, Princess. Like I said before, you're not getting rid of me that easily."

Was it really only yesterday I met this brute of a man?

A sexy brute, but a brute, nonetheless.

I ignore all three of them and do my usual stretches so I don't have a muscle spasm on my run. I don't need to add "go to the ER again" to my to-do list.

When I'm done, I refuse to acknowledge their presence. Even though normal is a thing of the past, I can still pretend. *All Around Me* by Flyleaf blasts in my headphones, but I can't focus on anything except how fucking awkward this all feels. It's like I'm being escorted by the Secret Service. All that's missing are the black sunglasses and the earpieces.

Before I know it, I realize I'm running towards Joey's and decide I might as well keep going. He's not going to be happy to see me, but tough luck. He deserves a goodbye too.

We finally arrive and Rio walks right on in then lays on the ground in the entryway. Zane enters and leans against the wall laughing at Rio's dramatics. Asher is hardly out of breath. Chuckling, he steps over Rio and says, "Pussy."

I whip around, hold up my finger, and scold him. "Take it back."

"What? No."

"Yes. Take it back," I insist firmly.

"No. He's acting like a wuss."

"Your logic is flawed. A pussy is not a wuss. A pussy can take a fucking beating. A set of balls cannot." I end my argument by glancing at the lower half of his body and forming a fist. He immediately takes a step back and covers my target with his hands.

"No need to test your theory. It's fact, but I'm not taking it back."

If looks could kill he'd be dead ten times over from my glare. "Fuck you, big guy."

He just rolls his eyes at me as if I'm a cranky hormonal woman about to start her period. Yeah, definitely fuck him even if he looks sexy as hell with a light sheen of sweat covering his body.

"What the hell are you doing here?"

I whirl around and see Joey in his usual spot. I approach him with guarded steps as if I'm being reprimanded by a parent, but I pray my voice and body language seem normal and at ease. "I know you missed me."

"I told you not to come back for a week," Joey states unrelenting.

Once I'm at the desk, I lean towards him and lower my voice. "I came to say goodbye."

Joey keeps his expression schooled, proving he picks up on more than most. "Call me when you get where you're going, kid," then louder so the men behind me can hear, he asks, "You good to train today?"

"Yep. Doc signed off on it and everything." I give him a grateful smile.

"You're a shit liar," he leans to the side and eyes the guys. "You killed two of them and brought an extra."

Loud enough for Asher to hear I say, "That's Asher. He's not one for pleasantries. He's a caveman and only communicates with grunts and hand gestures."

"Whatever he is, he still has to pay. You know I don't give discounts for recruitment, right?"

"Ha. Ha. Very funny old man."

"By the way, you look like shit." The corner of his mouth twitches. My heart warms because again, Joey knows what I need.

"And you look like a shriveled up dick."

CHAPTER 28

SPENCER

*A*sher did indeed sign up for a gym membership which is inconvenient, but at least Joey is getting more business. That's probably the only upside of being attacked.

Maybe not the only upside.

Inner Spencer is in full sass mode today.

Okay, fine. I admit that maybe there are other positive things. Specifically three things. Or three persons who will remain forever nameless, but nothing can come of it. I'm leaving. I have my plan drawn out. I just hope I don't fuck up the execution.

With our workouts complete, we make a pitstop at the Starry Night Smoothies. Surprisingly, Asher ordered a green smoothie. Unsurprisingly, Rio ordered a peanut butter chocolate smoothie. Zane got the same as I did, a fruit smoothie, to which Rio called Zane a suck up while pretending to cough. I smacked his back while sipping his smoothie causing him to actually cough from choking.

My phone rings when I'm halfway done with my fruit-filled

deliciousness. As I tap the answer button, I lower my voice and prepare myself for the conversation.

"Mom, is everything okay?"

Her concern pours from her tone. "It's been so long since I've heard from you. I was worried. Are you okay?"

"It's only been a couple weeks." I sigh.

"I'm your mother, I'm allowed to worry," she raises her voice as she continues and I wince. "You left three years ago without giving me an explanation as to why, and now all I get are these short phone calls."

"I know, Mom. I'm sorry." I deflate.

"Tell me where you are, so I can come be with you."

My chin quivers. "You know I can't do that."

"I deserve to know!"

My head shakes back and forth and my eyes blink rapidly. She's never gotten aggressive like that before.

I slump in my seat and rub my forehead. "I'm so sorry."

A hand grabs my phone and ends the call while Mom's voice still blares through the phone. My jaw drops in Rio's direction and his head turns to Asher and Zane. Zane's lips are pressed flat, Asher's jaw is set tight, and Rio's arms are crossed.

"What the hell guys?"

"Yeah, what the hell, Spence? Does she always talk to you like that?" Rio's gaze narrows.

"She's just concerned." Each of their expressions prove they don't believe my answer.

"She seemed pretty adamant to know where you are," Zane says.

"Any mother would do the same," I argue.

They each give me a speculative glance and drop the topic. We finish our smoothies in silence and jog back to my apartment. Once there, Rio and Zane each kiss my cheek and leave for work, and Asher sticks around.

I'm in my shower while Asher relaxes in my living room. The only barrier between us while I'm naked, covered in soap, is a simple door. The knowledge is unnerving yet intoxicating. I shouldn't be thinking about him while I'm in here. Not like that, but I can't help it. Watching him at the gym has awoken a carnal woman inside, and she isn't going to sleep any time soon.

My thighs clench together, and I feel a flush taking over my body that has nothing to do with the hot water raining down on me. My skin begins to itch and my pussy aches.

"Fuck it." My hand glides down my wet body. My finger rubs teasing circles around my clit, wishing it was a different hand bringing me pleasure.

Asher looks like a man who knows how to make me scream. He would play my body like a fiddle and whisper filthy words in my ear, setting my skin on fire.

"Work that greedy pussy on my fingers, Princess," he'd say.

I would lean against the wall for support and open my legs for him while he guides his knee between my thighs. His massive fingers would be too big to fit, but he'd work them in.

My finger flicks over my sensitive bud causing a whimper to slip free. I bite my lip to prevent any more sounds escaping, but it's not enough. My other hand cups my heavy breast, and I swipe my thumb over my pebbled nipple still wishing it was a large calloused hand instead.

Slipping my fingers inside my pussy I gasp and swipe my thumb back and forth over that little bundle of nerves.

"Come for me, baby. Squeeze the life out of my fingers like you would my cock." He would growl at me.

Imaginary Asher is too much to handle. When I pinch my nipple and give a little twist, I detonate. I open my mouth with his name on my lips and sink down to my knees as I draw out my orgasm.

"Asher."

My fingers don't stop until I've come back down to Earth.

A creek outside the bathroom door makes me freeze, fingers still buried inside my core and hand still cupping my boob.

There's a light knock. "Everything okay in there?"

"Yep!" I shout.

"I thought I heard noises."

Shit. Was I really that loud?

No. There's no way. Wait. Was he listening?

"Nope! All good here!" I reply hoping he'll drop it and never ask again. Instead of acknowledging me, he stomps away.

With a towel wrapped around my body, I look in the mirror and notice the pink that has taken over my cheeks. An orgasm does the body and mind good, but this orgasm has only made me hungry for a touch that's not my own. A touch I have no right wanting.

CHAPTER 29

ASHER

Spencer is a screamer.

My pacing across the hardwood floor was interrupted when I heard a cry. Not that I would have burst into the bathroom, but I figured I should stand by the door in case she needed me. The last thing I expected to hear was Spencer shouting my name in ecstasy.

Her little moans and whimpers seeped through the door, and my dick was instantly hard. No matter how much will power I possess, I was unable to make my feet carry me away. My hand wandered to my stiff cock and gave it a squeeze.

I have no business lusting after this woman. The energy and time required is not there. Not to mention I'm eleven years her senior and she has no idea.

My voice finally decided to work and I shouted through the door. If I have to suffer with a fucking woody then she can live through the day in embarrassment. I know she knows I heard her, and man, does Princess blush easily.

I return to my pacing in the living room and call up my boss, Supervisory Special Agent Aaron Marreli.

"Dawson. What do you have for me?" His voice is raspy as if he eats nails for breakfast even though he's never smoked a day in his life.

"Marreli," I greet. "I don't have any more than what I've reported, but something is nagging at me. I feel like this woman is the key."

"Spencer Gray?"

"Yeah. She says she thinks her attacker is her ex, but this feels like more than a jilted lover."

"Nothing much has come from the evidence Berkowitz and Kowalski collected. They followed up with the florist. The shop doesn't have cameras and the customer paid cash. The owner said the man wore sunglasses and a hat. The usual disguise." His annoyance only adds to my own.

"Dammit," I sigh and lean my head back to stare at the ceiling. "Detective Zane Kingston said Spencer scratched her attacker and the DNA was collected at the hospital. Our guy has never left any DNA on the bodies, but I think we should still get the evidence from the NYPD and run our own test."

"That may not go over well with the local PD, even with your friend being the lead detective."

Fucking assholes with delicate egos. My patience for that kind of territorial bullshit is nonexistent. "I know. I'll talk to Zane. He'll be able to smooth things over with his Captain."

"I hope so. We don't need to burn any bridges." His comment, though true, holds a warning. I can't fuck this up.

"Got it." The dial tone meets my ear.

Fuck. This is not how I saw my trip home going. I figured I'd get here, relax, then get back to working on the case.

From the moment my feet touched New York soil, I've been on bodyguard duty. Fortunately, this favor for Rio and Z might just be the key to stopping this killer.

The turn of a knob makes me pause and I face Spencer's

bedroom. She walks out in her usual studio attire, but my mouth still salivates at the sight of her curves. Her cheeks are still flushed from her *steamy* shower. When her gaze meets mine, her eyes go wide. I don't know what she sees, but hopefully it isn't the bulge in my shorts.

CHAPTER 30

SPENCER

*A*fter showering and dressing in my ratty studio clothes, Asher uses my bathroom to take the fastest shower known to man, changing into an outfit he had laying in his car for work. With Asher looking yummy enough to eat and me looking homeless, we walk down to The Mudhouse in comfortable silence.

Ha. Yeah right. It's awkward as fuck.

When I exited my room with wet hair, no makeup, and my normal work outfit, Asher's eyes held a fire in them that told me everything I needed to know. He heard me. He knows what I did. I shouldn't be ashamed. I can do what I want. I'm a woman with needs, but the fact that he may have heard me say his name…Oh God. Bury me in my overcrowded storage closet please.

It doesn't matter. You'll be gone soon.

The thought is sobering. I won't be around long enough to ask him how he feels about my little self care shower. Not that I have the lady balls to do that anyway, but the opportunity isn't there. It'll never be there.

I order our drinks, black coffee for Asher and a mocha with whipped cream for me, and we wait for our morning fuel in—you guessed it—silence. His muscles are taut and the burning embers still alight in his eyes. The tension between us could be cut with a fucking knife, but I can't tell if he's happy about it or annoyed.

Focus. It's go time soon.

Right. Go time. I can't get caught up in my attraction for Asher, and I can't even begin to think about how Zane and Rio will react. My self-loathing overwhelms me every time I imagine their devastation.

We've grown close. They want to start something with me, but I'm running just as the seeds are being planted. I'll let myself mourn the relationship we could've had when I get to the west coast.

Our coffee is taking longer than usual, but I'm content to wait. I want to savor my last moments in The Mudhouse.

My nostrils fill with the rich smell of coffee beans followed by a sickly-sweet vanilla aroma as a blonde bombshell walks by. She looks like she just got off the runway with her perfectly styled hair, extra plump lips, and full face of makeup. She's wearing an overly tight skirt and a Marc Jacobs tote bag hangs from her arm while she types away on her phone.

As a girl's girl, I give props to her power outfit, but then her gaze wanders a little too far this way and lands on my bodyguard. I know the juxtaposition between Asher and me is immense. He looks ready to fight crime with his FBI badge on his belt with his dress shirt and slacks sitting perfectly on his fit frame. Meanwhile, I'm ready for a soup kitchen.

If Asher notices her, he doesn't give any indication. This probably happens to him often. Hot women in coffee shops must walk right up and give him their number all the time. But we're standing so close our shoulders are brushing with each breath. Surely she wouldn't…

As the woman begins to sidle up to Asher's side, I clear my throat drawing his attention. Then I do what I do best. I babble and make shit up as I go. "I have a lot of traveling back and forth between the gallery and studio today. I have to make sure some sales go out for delivery and then there's a shipment of clay coming in today. Would you mind helping me unload that? Then there's counting all the new inventory. Hayes usually has that under control, but I feel bad, it's a lot to handle. The day camp is coming by. Oh, and I need to—"

He sighs and interjects, "I get it. Lots of moving around, but I can guarantee you, Princess, I'll be right there with you."

As he speaks I lean forward subtly, checking to see if the bombshell got the hint. I let out a sigh of relief as I see her grab her coffee and leave.

Then it's Asher's turn to clear his throat. Embarrassed that he may have caught on to my scheme, I fumble to reply, "Oh. Um. It's no trouble. Really. You don't have to go with me *everywhere* everywhere." I do my best to pacify him.

His ego might still be bruised from my excursion to the coffee shop yesterday, but geez. Get over it.

"Yes, I do."

Surely he doesn't mean that.

An hour later after I've downed my coffee and I'm about to pee my pants, it's time to test the theory.

"Where do you think you're going?" Asher asks as I walk away from the worktable.

I drop my shoulders in frustration. "To the bathroom."

"Not without me," he simply states as he stands from his perch on a stool.

"You've got to be joking." There's no way. He's bluffing.

"Not even a little bit, Princess."

I narrow my eyes at him and walk to the back of the studio ignoring the questioning glance from Hayes. Turning to shut the door, I attempt to slam it in Asher's face but he holds it open with his hand. I push back repeatedly and feel like a younger child fighting with their older sibling as my feet slide across the floor while trying to get a good grip.

With the next two shoves I grunt out, "Get. Out." I stop and huff a big breath. "Move you overgrown man-child!"

He just stands there unphased, not even bracing his legs. He's just nonchalantly leaning on the door as if it's any other normal day. He's not even breathing hard, meanwhile I'm panting from all the exertion with a drop of sweat trickling down my back.

You've got to be kidding me.

"Are you done throwing your fit?" he asks, annoyed.

"You're not coming in here. One, it's a small single bathroom. There's not enough room for you and me. And two, I have to pee."

Why do I even have to explain this to him? You don't pee in front of the guy you pictured while masturbating in the shower. I know he heard me. He knows I know he heard me. We both know I did what I did! There's no way I can pee in front of him.

Instead of answering me, Asher pushes me backward until my calves hit the toilet seat. Then he steps in further and the door shuts behind him with a snick.

"Your throne, Princess. Have a seat." He flourishes his hand and does a slight bend in a mock bow.

Blood rushes to my cheeks and I fold my arms. I'm trapped with nowhere to go, but the dread of what could happen next, never comes. I can't take this. This familiarity my body and subconscious mind have with him. This can't be the life I leave behind.

My face remains neutral and I cross my arms. "No."

"Fine. We can just chill here. Make small talk."

"Whatever," I scoff at him.

You sure showed him.

Fucking hell. I roll my eyes and remain upright. No way am I caving. I'd rather die than pee in front of him.

"Enjoy your shower this morning?" he asks with a smirk.

My jaw drops. The audacity of this asshole! I swear steam is coming out of my ears as I mentally shoot serrated daggers at his gorgeous fucking face.

Damn him! My face is heating even more. I'm sure I'm as red as a tomato now.

"The least you can do is turn around," I grit out through clenched teeth.

With a smile resembling the cheshire cat, he spins to face the door.

"If anyone asks, this never happened. Got it?" I say lacing each word with unspoken threats.

"As you wish, Princess."

Is it possible to actually see red? Because if so, that's me right now. If I had a brick, I'd hit his obnoxiously thick skull with it.

"Don't you dare turn back around." Sometimes you have to voice the things that could be left unsaid, but some people are stupid like the lump of muscle in front of me.

"As you wish, Princess," he repeats. I can hear the laughter in his voice. His smile is beautiful, but right now, I'd rather it not be present for this mortifying experience. It only adds salt to my gaping wound.

I quickly slide my leggings down to my knees and sit my ass down on the seat. If he does turn around, he's going to see as little as possible. Closing my eyes, I focus on the sound of nothing and will my bladder to empty. After what feels like an eternity, I let out a sigh.

"Pee shy?" There's still that smirk in his tone. God. I want to smack that panty-dropping smile right off his gorgeous face.

"I need you to make noise."

"What, like sex sounds?" He teases. I wouldn't complain if I heard his sex noises, but not while I'm trying to pee.

"No, you idiot. Just sounds to drown out the sound of me peeing."

"Seriously? Just pee." He sounds like he's well on his way to aggravation.

"I can't. Please, Asher." I plead with him.

"Fine," he concedes. "*Whooshhhhhhhh. Whooshhhhhhh. Whooshhhhhhhh.*"

I giggle and force myself to hold in the pee begging to come out. "What the fuck is that?"

"Water sounds," he states as if it's obvious.

"That's what you think water sounds like?" I tease back giving him a taste of his own medicine.

"Do you want the noises or not?"

"Yes, please," I say pretending to be chastised.

"*Whooshhhhhhh. Whooshhhhhhh.*"

I finally pee and sweet relief washes through me. My bladder thanks me, my abs thank me, and my urinary tract thanks me. When I'm done, I flush and nudge Asher with my foot. He smirks at me over his shoulder and my face gets hot all over again.

After I wash my hands, I head back to the worktable where I have a lump of clay I've yet to shape. Hayes motions to get my attention, but I refuse to look. He resorts to putting his hand in my face, so I make eye contact. He raises his brows and widens his eyes as if it's enough to convey a whole message, which it is.

211

"Do not. We will never talk about this. Ever." I threaten.

He busts up laughing causing giggles from Alma and Paul. I bury my face in my hands and wait for the laughing to subside.

I'm going to miss this. I'm going to miss Alma's warm heart, Paul's tender soul, mine and Hayes' comfortable companionship, and Iris' humor. I'll mourn the loss of Zane's attention to detail, Rio's lively spirit, and even Asher's grumpy demeanor, but I've endangered everyone here enough.

Anthony's message was clear. *Come back*. That's not happening. Never. My only choice is obvious.

I have to go and leave my heart behind with these people who have done nothing but show me love.

CHAPTER 31

SPENCER

For the next hour, the joke of the humiliating bathroom incident doesn't die. Every time I make eye contact with Hayes, he starts chuckling. A few times it turned into a full belly laugh. I swear if I didn't love that kid like the brother I never wanted, I would punch him in the face.

His laughter makes me feel like I'm reliving the experience all over again which was horrifying enough the first time around. Remembering it makes me all the more angry with Asher. I know he sees my death glares, but they just make him smile like the fucking cat that ate the canary.

I'm finally given a reprieve from being the butt of the joke when a loud knock sounds on the back door of the studio signaling the clay shipment.

Now is my time to run. I have to go about this carefully and pray that Asher doesn't catch on. With shaky legs and sweaty palms, I go to open the heavy metal door, but Asher nudges me out of the way. Before he turns the handle he peers down at me and says, "Whatever you're thinking, don't."

"I don't know what you're talking about." My throat has gone dry so my voice has a slight rasp.

"Don't play games with me, Spencer," he warns.

"I'm not," I say with as much force as I can muster. "Now if you don't mind, I have a business to run. Please open the door. That clay is very expensive." Reluctantly he greets the truck driver, and allows me to move in front so I can sign for the order. I drop the pen twice, and when I finally sign, my signature is filled with bumps and squiggles from how bad my hand is shaking.

While unloading the palettes of clay and supplies, a herd of children storm into the studio. Alma's two children stick out from the bunch. They number among the more *spirited* of the kids.

Shit. I should have planned this out better…or maybe not.

An idea forms in my mind and I know I'm going to Hell for this.

I get the students started on painting their pinch pots as the patrons and the delivery guys fill the dank alleyway. It's gross back here and smells like piss so I avoid it at all costs. Plus, the dumpsters are always overflowing, the ground is constantly sticky and there's little to no lighting at night, just another perk of New York living.

Everyone begins the process of moving the clay into the storage closet and stacking the excess along the back wall. We've done this song and dance only a couple times before, so Hayes and I have to direct what goes where. I keep an eye on Asher who is helping amongst everyone else. Each time he loses sight of me, he maneuvers around the crowd swiftly to catch up with me again. He's not going to make this easy.

I send up a last prayer of forgiveness when I trip a delivery worker and he drops a bag of sand. The paper bursts open and sand spreads all over the floor. My chest pounds and my senses go on high alert.

All at once everyone springs into action. Hayes grabs a couple brooms, Alma and a few of the delivery guys get down on their hands and knees to scoop the sand back in the bag. But Asher's attention zeroes in on me.

"SAND BOX!" one child shouts and then they all converge on the granular rock like ants at a picnic.

"Come on, Viking Hottie. I need your help," Alma says with a sigh as she tries to tug Asher with her into the fray, ignoring the fact that he's in dress pants. "We need your big hands," she adds with a wink.

Asher looks like a deer caught in the headlights watching the children roll around in the sand. I almost feel guilty.

As soon as he turns his back, I scurry away to the gallery and send up a silent thank you to the universe and Alma. I could not have planned that better myself.

My heart pounds as I race against time. This feels all too familiar. Like the night I left Texas, but this time I'm leaving to save others and not just myself. But yet again, I don't have the luxury of time.

I left my purse and phone at the front desk of Abstract Creations earlier and rush to grab them.

"Oh hey! Whatcha doing over here?" Iris' question has me jumping out of my skin.

"You scared me." I throw my hand over my chest. My heart is now slamming against my rib cage and the hairs on the back of my neck stand.

Is Anthony watching me now? Is he out there waiting for me to leave? Is that a risk I can take?

What other choice do you have if he is?

Fuck. None. I will be the wall between Anthony and those I care about. He can't touch them.

215

"My bad. Is everything okay?" Iris asks with a tilt of her head. I take a brief moment to remember. Remember the day we met, all our times out at Moonlit, the lunches we shared in the breakroom, the laughs, the memories. Pain radiates from my chest, but I can't let it slow me down.

Before I can stop myself, I pull her into a hug. Shocked, she takes a moment to wrap her arms around me. I soak in her kindness, her strength. I can only hope she doesn't hate me after this.

"Thank you," I whisper.

"Huh?"

I pull back, but keep a hold of her shoulders. "They need help next door. A bag of sand broke. I'm going to run upstairs to grab an extra broom."

"Oh, shit. I'll meet you over there." She rushes away in her high heels to the studio without a goodbye. I wish she would've at least waved, but why would she? All it would've done is eased my guilty conscience.

As soon as the door closes with a snick, I snap back to it. My breaths saw in and out of my lungs as I neatly place the envelopes on the desk and dash out the door. I take a moment to throw on a baseball cap and large jacket before casually strolling on the sidewalk in front of Clay Creations. Once I'm past the windows, I dart up the stairs and into my apartment.

I barely step inside my room to grab my backpack and duffle bag filled with essentials. After I sling the bags across my body, I quickly adjust the cap so it covers more of my hair. My ponytail is sticking out of the back, but it'll do for now.

Striding back to the front door, I rip it open, but am met with a wall of muscle. My breaths stop and my heart sinks.

"Now where do you think you're off to, Princess?"

Shit.

CHAPTER 32

SPENCER

I blew it. My one chance and I fucking blew it. They're all still in danger. I was supposed to take the threat with me when I left.

Asher steps into my apartment, causing me to take a few steps back. I almost tumble onto my ass from how bad my knees are shaking. My breathing picks back up again. Asher pauses a few feet inside, but I keep inching backwards.

His face is furious. His anger is thundering out of him and crashing into me. My thighs finally hit the back of the couch, and I attempt to sink further away from Asher's wrath.

"I said, where the fuck do you think you're going?" I expect his voice to boom, his hand to rear back. But neither happens. His fury is contained, but nonetheless frightening.

I hear a crinkle of paper and glance down to Asher's fist. He's holding my letters. All of them. In his other fist, one is opened.

Double shit.

He lifts it up and begins to read as he stalks toward me. "I won't let him get to you. I know you probably hate me, but in the short time I've known you, you've made me feel safe and cared for. You, Rio, and Zane have given me something I've been missing."

"Stop." I lift my hands in front of me, pleading. I can't hear anymore. It ripped my heart to write the letters, I don't need to hear my deepest thoughts expressed out loud. Asher ignores my hands and continues forward. "What? Can't take it?"

"I get it, okay?"

"Do you? Do you get it?" His voice stays even. The calm before the storm.

"Yes!" I shout.

"I don't think you do. I don't think you know what it was like for those three minutes that I couldn't find you," his voice begins to waver. "One hundred and eighty seconds of pure torture, thinking I failed you. Thinking the psycho coming for you, finally got his hands on you. So no, you don't fucking get it, Spencer."

"I'm sorry." My voice cracks and the dam breaks. Tears flow freely down my face. I scared him. This giant man with the hard exterior. I frightened him. He doesn't strike me as someone who scares easily or someone who handles it well. His carefully composed facade is cracking in front of me. The mask is fracturing and the glimpse I'm getting behind it breaks my heart.

"Who is 'him' and why do you think he would come for us? What has you so afraid?"

His question sucks all the oxygen from my lungs. I won't go back. Never again.

I steel my spine, and remind myself the less they know the better. "That's none of your business."

"Excuse me? I'd say that it damn well is my business. What has you so spooked that you think running is the answer? What was it about the flowers yesterday that freaked you out?" He's only inches away from me now and I have to crane my neck to see his face. He's rebuilt his mask and the cold facade is firmly back in place.

I cool my features to match his. He's already on the right trail. I can't let him figure it out. I'd like to think I mask my emotions well, but the truth is I know I'm an open book to these guys. "It's nothing," I answer him. His nostrils flare and he lets out a frustrated sigh.

"Did you stop to think what running would do to Rio and Z?" His question makes me flinch.

"Of course I did." He's pushing my buttons and he knows he hit the right spot.

"Really? Because it seems like you couldn't wait to leave."

"That's not fair. I don't have a choice," he's itching for a fight and lucky for him I'm willing to give him one because never again will I be someone's punching bag. "Do you actually think I wanted this? That I wanted to leave you all behind? Writing those letters, walking out the door. It killed me." I didn't realize I was shouting until I was done. My chest heaving with the anger of the moment. He pushed and now he gets to live with the consequences.

"You really want to know why?" I ask. He says nothing. "I'm terrified of Anthony. Just the thought of him being here has me trembling head to toe. He'll kill anyone who gets close to me without batting an eye. He wants me back, but I'll never go with him. Over my dead fucking body." Asher winces, but I don't feel bad.

Don't corner a wounded animal. She'll snap right back at you.

"So yes, I know he'll come here and take you all from me. I am willing to do the one thing that'll prevent that from happening. I'll leave."

"Just like that?"

I nod my head. "Just like that. I already have things arranged so Hayes will get everything. Clay Creations, Abstract Dreams, my apartment. I left a letter for everyone. All you have to do is step aside and I'll be on my way."

Asher's face is stuck on an expression of rage, and he says nothing. The silence stretches between us. The only sound is our heavy breaths.

When he speaks again it's with finality. "You're not fucking leaving." Before I can get another word out he's dropped the letters, knocked my hat off my head, and smashes his lips to mine.

It takes me a moment to realize what's happening. We went from shouting to kissing within minutes, but I would expect nothing less from us. We get under each other's skin in a way that drives the other mad. The stolen glances, the lingering touches. We were a ticking time bomb, and now that we have detonated it's nothing but exploding fireworks.

His hands land on my hips and his tongue sweeps across the seam of my lips, demanding entry. I bring my hands up to his chest thinking I'll push him away, but instead my body reacts on instinct.

I grip his neatly pressed shirt pulling him closer and opening my mouth to him. Our tongues and teeth clash, punishing each other. I've never been kissed like this before. My panties flood and my core throbs.

He removes my bags from my shoulders, and groans as his tongue invades my mouth again. Each swipe ratchets my need higher and higher. His hand snakes up my back and dives into my hair. He uses his grip to tilt my head to the side for a better angle, plunging his tongue deeper. His other hand moves south, seizing my ass. He pulls me closer and grinds into me. His slacks don't hide his thick length. I moan and writhe against him.

I need more. I need him inside me. My pussy aches to be filled.

My sounds spur him on and the next thing I know he's gripping my thighs and lifting me up. My ankles lock at the small of his back and my hands clutch his shoulders. His lips meet mine again and we battle each other for control, neither willing to give it to the other.

I glide my hands up his neck and to his luscious, thick hair. I undo his bun and cast aside his hair tie. His hair is shoulder length and soft to the touch. I scrape my short nails along his scalp which makes him moan.

"Do that again," he orders.

I grin at him and tug on his hair instead.

"Not what I said, Princess."

"I know," I say smugly, and then smash my lips back to this and run my nails along his scalp again.

The front door bangs open causing Asher and I to break apart. Rio is standing there frantically scanning the room. When he finally registers mine and Asher's precarious position, a smile slowly slides into place. "Why wasn't I invited to the party?"

Before I can explain, I yelp as I'm crashing into the couch with a bounce.

That fucker dropped me.

CHAPTER 33

SPENCER

"That's not what it looked like. It was nothing," Asher says.

Well that was a blow to my ego. Unfortunately for Asher, I don't forget easily. "Yeah the way you shoved your tongue down my throat really felt like nothing."

Even though he won't look at me, I can see how my words affect him. His jaw ticks and the muscles in his back tense. I know I'm being a brat, but he doesn't get to kiss me like *that* and then say it was nothing.

I'm a tangle of arms and legs as I try to stand up from the couch. I love this couch, but comfortable cushions do not make good stepping stones.

"If you say so," Rio says unconvinced. "Now, Mama. What's this I hear about you running?"

Frozen in my awkward position, I reluctantly meet Rio's gaze. He's trying to be his normal playful self, but I can see the hurt. He thought I was leaving him when it was the opposite. Accepting what they mean to me, means I have to go.

He nods to the envelopes scattered at Asher's feet. "What are those?"

"Nothing," I answer quickly. At the same time Asher says, "Goodbye letters."

I scramble over the edge of the couch and immediately go to my hands and knees to gather the envelopes before any more can be read. "They're nothing," I say more firmly. Before I can reach Rio's, he swipes it off the floor.

"I believe this belongs to me. I mean it has my name on it and everything. So I would say it's safe to assume it's mine," Rio says the last part to Asher.

"I would agree with that reasoning," Asher replies.

I jump to my feet and snatch the letter from Rio. "No, it's mine until I decide to give it to you."

"I think that was the plan when you left it on the desk downstairs," Asher snaps. I glare at him over my shoulder.

"I apologized for that." It's a shitty comeback, and we both know I'll be apologizing for a long time.

Until you're able to actually leave.

While I'm arguing with Asher, Rio slips up and grabs the rest of the letters from my hands.

"Hey!" I shout and dive at him, but Asher's arms circle my waist and lift me up against his chest.

"No you don't, Princess."

"Stop calling me that!" I shout as I kick my feet wildly. I don't want to hurt him, but I wouldn't be upset if I did.

"You didn't seem to mind it earlier."

"Oh, now it's not *nothing*, huh? Well fuck you, you asshole!" I flail about in his arms to no avail, and I'm not entirely sure I want to leave the warmth of his embrace. Even if it's not entirely comforting at the moment.

No, bad Spencer. We do not cave to the grumpy overgrown man who has the emotional capacity of a teaspoon.

223

I hear a rip and my attention jerks to Rio opening all of the letters. "Oh my God! Stop!"

"What's the big deal? It's not like I'm reading your diary."

"Yes, it is!"

"Eh. Not really," he is silent while he reads. "That's really nice of you to leave everything to Hayes, but that won't be necessary. You're not going anywhere, *chica*." He crumples the letter and tosses it to the floor.

"Rio!" I'm tired of explaining this. Once is enough. Asher can go spill to the other two over some tea like the meddling old ladies they are.

Very hot and sexy old ladies though.

Ugh. Not now. My vagina cannot be the one in control right now.

"SPENCER!"

All our heads snap to the door which is still open. Footsteps thunder up the stairs. Why are Rio and Asher not alarmed by the angry man charging up here?

"SPENCER!"

"Somebody's in trouble," Rio singsongs from the kitchen.

"What?" Asher's arms fall away from my waist and my gaze zaps around the room, looking for something I could use as a weapon. I really should buy some candlesticks. One of those would be perfect right about now.

I breathe a sigh of relief when I see Zane appear in the doorway, but my relief is short-lived. His hair is disheveled, his shirt is untucked and wrinkled, and his eyes are plagued. His gaze snaps to me and takes in my appearance. I know what he sees. Studio clothes, flushed cheeks, swollen lips, but then he glances down and sees the bags I packed; the rage in his voice comes back

"You thought you could leave me?" His nostrils flares and

he advances on me kicking the door shut behind him. "What was your plan, Spence? Huh?"

Slow steps carry me backwards down the hall. I'm tired of these men backing me into a corner, but when approached by a predator you back away, and that's exactly what he is right now. A predator.

The hurt I caused is there, but he's covering it with the anger radiating from him.

Isn't that what anger usually is? Hurt that we try to hide. We think no one will see what we deem as weakness, but it couldn't be more obvious with a flashing neon sign.

Instinctively I bring my hands up in front of me, but my subtle sign doesn't deter him. He's on me before I reach my bedroom. He grasps my hands in his and brings them to his hard chest. The pounding of his heart underneath his sculpted muscle hammers against my palm.

"Why? Tell me why." Zane pleads. His voice is wrought with emotion, but is still harsh.

"I was trying to keep you all safe. Damn you fucking stubborn men! Just let me go and you'll all be safe!" I'm losing it. I can't keep explaining myself like a broken record. How many times do I have to tell them until they fucking get it? They're not safe with me around. Anthony will always follow me.

"She thought she was protecting us from Anthony," Asher chimes in.

"You were going to leave us because of him? That pathetic waste of space?" Zane asks even more enraged, but his solid grip on my hands doesn't turn painful. Even in his anger, he's mindful of me.

"Why does it feel like y'all know him?" I ask skeptically.

"We looked him up last night after we left," Rio says like it's no big deal as he keeps reading my letters.

"You had no right! What if he finds out? If he wasn't

already here, he definitely is now. I really have to go. I can't stay here." My mind begins to spiral.

Before, I could at least lie to myself saying that he had the flowers delivered meaning I still had time to get away, but now there's no fooling myself. He had a private jet that he used so he could travel at the last minute if needed.

"Not fucking happening, Angel." With Zane's declaration he bends down and throws me over his shoulder. One moment I'm upright and the next I'm staring at his in-shape ass.

"Zane! What the hell? Put me down!" He ignores me and continues his march while I carry on with my futile attempts. Then, for the second time today, I land with a bounce on the couch as Zane plops me down.

When I try to sit up, he's on me. He has my arms pinned above my head and my legs wrapped up in his before I can even blink. So much for all those boxing and self defense lessons. Why can't my traitorous body be on my side for once when it comes to these men?

"Zane, get off of me." I buck my hips, but he doesn't budge.

"No. Not until you promise."

"Seriously?" My question comes out as a screech. This is ridiculous. Pin me down until I agree? We'll be here for a while then. They want to be headstrong cavemen? Well, two can play at that game. Or four. Whatever.

"Promise you won't try to leave."

Oh my God. They've lost their minds. Is no one else seeing the huge bubble of danger surrounding me? It's like they want a ticket for this crazy ride that leads straight to their deaths.

"She's never going to agree to that," Asher says with a sigh as if I'm the one being difficult. Well fuck him. *They're* the difficult ones.

"Promise me. Please." It's not Zane's words that have the

guilt eating at me. It's the pain in his tone. My soft, quiet Zane is begging me not to break what we have built, what I have actively tried to avoid building with him. It's hard to resist when the other party is so pushy, but have I really tried resisting? They make me smile. The warmth and security I feel when in their arms is on a level I've never felt before. Why should I have to give that up?

So they live to see tomorrow.

"I can't," I choke out with tears gathering in my eyes.

For a moment I think he's going to let me go, save himself and his family. Part of my heart breaks at the thought. I want them to choose me. Fight for me. But that's Selfish Spencer talking. I can't be selfish here. They come first.

Zane lets out a breath rebuilding his resolve. He's not letting me go. I'm half relieved, half scared. Relieved because he really does want me. He's willing to fight for me. I've never had that before. Even Abuela was only able to do so much. I'd beg and plead to be able to stay with her when the summers would end, but she'd always send me back to Mom.

The other half is scared because these men may as well have signed their own death certificates. Anthony will do whatever it takes to get to me. It's a miracle he's left Mom alone all these years, but I know it's her lack of knowledge that has saved her.

"I can do tonight. Asher, you still good for the rest of the day?" Zane asks.

"Yeah, I have a few more days until I have to be back at the office."

"Rio?" Zane asks.

"I'll come with you tonight. It'll be nice to finally sleep without my legs being crammed against my chest in your car. I'm afraid that one day I won't be able to stand up straight anymore," Rio jests.

"What are y'all talking about?" I interject, but they ignore me and keep discussing amongst themselves.

"When I go back to work, Rio, can you be here?" Asher takes over the directions.

"*No hay lugar donde prefiera estar,*" Rio answers with a smile.

"Z, you got the weekend?"

"I'm all over it," Zane gives my wrists a squeeze. "I can have some patrols drive by during the day as well," he adds.

"Stop talking about me like I'm not here!"

They all look at me. Their attention is almost too much. Having the attention of these three powerful men is intoxicating. I don't know if I ever felt anything else quite like it. It's like they're moments away from pouncing, but at the same time I'm the one in charge here. My next sentence comes out breathy even though I'm going for assertive. "No one is staying the night, and I don't need a bodyguard."

"Could have fooled me," Asher scoffs.

"You really think we're going to leave you alone after this stunt today? *Estás más loca de lo que pensé.*"

"Ugh! You infuriating, dumb, alpha men!"

"I take that as a compliment," Asher comments.

"Angel, look at me," Zane's plea tugs at my heart and I can't stop myself from complying. "Don't deny me this. I need to protect you. *We* need to protect you. We're going to do it whether you like it or not. It's up to you if this goes smoothly or we handcuff you to one of us twenty-four-seven."

I narrow my eyes at him and challenge, "You wouldn't."

"Try me. You think it was fun getting Asher's text that he couldn't find you? I broke every traffic law in this fucking state to get here. You won't be without one of us until you can promise you won't run. Even then, one of us will still be here, but without the threat of handcuffs."

He better fucking not. Fuck no. "Try it Zane Kingston, and

see what fucking happens." I hope my threat actually comes across as threatening.

It doesn't.

A wide smile spreads across Zane's mouth, lighting up his face. "Does my Angel have claws?"

"I'm not joking here."

"Neither am I." He shifts my wrists into one hand and reaches back behind him with his free hand. When that hand comes back into view, the clink of metal rings in my ears. Dangling from his index finger is a set of handcuffs.

"Fine," I spew through gritted teeth.

CHAPTER 34

SPENCER

Going back downstairs was weird as hell. I already said my goodbyes even if no one else knew it. Seeing everyone after I was prepared to leave them all behind was too much. I may have cried a few times. Iris thought Asher did something and threatened to chop off his balls.

Zane and Rio went back to work with a promise to be back later with dinner. I don't like that they know food is the way into my apartment, but love the familiarity that means they know me.

At the end of the day everyone leaves, except Asher. The normality leaves behind a bittersweet feeling festering in my chest. If I would have been able to get away earlier, my day would not have ended this way. I love being able to live it even if these experiences are numbered.

I'm startled when Asher appears next to me with my purse in hand. "Come on, Spencer. Let's get you home." He hands over my bag and places one of his hands on my lower back, guiding me out the door. The simple touch shouldn't get me all hot and bothered, but now that I know what those hands feel like exploring my body, I can't help clenching my thighs together.

I refuse to forget his earlier comment. Was our kiss really nothing to him? I have only kissed a few men in my life, so to say I'm inexperienced is an understatement. Maybe it really was awful for him. Embarrassment colors my cheeks on our short walk to my apartment.

If Asher notices my change in mood he doesn't mention it, which is probably for the best. I'm not going to argue with him over it, I know when I'm not wanted. I may make a fool of myself and stumble over my words, but I still have some pride.

After checking all the rooms, Asher makes his way to the kitchen and starts to pull things from the fridge. Things I definitely did not buy.

"What are you doing?"

"What does it look like I'm doing?"

"It looks like you turned my fridge into a Mary Poppins bag and are magically making groceries appear."

Asher lightly chuckles, shaking his head. I guess Kind Asher is back. "Rio picked some things up while we were in the studio and stocked up for you."

I scrunch my nose in confusion. "Why? I don't cook."

"I noticed."

I plop myself in a stool and wait for him to elaborate.

He doesn't. What a shocker.

We transition into a comfortable silence as he moves around the kitchen with ease. Chopping veggies and pan searing chicken on the stove.

"What are you making?"

Instead of answering, Asher taps the screen on his phone and a mix of jazz and R&B streams from the speaker. He turns the volume up all the way, drowning out the verbal beatdown I'm giving him in my head. He sways across the tile, getting lost in a rhythm he has set. Not a skilled dancer, but that doesn't make the movement of his hips any less enticing.

Finally choosing to bless me with his baritone voice he says, "Rio got stuck helping our neighbor and Zane is going to be late, so I'm making dinner. That way we don't starve."

I'm done trying to understand this man. First, it's "I don't do bullshit" then he makes me pee in front of him. Then after he stops me from running, he gives me a crazy intense kiss and says it was nothing. Now he's dancing in my kitchen cooking me dinner.

I give up.

Choosing to ignore the mood swings of the giant, I pull out my tablet, put on my accounting hat, and crunch some numbers. Such is the life of a small business owner.

"Bon appètit," Asher says, placing a bowl of stir fry in front of me.

"Is it edible?"

Okay, so maybe the brat attitude is going to take a while to go away.

Again, I get no verbal answer. His reply is to grab his own bowl and eat beside me. The intimacy of the situation is too much to handle.

Fine. If he can act like our kiss was no big deal, so can I. I'm a grown ass woman. I can kiss whoever the fuck I want.

I take a bite of the food in front of me and a small moan slips free. Of course, he can actually cook. The fucking cherry on top of the disaster sundae that is us.

I continue eating, acting like this isn't the best home cooked meal I've had since Alma dropped off a container of her tamales last Christmas. Before I know it, I have devoured the whole bowl. When I stand with my bowl, Asher stands and takes my dish from my hands. Wordlessly, he takes his bowl and mine to the sink and washes them by hand, dries them, and puts them away.

I should not swoon at how he takes charge and cares for me in situations like this. I'm an independent woman, dammit. I do not need a man to complete me. But fucking hell, if he wanted to replay our kiss earlier, I would not oppose.

No, Horny Spencer! He said the kiss meant *nothing*. We're above the urges of our hormones.

As if he can read my thoughts, Asher crowds me until I'm backed against the high countertop. He brings his hand to my face and tucks an errant strand of hair behind my ear. His hand then trails down the curve of my neck causing goosebumps to rise in its wake. An involuntary shiver makes my shoulders shake imperceptibly. He notices and smirks then takes his motions a step further.

His hand doesn't deter from its path and sweeps across my chest, brushing the outer swell of my breast. Having chosen a simple bralette over an underwire torture device earlier, I can feel his touch even though it's light. My core pulses and I subtly rub my thighs together. Again he sees. He always sees. It's annoying yet exhilarating.

He leans down and brings his mouth to my ear. "What are you doing to me, Princess?"

"The same thing you're doing to me."

"And what's that?"

"Driving me crazy."

At my confession, he licks the shell of my ear then takes it into his mouth and drags his teeth over it. The thrill of it sends a jolt to my clit. This time I allow the moan to escape from my mouth.

His hands grip my waist and place me on the bar stool. I eagerly open my thighs and allow him to step between them. Even though I'm elevated, he's still taller than me. Wasting no time, he grabs my face and attacks my mouth with an urgent need. A need I'm feeling as I pour my intense desire into the kiss.

When his hands drop down to my breasts and give them a squeeze, I arch into his hands but pull back.

"Asher, wait."

He goes unnaturally still and slowly places enough space between us that his scent no longer clouds all logical thought.

I wait for his eyes to connect with mine before I ask, "Was it really nothing?"

He locks his jaw tight and I can see the muscles in his neck work as he struggles with his answer. I hold my breath and wait, but whatever he has to say he refuses to voice.

"No bullshit, right?" I ask with lifeless humor.

He gives me a slight nod. "No bullshit."

"So?" I ask hopefully. Getting an answer from this man is like pulling teeth. I don't know where this patience is coming from, but I'm going to need more of it to get through this fucking conversation.

"It wasn't nothing," he answers and I finally release my breath. "But it can't happen again. It's complicated."

Fury like I've never felt before clouds my vision. *He* kissed *me*. Both times! I'm sure he can feel the undiluted rage radiating from me because he takes the smallest step back.

"Is it my job to keep your hands off me?"

Confused, he answers, "Of course not."

"Then control yourself and keep your hands away from me. I'm not doing this hot and cold mood swing shit with you anymore. Think with more than just your tiny dick!" I shove him aside, knowing I moved him because he let me. There's no way I could move that boulder on my own.

As I stomp to my room, I leave Asher behind dumbfounded and, hopefully, feeling a little guilty.

Screw him.

I know I shouldn't have lashed out. Maybe we could have had an adult conversation, but that man maddens me more than anyone I have ever encountered.

Slamming my door shut, I go straight to the shower to wash away Asher's touch and the conflicting feelings stirring inside.

CHAPTER 35

SPENCER

*A*fter I've scrubbed my skin raw and done some self care, not *that* kind, I exit my steam-filled bathroom wrapped in a soft towel. Feeling refreshed and relaxed, I'm ready to dive into bed and forget the Viking incubus who draws pleasure from my body like he was made to do it.

A squeak escapes my lips when I find that I'm not alone in my room. "Zane! How did you get in here?"

"It's not like you locked the door," he comments without looking up.

I take him in and my jaw drops. Drool probably drips from my mouth. He's shirtless with a pair of gray sweatpants hanging low on his hips. He has a fucking six pack and that glorious Adonis belt. His skin is smooth with a smattering of chest hair. He has a small tattoo that I can't quite make out across the right side of his ribs. His ankles are crossed as he leans back leisurely against my pillows, and he's reading a book on the far side of my bed. Not just any book. He's reading *New Moon*. A pair of simple, black rimmed glasses sit perfectly on his perfect face.

It's like he was put on this Earth to draw me in, to pull me closer. I almost go to him, but then I remember I am wearing less than he is.

My hand tightens around my towel and he finally notices it's all I'm wearing. His perusal sets my skin on fire. My legs are on full display as my towel only goes to my upper thigh, barely covering my ass. My hair is combed but still dripping. I feel a droplet part from my hair, landing on my chest and sliding down between my cleavage. Zane's gaze follows its path and his eyes darken with desire.

Breaking the moment, I clear my throat. "*New Moon*, huh?"

"Yeah. Have you read it?"

"That's like asking if I was a teenager," I scoff. Zane just stares back waiting for my answer. "Yes, I read it when I was fifteen." He nods his head in understanding. Needing more information, I ask, "What made you want to read the series?"

"Solana asked me to read it."

Jealousy quickly makes its way into my bloodstream. I want to ask who the fuck Solana is and how she could get a grown man to read a YA fantasy romance series, but I resist. I have no claim over him, and I can't just ask questions about the women in his life.

He smiles to himself, but doesn't ask why my face looks like I ate a lemon. Instead he asks, "Are you team Edward or team Jacob?"

"Neither."

He gives me a confused look. "How does that work? You wanted her to end up with Mike?"

I bust out laughing. "Oh God, no. He was sweet, but in romance books no one wants the sweet guy when you can have a billionaire vampire or a warm-blooded werewolf. No, I'm all for Charlie."

"The dad?" His eyebrows raise so high it's like they're trying to disappear into his perfect curls.

"He's a small town, grumpy sheriff and he's a single dad. He's what smut is made of."

Zane smirks and lets out a small chuckle. "You looking for someone to call daddy?"

"What? That's not what I said." My toes curl at the thought and I can feel the tips of my ears turn red.

A predatory look spreads across his face. "You can call me daddy."

My feet shuffle side to side and my toes curl. I would totally call him daddy, but I will never admit to it.

He rises from the bed and approaches me like he's getting ready to pounce. The simple act of him walking to me has me hypnotized. His muscles are strained as he stands a breath away as if it's taking all his willpower to keep himself from touching me.

Does he think I wouldn't welcome his touch? Did he find out about my kiss with Asher? Oh God. Did he find out about the second kiss? Does that mean I'm off limits? He said he was fine with me and Rio. Is he not okay with me and Asher? Not that there's a *me and Asher*, or even a *me and Zane and Rio*.

How long can I resist these men? The answer is, not much longer. It's going to make leaving all that more painful.

"Hey. Where did you go?" Zane searches my face for the answer.

Clearing my throat, I reply, "I'm right here." I plaster a halfhearted smile on my face.

"I'm talking about here," he cups the side of my head and soothingly rubs his thumb over my temple. "You left me for a second there, Angel. Where did you go?"

"You can't keep doing that." I sigh, enjoying the feel of his warm hand.

"Doing what?"

"Reading me so easily. I'm not an open book," I argue

"I'm sorry to break it to you, Spencer, but you couldn't be more open if you tried. I notice everything about you. Every flinch, every smile, every lustful gaze. You have pulled me in without even trying. I'm locked in your orbit and I'm not going anywhere."

He brings his other hand up to cradle my face. My knuckles turn white with how hard I'm gripping my measly towel. His eyes drop to my lips, and I lick them on instinct. Slowly, ever so slowly, he lowers his face to mine.

The kiss is barely there, but butterflies still take flight in my stomach. He lightly moves his soft lips over mine. When I finally move my mouth in time with his, a groan echoes in his throat. I grip his waist and pull him closer.

Our kiss turns into a dance. He leads and I happily follow. Giving up control has never made me feel so safe.

His tongue swipes across my lips, seeking entry. I ravenously open my mouth to give him access. Our kiss gets hotter as his teeth clamp my lower lip and scrape over it. I grip his shoulders, and I feel my slick desire start to slide down my inner thigh. One of his hands trails down my back and grips my bare ass while the other slides down the front of my body. He flattens his hand over my chest and drags it down between my breasts. When his hand reaches my leg, he dips under my towel and grabs my pussy possessively.

I gasp into his mouth as his fingers easily glide through my slit. "Is that all for me, Angel?" Another gasp leaves me when he slips a single digit inside. "Answer me."

"Y-yes. It's for you."

He pumps his finger in and out, hitting that spot and causing my knees to shake. Zanc walks us backward until we reach my closet door. He inserts another finger, stretching me.

"Ride my fingers, Spencer," he rasps then covers his mouth with mine in a brutal kiss.

My hands roam to his back. He stiffens and abruptly pauses the kiss. I feel it in my gut that something is wrong.

Before I can ask if he's okay, he slams me into the door and traps my wrists in a harsh grip above my head. He pushes his body into mine, which is the only thing holding my towel up. If he steps back, he'll get a full-frontal view of all my bits, but my embarrassment dissipates when I see the pain etched on his face.

"Zane?"

His eyes are closed, brows furrowed and his breathing intensifies. He's trapped in his own mind and struggling to stay with me. I know the feeling all too well.

"Baby, look at me. I'm right here. You're with me." After more kindly whispered words he finally gifts me with his beautiful emerald irises, but his demons are still circling, waiting to dive in and take a piece of him. But they don't get him. They don't get to take his goodness, his happiness. They have already taken enough from him.

I don't need to know what haunts him to know he's hurting. I don't need details. I'll never ask. His past is his own. I have no right to it, but that doesn't mean I can't be here for him.

"Breathe with me. In your nose," I do a dramatic inhale. "Out your mouth." Then a big exhale. He doesn't do it with me the first time, but joins in on the second. After a minute or two of our deep breaths, his demons retreat and his eyes focus on me. Shame colors his features.

Zane averts his gaze. "I'm so sorry."

"No. Don't apologize. You have nothing to be sorry for." I give him a reassuring smile.

He inhales deep one more time and lets it out while searching my face. He releases his grip on my hands and inspect them. I didn't realize how tight his hold was until he lets go and the blood rushes back.

As he leans back my towel starts to drop. I pull my hands away, but he doesn't let them go far. His focus remains on my nonexistent injury. I let out a squeak and try pulling away harder, but it's too late. The towel has dropped and Zane's eyes lift. He zeroes in on my very exposed breasts. My nipples harden under his gaze.

"Oh shit!" I slam my front against his.

Zane's eyebrows raise and he asks, "You want me to feel them too?"

"I didn't know what else to do to cover up." I bury my heated face in his chest. A moment of silence passes and I feel a rumble from Zane that quickly turns into a full blown laugh.

"I'm glad I amuse you, but can we forget this ever happened?"

Zane sobers enough to answer me. "Absolutely not. I will never forget that sight for the rest of my life."

I let out a frustrated groan. "Then could you at least cover your eyes so I can go in my closet and change?"

"You want my honest answer?"

"Yes."

"No," he answers unabashedly.

I roll my eyes at him and come up with a plan. I do an awkward side bend grabbing the towel and throw it over his head. With his gaze obstructed, I dart away seeking refuge in my closet. I slam the door behind me and lean against it.

His laugh echoes from the other side and he calls out, "Nice ass, Angel."

I heave out a breath and place my embarrassment in a tiny box with ten locks and shove it to the back of my mind.

Looking through my drawers I stumble upon a crucial predicament.

What. Do. I. Fucking. Wear. To. Bed? Nightie, shorts and a tank, or an oversized tee? When did picking out what to wear to bed become so hard?

When the sexy ass men decided they'd stay for a sleepover.

The plain nightie says "I want sex" which I don't. I think. The shorts and tank are safe, but I hate wearing pants to bed. The oversized tee would cover my ass so I could go sans pants, and I could wear granny panties to deter their mischievous side.

Who am I kidding? Nothing would deter these headstrong men. Maybe I need a chastity belt.

Fuck it. Oversized tee paired with granny panties it is. Or… I reach for my favorite black lace thong.

Dressed and ready for bed I gather my courage, ready to rip off the band aid. Stepping into my bedroom I'm taken aback. I was prepared for one sexy shirtless man. Not two.

Rio now sits on my bed with Zane. Shirtless, basketball shorts, and his tattoos in full view. They don't notice me, so I take the opportunity to drink them in.

Rio's tattoos are a work of art. They flow across his skin beautifully. Amongst all the ink I'm able to make out a devil with a pitchfork on Rio's ribs. His eyes promise death and destruction, making me shiver. I also spot a portrait of a young girl on his bicep. There's some script as well, but I can't make out the words.

Zane has discarded his book and glasses on my nightstand. I wish he'd put them back on. I'm a glutton for punishment.

Their heads are bent together as they talk in hushed voices amongst themselves. I catch a few words.

Cain. Kidnap. Hunt. Kill.

The last word causes a chill to erupt over my skin.

Making myself known I ask, "What are you two gentlemen talking about?" Immediately they both go silent and eye my chosen attire.

Rio ignores my question. "Let's get this slumber party going!"

"Maybe we should discuss sleeping arrangements," I suggest, not wanting them to get the wrong idea. I need my bed to myself in order to get quality sleep. I have a blow up bed they can use and my couch is comfortable.

"I agree," Rio says. "Z, which side of the bed do you prefer?"

Zane looks like he's actually mulling over Rio's question. "Window."

"Sweet that leaves me by the door and Spencer smack dab in the middle."

"Ha ha. Very funny," I deadpan. "Seriously. I have sheets and blankets in the hall closet you can use—"

My hospitality speech is cut short when Rio interrupts. "We're sleeping right here with you, Mama. *En serio.*"

"No. I need my room empty of people, and I roll around a lot. I didn't ask for this sleepover, so y'all can deal with finding another room to crash in."

"We're not moving," Zane argues.

"I can't sleep with you two in my room!"

They glance at each other, both wearing a knowing smirk like they are secretly sharing a joke I'm not privy to.

I sigh and turn to make my way to the couch. They can share my queen size mattress and I'll get cozy out there. Before I can reach the door, I'm thrown over a shoulder. By the sweatpants and ass that meets my face, I know it's Zane.

What is with him and carting me around like a sack of potatoes?

"Really, Zane? Hauling me around like this is not the solution to everything." Zane says nothing, and I hear Rio chuckle. I'm deposited on my bed and a pair of inked arms wrap around my middle dragging me backwards. I try to push Rio away, but he tightens his grip.

These. Damn. Men.

Without speaking, Zane lays on the bed next to me and throws a blanket over us. Then he switches off the lamp, coating the room in complete darkness, and falls onto his back.

Rio wraps himself around me from behind in a huge bear hug as I lay on my side facing the window. I bask in his warmth and his breath on my neck. I've never cuddled like this before, and I can't say I hate it especially when it makes me feel secure. Safe. Ready to battle the demented shit my subconscious will no doubt conjure up.

As much as I love this feeling, I can't sleep like this. I wait a minute thinking I can take them by surprise and run out of the room. As if he can read my mind Zane says, "Don't you dare, Angel."

"*Intenta correr. A ver qué pasa.*"

I may not understand what Rio said, but the sentiment is loud and clear. It also makes me shiver a little. Every time he speaks Spanish to me in that sultry tone my body yearns for his.

Zane turns on his side and moves closer so our bodies are almost touching. He brings his hand to mine and clasps it in a desperate hold. It's a simple gesture, but it speaks a thousand words.

Once again I'm hit with how hurt he was at my attempt to leave. Giving him the reassurance he seeks, I squeeze his hand back.

Rio leans into me so his mouth reaches my ear. "Next time you flaunt your black lace panties like that, I'm going to tan your ass."

My eyes go wide and my cheeks burn. I completely forgot what I was wearing under my shirt when Zane went all caveman on me.

With my rebuttal on my lips, Zane silences me before I can get a word out. "Sleep, Angel. Your nightmares won't get you while we're here."

I'm not going to win with these two tonight, so I give in to the allure of sleep.

As I drift off a thought occurs to me...

How do they know I have nightmares?

CHAPTER 36

SPENCER

*W*aking up hot and sweaty is not recommended. I thought I might have gotten a fever and was sweating it out, but no. Just surrounded by two very warm, very *hot* bodies.

I wake on my own when light filters through my sheer curtains. What time is it?

My arm reaches over a man made of solid muscle while another has his arms of steel locked around my torso. Snagging my phone off my nightstand is next to impossible. My breasts end up in Zane's face and I try not to suffocate him while he's unconscious. I tap my phone screen and see it's seven a.m.

How did I sleep so late?

Fucking hell. I missed my run.

Slowly lowering myself back down in the middle of the bed, I resign myself to the fact that a workout is not happening today. Now to figure out how to peel away Rio's iron grip. His hands are clenched together as if even in his sleep he was worried I would slip away. The thought makes my heart hurt.

I trace the designs swirling around his rough hands and

glide my finger over the art. The ink is slightly faded indicating he got these done some time ago. The Devil's face on the back of his right hand is chilling. His horns rise above his head and extend onto Rio's wrist. The Devil is smiling too wide, but the glint of trouble in his eyes makes me smile to myself.

He's clearly a fan of Devil tattoos.

Rio. My troublemaker.

Next, I track the words across his knuckles. The word *vive* stands out on his right hand.

Live.

Switching to the other hand I trace over the other word. *Pelea.*

Fight.

Is that the creed he lives by? Live and fight.

Heaving a sigh, I decide it's time to get up. I peel Rio's fingers apart one at a time, miraculously not waking him in the process. Now for the difficult part. Getting up without waking the logs on either side of me.

Without even an inch of space on either side, I'm somehow able to get one knee under me and extend my arm on the same side. I will never again complain about the yoga I do every night.

My other arm goes over Zane, and I place my hand on the mattress next to his head. My other leg also goes over him and my knee lands right above his hip.

My boobs are once again right in his face.

Oh well. Girl's gotta go what a girl's gotta do.

Straddling him, I shift my weight and begin lowering my leg to the ground.

Zane must finally feel all the movement around him because his eyes snap open. Panic clouds his gaze, but then he focuses on what's in front of him and he smiles.

"You didn't need to go to such extreme measures to seduce me, Angel."

Mortified, heat rises in my cheeks. "This isn't what it looks like."

"Oh?" he asks with a raised brow. Without waiting for further explanation, he grips my hips, snapping them down to meet his and dragging my pussy over his hard cock. I bite my lip to prevent any sounds from escaping, but my efforts are unsuccessful as a small moan slips free.

Zane raises his head to meet my neck and inhales then licks a line up to my ear where he places an open mouth kiss. "I could wake up like this every day."

All the air leaves my lungs at his confession and the need his actions are stirring in me. He continues to move my hips, so my pussy rubs up and down his length. I throw my head back and let out a needy groan.

"That's it. Use me, Spencer. Come all over my cock."

Zane releases my hips and I realize I'm moving my hips all on my own. I want this. My body wants this.

He glides his hands up my stomach bringing my shirt up with them to reach my breasts. He cups them and pinches my hard nipples. The sizzling feeling in my core builds and builds waiting to explode free.

"*Mierda*. I'll never say no to this sight in the morning," Rio says in a groggy voice.

I squeak and attempt to pull away at the same time Zane reaches for me to keep me in place. I dodge his hands, but lose my balance in the process and end up sprawled on the floor twisted in the blanket.

Rio and Zane poke their heads over the side of the bed and spot me in a slightly compromising position. The blanket is tangled around my legs, and my shirt is still somehow above my boobs. Rio's eyes go wide and his mouth gapes open. Zane's stare has the same heat as before.

They scramble off the bed in a race to get to me, and I shove my shirt down making myself decent.

Each holding out a hand to me, they wait for me to take their offer. Instead, I pull the blanket over my head. "I'll just stay under here until y'all leave. Thanks."

My ears are met with snicking. Curious, I bring the blanket down a few inches and see Rio swiping at his eyes while Zane covers his mouth.

"Y'all are mean," I say with mock anger.

"I'm sorry, Mama. You're just so cute."

"Cute?" I ask, affronted.

"Very cute," Rio answers.

I narrow my eyes. "No woman wants to be called cute by the guy she…" I say trailing off.

"The guy she what?" Rio pushes.

I shake my head violently refusing to answer. He leans down grabbing my arms and stands me up easily.

"The guy she dates? The guy she wants? The guy she wishes she'd just give in to and fuck?" Rio inquires, still seeking the answer I'm reluctant to give.

I bite my lower lip, holding in my reply as if it would slip free without my consent.

Rio's focus zeroes in on my lip. He brings his mouth to mine, stealing my air. But instead of kissing me, he uses his teeth to release my lip.

"If anyone gets to bite your lip, Mama, it's me."

If I thought my panties were wet before, they're drenched now. I jump back only to collide with another body. Zane's body.

Throwing ice on the inferno, I back away from the sexy

men intent on ruining every last pair of panties I own. I ask, "Why didn't my alarm go off?"

"I turned it off," Zane states.

"What? Why?"

"You needed the rest."

"I wanted to go for a run," I argue.

"Not today." Zane's face is completely blank, but his arms are crossed ready to fight me on this. Where did all this bossiness come from?

"Why the hell not?" I am outraged.

"You work too hard. You're going to wear yourself into the ground."

"You don't get to make that choice for me, Zane." I know my voice is getting louder with each reply, but I don't give a flying fuck.

"Yes, I do," he says it so casually like it's no big deal.

"No, you don't. What makes you think this is okay? What gives you the right?"

His face turns hard. "You trying to run away. That's what gives me the right."

My mouth drops open.

Reading my expression, Rio adds with a shrug of his shoulders, "You should have promised."

"Y'all can't be serious. If I promise I won't run now, can I go workout?"

"Nope," Zane answers.

"Again. Why the hell not?"

"Because then it wouldn't be a genuine promise, and you'd probably break it."

He's right, but I won't admit that to him. I won't give him the satisfaction of letting him know he's right. His lack of trust in me hurts, but I won't admit to that either.

"Y'all could just come with me like you normally do," I suggest.

"No, can do. We both have to get to work," Zane says.

Letting out a frustrated sigh I glare at the both of them. "This is not okay. You have to know that."

Zane approaches me and softly cradles my face in his hands. "I won't lose you, Spencer. I can't. You've possessed me. Body, mind, and soul. I can't breathe without you. If you were to go, you would leave me suffocating."

Tears swim in my eyes blurring Zane's face, but his words ring in my heart. I scared him more than I realized. Leaving wouldn't just shake my foundation, but his as well.

Can I do that to him? To them?

My options are: break their hearts or be the cause of their death.

I can only live with one of those.

CHAPTER 37

ZANE

Walking away from Spencer this morning took a strength I don't have. Each step was like walking through mud, but to keep her safe I had to keep going. Reaching down deep inside myself, I grasped the critical need I have to just exist in her vicinity and shoved it aside.

Now I'm sitting at my dismal desk, pretending to work while I wait. Waiting is my specialty. Most in my field hate stakeouts, but I enjoy them. I love the moment the fucker realizes I'm there for *them*. I love it even more when they run. The thrill of the chase feels like lightning coursing through my veins.

Patiently, I'll sit here until those two fuckups walk through the door. They were called out for a convenient store robbery first thing this morning but should be back soon.

I feel the grin stretch the skin around my mouth as I pretend to scan Ava Thomas' case file. Probably shouldn't be caught smiling while going over the details of a girl's abduction.

"I'm looking over the Gray file and I'm not so sure it's

connected to the string of kidnappings we've been looking into," Liam says, taking my attention away from my objective.

My background check on Liam came back clean. No skeletons in his closet. Not even a fucking parking ticket. He's practically a boy scout. He grew up on a cul-de-sac in Pennsylvania, did well in school, brings a bouquet of flowers to his wife every Friday. Even if he isn't able to come home, he will have them delivered. An all around good guy. The poster child for American living.

In response to Liam's observation, I just raise my eyebrows. The newbie stammers and tilts his head back down to the file in his hand. Poor guy will get used to my nonverbal communication. It makes him nervous, but oh well. Not my problem he scares easily. I just hope he doesn't get this worked up when truly under pressure, when bullets start flying. That's how I will know if the kid is worth his salt.

"Ms. Gray recalls seeing a sedan, but Ava's sister said she saw a white van, and the guy didn't use chloroform. He didn't even cover her mouth. It's like he knew no one would come help her. Whoever this guy is, he's cocky."

I nod my head. I already put that together, but I can tell he's onto something. The way his brow furrows and his mouth tightens into a straight line as he looks over Spencer's statement, which I had her sign this morning before I left, suggests he is connecting the dots.

"Ms. Gray's attacker is confident as if he's done this before. She doesn't mention his steps faltering or anything. He grabbed her, attempted to subdue her, and went straight for his car. As if it's a routine."

"Keep going, James," I encourage him.

"We should reach out to other precincts or maybe even the FBI and see if they have any open cases with a similar MO."

Bingo. Exactly what I was thinking.

"I agree. Run with it."

"What?" he asks, taken aback.

"It's your idea. Follow it. In fact," I reach into my top drawer and pull out one of Ash's cards and hand it to a stunned Liam. I'm not proud that I do this, but it comes in handy and I don't do it often. "Here. My friend works out of the FBI New York field office. Start there."

Liam stares at me, then the card, then back to me with his mouth wide open ready to catch some flies.

"Uh. Yeah. I'll get right on it."

Newbie needs to learn that I'm sure as fuck not going to hold his hand. Besides, I hate calling the New York field office.

"Where is the lab on the DNA test?"

"My friend actually asked for the evidence to be released into FBI custody. He thinks the attacker may be a serial. They're running it themselves."

Liam frowns. "And I'm still pursuing my idea why?"

"We're thorough."

"Okay. I'll make some calls."

"You do that," I glance towards the doors and lo and behold, Fuckup one and Fuckup two stroll through the door like they're hot shit. "And while you do, I have a few things to follow up on. I probably won't be back in until tomorrow."

I stand up and think about patting him on the back to let him know he's doing a good job, but the thought makes my shoulders tense. Instead I say, "Good work."

That'll have to do.

I shoot off a quick text to Rio and put on a charming smile while I approach the dimwitted duo ready to enact my plan.

"Hey guys." I give a quick chin lift in greeting. Troy is a well-built man who clearly spends too much time in the gym ogling his muscles. His fake tan and overly white teeth make for one very punchable face. Dustin, aka Fuckup two, is practically Troy's twin minus a few inches in height.

"Hey Kingston! How's it going?" Troy says, but clearly doesn't give a fuck about my answer.

"Can't complain." I hate small talk, but sometimes you have to blend in.

"Yeah, I heard about your arrest of the Midnight Rose Rapist. Nice work. Wish we could've been on the takedown team," Dustin chimes in.

"Yeah, couldn't have done it without you boys in blue. I can't take credit for all the leg work."

With shitheads like these you have to stroke their slimy ego. They think because they were the star quarterback in high school, but gave up their scholarship to a big university to be a cop, that somehow means they are above everyone else. Unfortunately for them, that's not how this works. They peaked in high school and are unable to hold onto that fame so they carry themselves like they're gods in hopes that someone will recognize their perceived greatness.

What a joke.

There's a reason both of them have been passed up multiple times for promotions and never get tasked with the big assignments.

"I need your help with a case. My witness is out in the Bronx, and I need to go interview her again. My partner is…" I trail off and chuckle to make them think I'm a member of their cool boys club. "Let's just say he's new." I almost feel bad for making them think Liam isn't capable, but I will do and say whatever is necessary to make Spencer safe. Even if it hurts someone's ego along the way. Not my problem.

Troy perks up and nods at my implication that I trust them to have my back more than I trust my own partner. "We got your back."

Yeah, I'm sure you do. More like you'd like to use my back for target practice with your knife.

"Thanks, man," I give them an appreciative smile and fake sigh in relief. More stroking of the slimy ego. "Follow me in your squad car. No lights or sirens, no matter what. I'll text you the details of the case on the way."

As I turn to walk away, I let the mask fall off. I despise men like them. They took the oath to protect and serve, but it means absolutely nothing to them. They dishonor it and are a disgrace to those who have lost their lives doing this job.

※ ※ ※

I PARK my car a few doors down and glance in my rearview mirror making sure these idiots in blue follow my lead. The drive here was slow. I wanted to make sure they didn't get lost in all the traffic.

I get out of my car and wait for them by my door. Rio replied to my text on my way here saying he was ready.

"Hey, Kingston. We never got the case details," Troy says as he walks to me with what he thinks is swagger. His hands rest lazily on his utility belt.

"My bad," I pretend to pull up my texts to them, but really I opened Solitaire. "Oh, the text didn't send. I'll resend it real quick." Again, pretending to send a text when really I'm continuing my game from earlier. "It's sending. Come on. Let's get inside."

I walk up those familiar concrete steps and knock. Rio opens the door with a jerk.

Fucking door always getting stuck.

"What can I do for you boys?" he asks.

"Detective Kingston with the 10th. These are Officers Troy

and Dustin. We're here to talk to Carmen. Is she around?" I respond.

"Yeah, yeah. Come on in."

Rio opens the door wider and stands to the side while I lead Fuckup one and Fuckup two into the living room.

"Where is—"

Before Troy can finish, I spin on my heel and punch him in the face, knocking him out cold. Fucking pansy ass. Can't even take a hit like a man.

Dustin reaches for his gun. Before he can unholster it, Rio is right there with a red brick and hits Dustin over the head.

"Where the fuck did you get that?' I ask.

"From Mrs. Romero's yard," he answers matter-of-factly.

"You haven't been there for days. When did you take it?"

"When I was there last. She had bricks surrounding her planters and she said she wanted them gone so I took a few. Want one?"

"You have more than one?" I ask confused as fuck.

"Of course. I got one for each of us. There's even one for Spencer."

"Why?" I throw my hands up in frustration.

"I think the appropriate response would be 'Thanks Rio! That's so kind of you to think of me while shopping for weapons.'"

"You weren't shopping for weapons! You were in an old lady's yard!"

"Shhhh," he exaggerates the shushing by putting a finger to his lips. "Lower your voice, *amigo*. You'll wake our guests before we even have time to show them to their room."

I shake my head and grab Troy under his armpits to haul him down to the basement.

Adding the basement to the place was not easy. Especially when Asher decided we could do it ourselves because we didn't need anyone else in our business. I agreed with his reasoning, but I campaigned for buying a warehouse by the docks. We eventually got the warehouse and occasionally use the space to *interrogate*, but we still use the basement of our brownstone every now and then.

Now is one of those times.

"*Estás gordo, hijo de puta.*"

I grunt in agreement with Rio. Troy is too jacked. I'm sure half of his gym time is spent staring at women who don't want the attention.

When we finally strip them down to their underwear and have them secured to the metal chairs, Rio shoots me a shit eating grin.

This is his domain.

He tosses ice cold water on the sleeping beauties, and they sputter awake.

"What the fuck!" Troy roars as he jerks on the handcuffs that have him strapped to the armrests.

Good thing we soundproofed this baby.

Dustin is still dazed and confused. He looks around, his eyes unfocused. When he tries to stand, he finally becomes aware of his situation.

"Good morning, Sunshine," Rio says with a maniacal smile.

The hairs on Dustin's arm visibly stand on end. Rio is a pro at putting the fear of God in people. Especially when we need answers.

"Kingston, what the fuck is going on?" Troy barks.

Half of getting information depends on how you approach the suspect. I learned how to interrogate someone on the job, but Rio taught me how to use pain and fear to get the answers faster.

Troy thinks he's the top dog in the room. Dustin already

knows where he stands in the pecking order. The question is, do we break Troy and scare Dustin further or do we just go for Dustin?

I eye Rio quizzically, he turns his eyes to Troy.

Breaking the dickwad it is.

We have done this enough that we don't need words to communicate here. It's even more fun with Asher.

I roll up my sleeves, undo my tie, and set it gently on the metal tray next to Rio's knives, drawing their attention to the sharp, shiny objects.

Oh, how Rio loves his knives.

Then I grab the wood baseball bat and flip it over in my hand a few times.

Cliche? Yes.

Badass? Also, yes.

All of my movements are intentional. We need them to know we mean business. We don't have time for a drawn out questioning. We need answers. Fast.

"Tell me, Troy. Are you a betting man?" I continue playing with the bat.

"What?"

"I think my question was quite clear, don't you?" I ask the rhetorical question to Rio.

"*Sí.*"

"What's your vice? Blackjack? Russian roulette?"

Troy turns red like he is ready to blow.

"Okay, I'll answer for you. Poker. Am I right?"

Still no answer.

"It's okay. I know I'm right, and judging by the second mortgage that you took out on your house, I'm willing to bet your poker face is shit. Does Denise know?"

"You leave my wife out of this, you bastard!" He bellows.

Rio picks up a carving knife and approaches Troy. Dustin looks on, quivering like the little bitch he is.

"Ahhh. I'm guessing she has no idea," Rio says, his smile never faltering.

"Is that what this is about, huh? Rico sent you to rough me up? He must really be scraping the bottom of the barrel."

Rio lets out a laugh that promises pain.

"This *puto* thinks this is about the money he owes the MS-13," Rio says to me. When he turns back to Troy he slices across his bare chest and blood immediately blooms from the wound. Troy hisses, clenching his teeth.

"No no, *amigo*. We just need you to know that we know everything about you. We know about the strip club you visit once a week, the gambling debt. We even know how little Mary likes her waffles in the morning," Rio says threateningly. We would never hurt his daughter, but he doesn't need to know that. "We're here because you fucked with some case files."

"I don't know what you're talking about," Troy says through a locked jaw.

Rio brings the knife down hard on Troy's thigh causing a scream to escape his throat.

"*Cállate*. That wasn't even that bad. Suck it up." Rio rolls his eyes at Troy as his head hangs forward and sweat drips from his forehead.

Rio slaps Troy to get his attention. "Don't you dare pass out on me."

Troy just grunts and Dustin's minor shivering has turned into a full body shake.

When Rio turns his attention to Dustin, the bitch sings like a canary.

"We were just told to make some stalking reports disappear. It was no big deal. The chick wasn't in any real danger. The texts weren't even threatening."

"Shut up, Dustin!"

"Oh no, Dustin, keep going. Tell us all about this *chick*," Rio says as he glides the sharp blade down Dustin's arm leaving a red line behind on his skin.

"W-we just threw 'em in the trash."

Lie. They're not in the trash.

"Why?" I finally chime in.

Dustin bites his lip, afraid to answer.

"Don't you dare!" Troy threatens Dustin.

"We d-didn't have a choice," he utters, still shaking like a fucking leaf.

I step in with the bat raised over my head and bring it down on Dustin's forearm. Not hard enough to break the bone. I think. Dustin howls and I narrow my eyes at him.

"Why!" I yell.

"They have pictures of us. I swear we didn't know they were—"

"I said shut up!"

Rearing my fist back, I nail Troy in the eye. He fucking did this. He didn't protect my Angel. With those thoughts, I let another fist fly. Then another. And another. Soon Troy's face is nothing but a swollen melon resting on a set of shoulders.

Turning back to a wide-eyed Dustin I grunt out, "Why?"

"Euphoria. A strip joint up in Yonkers. They employed some minors and got pictures of us with them," my face turns murderous and Dustin rambles on in defense. "I swear! I didn't know. I got a little girl of my own. I would never. I'm no pedo."

"Now tell me where the files really are," Rio demands as he settles the knife over Dustin's right pinky finger.

"They're in our squad car!"

Even though he answered, Rio doesn't care. He still presses down and severs the finger from Dustin's hand. Dustin wails, stirring Troy slightly.

"Do you know what we do to men who touch what they shouldn't?"

"No, man. I swear! I swear! We didn't know!" Dustin pleads.

"Too late, *amigo*." Then Rio takes each and every one of Dustin's fingers ensuring he can ever again touch what he shouldn't.

Troy is now fully awake. He can barely open his eyes thanks to me, but the split knuckles I sustained were worth it. Even though I can hardly see his eyes through the already swollen skin, I can still see them darting all over the place, looking for a way out.

I lean down and whisper in his ear, "You're never leaving this place. Say your peace, motherfucker. Your last words are mine."

There's a slight tremor in his hands anticipating what Rio took from Dustin.

"I'm not telling you shit." He manages to mumble.

"Loyal to the end. How cute. But your loyalty is misplaced. No one can protect you. You're going to die here trying to honor the men who blackmailed you. I'm going to find those pictures and I'm going to send them to your wife so she knows exactly who you are."

"You wouldn't dare." He hardens his voice, but I don't give it any stock.

"Wouldn't I? It wasn't hard to find out everything I needed to know about you. Just a few keystrokes and I had all I needed. Your wife is going to move on and find a *real man*. Your daughter will call someone else *dad*. They will forget all about you. Just like everyone else. It'll be like you never existed."

"I knew you were crazy. I told Captain not to let you transfer. You think I don't know about you? The fucked up detective who won't even shake someone's hand?" I don't flinch at his muffled words.

He's poking at old wounds that have long since healed. I am who I am. I have no apologies to make.

"Good to know Captain thinks your opinion is shit, seeing how he accepted my transfer and welcomed me with open arms."

Rio leans over Troy after discarding Dustin's fingers on the floor and says, "That's enough out of you, grumpy pants. Your turn. Time for your punishment."

Troy's energy renews and he thrashes violently, shaking the chair side to side. I move behind him to stabilize it.

"Stop moving. You're going to ruin my work," Rio chastises, but Troy continues to flail about. "Fine! See if I care if your stumpy hands look horrible afterwards!"

"No! No! Nooo!" Troy yells, but Rio isn't deterred. He slices off each finger slowly, drawing it out to the end.

With both guys passed out, Rio stands and wipes his forehead with the back of his hand. "Whew. Hard work," he looks down and notices a speck of blood. "Aw shit! Spencer really liked this shirt."

"You've never worn that around her."

"Well it would have been her favorite when I wore it today."

Tired of his antics and ready to move onto the next step, I stand in front of Troy with my gun raised and say, "Bye bye, motherfucker."

His brain matter blows out the back of his skull as I shoot him right between the eyes.

"Oh, come on! I'm not scrubbing this place again. You get clean-up duty this time."

CHAPTER 38

SPENCER

The day passes by at the pace of a sloth in New York traffic.

Extra. Fucking. Slow.

Laying down the law with Asher apparently has consequences. I don't know what is with this large man having such a delicate ego, but punishing me because I told him to keep his hands to himself? It's juvenile.

He hasn't spoken a word to me all day. Everyone else? That is a different story.

Asher told Hayes he got in touch with his tattoo artist and is able to get him in for an appointment if he's interested. He talked to Alma about her kids which had her batting her eyelashes at him as he fawned over the pictures she showed him on her phone. When Iris came by to eat lunch with Hayes, Asher charmed her with a smile that would make any woman swoon and willingly hand over her panties. He had her giggling like a preteen with uncontrollable hormones. The asshole even discussed the fucking economy with Paul. What started off as a conversation about Paul selling his teapots, turned into pricing and then morphed into supply and demand. The economy.

Are you kidding me?

But has the dimwitted giant uttered even a word in my direction? Nope. Not one.

Everyone can tell something is going on between Asher and me, judging by their glances that bounce back and forth between us. Today has been fucking peachy. Everyone is acting like Mom and Dad are fighting, which I guess you could say we are.

Oh! And the cherry on top. When I do look at Asher, half the time he's staring at me with red hot lust in his eyes. Each time I felt electricity zap my chest and spread through my body causing my panties to dampen. I was tempted multiple times to go upstairs and change. I probably have a wet spot in between my legs. Just the reminder has my face turning bright red.

It doesn't help that Zane wasn't able to come by for lunch…again. He would have given me a reprieve from the man who suddenly turns mute when I'm within three feet of him.

When Asher came by my apartment this morning to walk me to work, he only nodded at Zane and Rio as they left. We didn't even stop at The Mudhouse for coffee.

Maybe that's what has me in such a state. Lack of caffeine. Yeah, that's it.

Rationalizing my frustrations doesn't do anything though. By the end of the day I am fuming. Fucking *fuming*.

How dare he? I'm the one who told him to make up his mind and here he is acting like I'm a pariah. Well fuck that and fuck him.

You know you would.

I roll my eyes at my inner voice and murmur to myself, "Fucking horny ass bitch."

"What was that?"

I blink and look up at Hayes. I didn't realize he was so close or I would have cursed Inner Spencer out loud.

"Nothing." I shake my head at Hayes and utilize the motion to jar the angry voice swirling around in my skull. That bitch in there is helping no one.

"Okay, well I'm going to take off then. I got everything wiped down and put away."

I blink again and realize everyone has gone home and it's getting late. I normally close later, but it was Asher's grand idea that I should close at five p.m. until my attacker is caught, and it wasn't a suggestion he even brought up to me. No, no. He went behind my back and discussed it with Hayes, Alma, Paul, and Iris. They all agreed and Iris made temporary signs to hang in the door. That's how I found out.

"Thanks, Hayes. See you tomorrow," I say with a tight smile.

"Night!"

And just like that, it's me and my mute bodyguard. I didn't realize how much of a buffer everyone else unknowingly offered until now. The silence booms in my ears and tension fills every nook and cranny in the studio.

Turning my focus Asher's way, I catch him once again giving me that look. The look that promises the most delicious punishment.

What the hell did I do to earn a punishment from him?

Nothing. That's what. Setting boundaries doesn't deserve punishment. It deserves fucking praise.

Instead of averting my eyes like I have all day, I hold his gaze and allow the burn to make my core ache, but I won't let it show. If I have to suffer through his temper tantrum, so does he. I won't give in. I am stronger than the urge of my ovaries to have this man's babies.

When his eyes dip to the apex of my thighs I freeze. Shit. I was rubbing my thighs together.

Way to stay strong. You showed him.

Fucking hell. Damn Asher and his ungodly good looks. As my bodyguard, I should require him to wear a bag over his head and an extra long potato sack. I know it won't do anything to quell my need. I already know the magic his lips hold and daydream about the way he could toss me around like a ragdoll.

Again, damn Asher for turning me into this sex-crazed woman I don't recognize.

My chest heaves with each breath I take. I may be burning inside, but dammit if I won't make him burn just as hot with me.

Knowing it will enrage him, I grab my things and head to the exit. He wants to be the first out the door, but I'm too angry to give him what he wants.

Suck it, big guy.

I throw the door open and dash out onto the pavement with Asher hot on my heels. He snags my elbow just as I make it outside. Ignoring his presence, like he did to me all damn day, I lock up and head up to my apartment. I can feel his eyes drilling holes into the back of my head.

I purposefully stomp my way up the stairs which serves twofold. First, it drowns out the sound of his heavy breathing. I thought the sound would satisfy me because then I would know he is right where I am—sexually frustrated and just plain angry—but instead it bumps my need to a new height. Specifically six feet and five inches high. Second, stomping will hopefully drain some energy thereby draining the desire clouding my senses.

I'm ready to head straight to my room and lock myself in there until the object of my pent up frustrations is gone.

Halting halfway there, I spin and come up with a new plan. I don't know where this sadistic Spencer is coming from, but here she is in her boots that were made for walkin'.

Beelining for the kitchen and dropping my purse on the counter, I renew my calm, indifferent exterior. I lean onto one hip hoping it draws his attention to my ass. I may not know exactly what I'm doing, but I know it's working when I hear the wrinkle of paper from behind me.

Scanning the contents in the fridge, my eyes land on the plastic container of red fruit and can of whipped cream. I do a quick rinse in the sink, place the strawberries in a bowl, and take my findings to the counter in front of Asher where he sits on a stool at the breakfast bar, leaving a good few feet between us.

Ripping off my oversized shirt leaves me in my plunge sports bra and leggings. I bought the bra because it gave my boobs an extra lift. I never thought I would wear it like this in front of another person, let alone a man like Asher, but now I'm high fiving myself for the purchase.

I know my plan is working when I see the paper from earlier take on more of Asher's aggression.

I give him a little smirk, pick up the juiciest looking strawberry and take a bite allowing a single dribble of juice to trail down my neck and cleavage. Asher's focus follows its path as it disappears in my bra. His attention makes me wish it was his hands, his mouth caressing me.

A flush breaks out across my skin and I suck in an audible breath as his eyes return to mine. If I thought they were burning before, it's got nothing on the inferno blazing in them now. His rough hands grip the counter as if it's his anchor keeping him from coming to me.

Pushing him further I take another bite and drag the remnants across my lower lip.

Abruptly, Asher jumps to his feet, kicking the chair behind him.

Oh shit.

Maybe I shouldn't have poked the beast?

CHAPTER 39

ASHER

This woman. She thinks she can tell me to stay away and then pull this shit with those fucking strawberries like there won't be consequences? Fuck that. I'm putting an end to the bullshit right here right now.

I have been half-hard in my slacks all goddamn day. It's a miracle no one noticed, and now she thinks she can play games. When she bit into the strawberry, all I could picture was biting into that plump ass of hers and slapping it so hard my palm print would be visible for days. Her tits in that sad excuse for a top, practically pushing her perfect mounds in my face. Does she expect me to not look?

This game of chicken she started has my cock twitching, begging to be let out to play. I have never been this hard without being inside a woman. My dick could pound nails and I haven't even touched her. Not even a whisper between us.

While games can be fun, I'm calling her bluff.

I jump to my feet and kick the stool back sending it crashing into the wall. Her eyes go wide and if possible, her breathing picks up even faster causing her cleavage to jiggle ever so slightly.

Yeah, fuck this distance.

I round the counter, and she immediately backs away, putting a hand up between us. Like I'd let a simple hand get in my way. She taunted me, waved the red flag at the agitated bull. If she didn't want me to act, she never should have stepped into the ring.

"Don't start what you can't finish, Princess." I growl at her.

"I–I…" Her focus darts around the kitchen. She won't find the escape she's looking for.

"It's too late, Spencer. You should have thought your little game through first."

The panic leaves her and rage takes its place. "Back up."

"I don't think I will. Not when I can see that you want me as much as you hate me right now." She gasps and shakes her head. She can deny it all she wants, but we both know it would be a lie.

She doesn't realize it, but she's been rubbing her lush thighs together all day. I'd rather her thighs rub up against my beard as I tongue fucked her sweet cunt.

"Take off the leggings."

With shaking hands she dips her thumbs into her waistband.

"Don't go all shy on me now, Spencer. Or are you giving up already?"

Just like I predicted, her resolve returns and she's more determined now to step up to my challenge. Spencer shucks her leggings and tosses them at my head. I duck and let them sail past me.

The sight in front of me leaves me stunned. Her black thong is simple, but on her it looks like it's worth a million bucks. Her body is what wet dreams are made of. Her golden skin is smooth, and she's soft in all the right places. There is a beautiful pink hue that has tinted her cheeks and spread across the top of her tits. I imagine the weight of them in my hand and how I would worship them, sucking the peaks in my mouth and lavishing them with my tongue.

"Drop those panties, Princess," I say through gritted teeth. If I unclench my jaw, I'm afraid I might beg her to let me fuck her all night long. And I would, all night long.

Without hesitation she bends, taking off her panties and then removing her bra without me telling her to.

Oh yeah. My sassy little Princess wants this.

Just like before, she launches both articles of clothing at my head, but instead of maneuvering out of the way I catch them. Bringing her panties to my nose, I inhale deep.

"Fucking heaven."

I shove the thong in my pocket and toss the bra over my shoulder. Taking a step towards her again, she holds her hands up to halt me.

"Wait. Wait."

"You can't be serious."

"Is it still complicated?" She raises a brow in my direction.

I sigh and place my hands on my hips. "Nothing has changed since yesterday."

Narrowing her gaze, she draws the line in the sand. "Then you keep your hands to yourself, big guy."

"Fine. Hands to myself it is." With a wicked gleam in my eye and a slow grin promising mischief, I undo my tie, unbutton my shirt, and let it fall from my shoulders. Making sure I have her captivated the same way she has me, I slowly unzip my pants and fist my hard cock.

I almost blow right then and there like a teenager having sex for the first time when she nibbles on her lower lip.

"Asher…"

"Hop up on the counter, Spencer, and spread those thighs. I want to see how wet you are for me."

All doubt leaves her with my dirty words. My Princess likes it when I talk dirty.

Saving that info for later.

No. Not later. There will be no later. This is a one-time deal. I can never let it go any further than this.

Spencer stalks toward me adding a little sway to her hips, then she pivots and goes to the countertop next to me. Leaning back on her elbows she opens her legs revealing her needy pussy. She looks perfect like this, spread open wide for me. I wish I could impale her on my dick and never leave. She looks so fucking tight.

"Have you been drenched like this all day? Aching for me?" My question is met with a deeper pink coloring her cheeks. I smirk at her.

Yeah, she isn't as unaffected as she pretends to be.

"Use your fingers and rub your clit. Show me how you made yourself come in the shower yesterday while you shouted my name."

Her eyes go wide. "I didn't—"

"Don't lie. We both know you did."

Embarrassment coats her skin, but she still follows my instructions. Gliding her hand between her perfect breasts and down her abdomen. When she reaches her core, she circles her bundle of nerves and moans.

"Good girl."

Careful not to end this too early, I squeeze the base of my dick. I'm close already and we haven't even gotten to the good stuff yet.

"Give it a little flick," I instruct. When she does, I give her more praise which has her preening. "Just like that. That's it," I say in a husky voice.

The back and forth motion of her finger has a flare of jealousy stir up. It should be my fingers there. Not hers. Her legs should be wrapped around my waist—or my head.

"Eyes open and on me, Princess. I want to see what you look like when you cum," her eyes snap open and connect with mine and I swear I feel the act tug on my cold, dead heart. "Take two of your fingers and feed them into your pussy."

When she does, she cries out, "Asher!"

My name. She screamed *my fucking name*. I shouldn't be itching to hear it again, but I fucking am. I need it.

I finally start to pump my shaft in time with her movements. I watch her pussy tighten around her fingers and know she is close, so damn close.

"Look at you. Look how you're soaking the counter for me. So fucking wet."

"Asher, please," she whines.

"Tell me what you need, Princess."

"I–I don't know. Just please."

Eyeing the can of whip cream, I snag it without losing the rhythm of fisting my dick in that delicious up and down motion.

I shake it and her eyes go wide. "What are you doing?"

"You said no hands. You didn't say anything about my mouth."

Heat flares in her eyes again, and I add a drop of whip cream to each of her nipples. I look back up at her, waiting for consent. When she gives her head a small nod, I dive in like a starving man. I take as much of her in my mouth as I can and suck. Her back bows off the island and my ears are met with that glorious sound again.

"Asher! Oh shit. Asher!"

Her enthusiasm spurs me on. Once her nipple is as hard as

a fucking diamond, I let her mound pop free from my mouth and I give the other the same attention.

"Yes, please. Please, Asher, please. I'm so close." Her hand between us moves faster now.

I let her breast fall from my mouth and straighten.

"Me too, Princess," I pant. "I'm going to paint your perfect little body with my cum."

Spencer must *really* like my filthy mouth because she cums right then and there. The sight is nothing short of a religious experience. Her muscles tighten and she screams again.

The next thing I know, I'm cuming with her and do just as I said, paint her with my cum. I ride the high for what feels like forever.

When I come back down to Earth, I'm leaning against the countertop between Spencer's legs and my free hand is planted on the marble next to her head. She's staring up at me bewildered and I'm betting my expression matches hers, because what the fuck? I've never cum so hard in my life and I wasn't even inside her.

Coming back to my senses, I stand up and tuck myself back in my pants. I wet a towel at the sink and begin wiping my cum from Spencer's body. Washing away any and all evidence of what we just did as if it never happened.

I should do the same, wash this memory from my mind. I can't say I regret it. I would be lying to myself, but my priorities need to come first. My job, my family. Spencer has wormed her way under my skin without even trying and it's vexing. I can't let her burrow any deeper.

Once I have her clean, I scoop her up in my arms and carry her to bed. On the short walk to her room, she passes out cold. I lay her on the bed and rummage through her closet for something to dress her in.

When dressed, I tuck her under the fluffy comforter, but

then I find myself reluctant to leave. It's like I have concrete blocks attached to my ankles. Each step away from her is difficult and it doesn't get easier the further I get.

AN HOUR LATER, Rio and Zane find me with a Corona in my hand as I sit on the couch staring out the window.

"Honey, I'm home! I even wore your favorite shirt."

"Shut up, idiot. She's sleeping," I hiss.

"Already? It's still early, and we brought Thai," Rio says with a frown and holds up the two bags of take out in his hands.

I ignore him and go back to sipping my drink, not in the mood to put up with their rowdiness right now. I'm mentally banging my head against a brick wall. I told Spencer it was complicated. Fuck. If it was complicated before then it's a fucking shitshow now.

The woman drives me fucking crazy, and not to mention Rio and Z are already head over heels for her like a pair of love sick puppies.

Interrupting my pity party of one, Z takes a seat next to me.

"We had a chat with the fuckup duo today."

Just what I need, to focus on something that *should* have my attention.

"Oh yeah? How'd that go?"

"We got what we needed."

Waiting for him to elaborate, I give him a look conveying I'm all out of patience for the day.

He leans back and explains, "They got rid of the files just like we thought. Well, 'got rid of' isn't right. More like they hid the physical copies and erased the digitals from the system."

"Assholes. They say why?"

"I said we got what we needed," Z reiterates.

I cross my arms and wait.

He sighs. "They frequent a strip joint called Euphoria up in Yonkers. Turns out some of those girls shouldn't be working there. They should be getting ready for prom, practicing for their driving test, planning for what they're going to do after they graduate…but no. These girls work there and the owner has pictures. I dug into their finances to find the owner, but it's a never ending trail of shell corporations owned by shell corporations."

"What's your take?" I ask.

"Rio and I think it reeks of Cain, but how Cain and a small-time consultant like Anthony Cole are connected, I haven't figured that out yet. If Cain is the owner, then that means Cain owed Anthony. What would a big fish like Cain need from a nobody like Anthony in the first place?"

Rio joins us on the couch with a plate of noodles. "Maybe Anthony is a supplier."

"What? Like Anthony kidnaps women and children and sells them to Cain?" Z asks, leaning back in his seat.

Rio shrugs a shoulder. "It's a possibility. We have to ask ourselves what does an asshole like Cain need? Product."

"We need more info on Anthony Cole," I state, eyeing my two best friends wondering if they're thinking what I am.

"Absolutely not," Z says.

Yep. He's reading my mind.

"She lived with him, Z. For months. Plus, she was romantically involved with him for way longer than that."

"Don't you dare say what that fucker did to her was romantic," Z seethes.

"You know what I mean."

"Rio? Back me up on this."

"I don't know, *muchacho*. She's our best source of information. Besides, talking about it will help her. And who better to be there while she lets herself break than us?"

Zane levels a glare at Rio. They don't argue often and it has never come to blows, but Zane looks like he could punch Rio in the face.

"You know I'm right, Z."

Zane's anger wavers as he stares down at his balled up fists. "Shit. I know."

Rio abandons his plate of food and sinks down next to Zane. "This is how we help her heal and move on."

Struggling with words, Zane just nods.

"So, what's our next step?" Rio asks.

Zane stares at his hands. "Well we let Dustin go, so next we follow him."

"More like dropped him in the dumpster," Rio mumbles.

We all let out a dark chuckle together because we know a dumpster is exactly where the trash belongs.

"It's going to take him some time to wake up and then get himself to the hospital, so I give us three or four days before we need to tail him," Zane assesses.

"Tracker?"

"Implanted in his back where he won't see it. I'm sure he won't even notice the pain."

I nod in approval. This isn't our first rodeo and it won't be our last. We all know our roles and our strengths. We utilize them where needed.

"How's your case coming?" Rio asks me.

"I'm up shit creek without a fucking paddle," I say as I drag my hand down my face. "The floral company said the order was paid for in cash and the guy wore a hoodie and sunglasses."

"So, no description," Rio adds.

"Yeah. No chance of prints on the box since it was delivered by the floral company, but I know it's him. I know it's this fucker that has had me chasing my tail for months."

"Spencer is convinced it was Anthony. Not your guy," Zane says unhelpfully.

"I know, man, but my gut is screaming at me. It's him. I know she thinks it's Anthony, but she hit her head multiple times. Not to mention the adrenaline that was pumping through her at the time. We all know how that can affect someone in the moment."

"She swears up and down it's Anthony though," Rio argues.

"Whose side are you fucking on?"

"The truth has no sides," Rio says firmly.

Fuck. Can't argue with that.

"Whatever," I raise from my spot and head to the door, discarding my beer on the way. "I'm heading out, I need to get some sleep. I'll see you shitheads in the morning."

"Sweet dreams, Wolf!" Rio calls after me.

Ignoring him, I finally leave Spencer's intoxicating scent behind. I'll be able to think more clearly without her near.

My shoulders droop from exhaustion as I stroll to my Camaro. I'm not looking forward to the long drive home. I'm only stopping there to pick up supplies before I head out again.

I told Rio and Z that I was going to get some sleep, but I never said where I'd be sleeping.

CHAPTER 40

SPENCER

*B*eing confused as to how I got in bed is not an experience I want to repeat. The last thing I remember is finger banging myself in front of the man that makes me want to punch things while he came all over my chest. It was the single hottest moment of my life, but he doesn't need to know that. In fact, I would prefer it if he never found out.

But the real question is, how did I get a shirt and panties on?

I have chosen to ignore that question and pretend it never existed, because like Asher said, "it's still complicated," therefore I see no reason in mentioning that last night happened.

Today is a gallery day, so I got dressed in my usual work get-up. I begrudgingly took a little extra time with my makeup and hair this morning, but that's only because Zane turned off my alarm and I missed out on my morning run, *again*.

My sour mood was quickly remedied when I left the bathroom and the sweet aroma of waffles, bacon, and eggs filled my nose. Rio had run out for breakfast, and Zane ran downstairs and got my favorite coffee. For a few minutes I allowed myself to envision my life if I stayed. If Anthony didn't exist. Rio, Zane, and I would live happily here, eat meals together, never cook, and have movie nights. I have more space in this apartment than I know what to do with, or maybe we'd buy a house outside the city and commute to work together every day.

Would Asher live with us? Would he want to?

As quickly as the picture appeared, it vanished. It's a fairy-tale, just a dream, not real.

Now I'm in the real world with Iris going over numbers, marketing strategies, and emails from artists who want to display their work. All the while Asher sits in a chair with his arms folded, looking even more grumpy than yesterday. Why he's grumpy in the first place, I have no idea. It's not like he didn't enjoy himself last night.

I sigh and remind myself that I'm not responsible for his mood. I can't control how he feels. That is his choice.

My day can't get any worse.

Famous last words. The universe loves proving me wrong, a fact that I'm reminded of when Lance walks in.

He's dressed to impress. Well, I assume he believes his outfit would impress someone, but that someone isn't me. It's also not Iris, judging by her muffled laugh. He's wearing a beige suit with an ivory shirt, the top few buttons undone, leaving all of our eyes with an awful view of his hairless chest. He has a fresh spray tan and his nails are perfectly manicured. In his hands he has a large bouquet of pink roses.

"Hello, Spencer. Don't you look lovely today!" The way my skin crawls is impossible to ignore.

"Hi, Lance. What can I do for you?" Asher perks up at my reply.

"Some lovely flowers for a lovely woman." Lance hands

over the obscenely large bundle. It's so tall, I can barely see over the top. Little does Lance know, I'm not a fan of roses.

"Ew. Don't ever say that again," Iris says.

Lance turns his nose up at Iris. "They're not for you, so your input is not needed here. Run along."

I drop the bouquet on the desk and glare at him. "Do not speak to her that way."

"I think it's time you leave, Lance Richards." Lance's shoulders tense at Asher's gruff tone. I don't know how I missed Asher standing right behind Lance.

"And who are you?"

"I'm Ms. Gray's bodyguard." Asher shoots me a grin.

"It's fine, Asher. I'm sure Lance was just going to have a quick look around and then be on his way," Lance narrows his eyes at Asher and walks to a painting on the back wall. "Lance is harmless."

"I don't like him." His words are for me, but his stare doesn't leave Lance.

"I'm with Viking Hottie on this," Iris adds.

My stomach grumbles just as Zane strolls through the door with a brown paper bag that smells like garlic, marinara, and grilled chicken.

"Hey, Angel. I brought lunch," he beams at me. He breaks eye contact with me for a moment to nod at Asher who tilts his head towards Lance. Zane follows Asher's gesture, and his eyes turn hard.

There should be a book on this shit, *How to Decipher the Grunts and Gestures of Cavemen.*

"Lance Richards," Zane seethes.

How do they both know his name?

I ignore their ridiculousness and a megawatt smile breaks out across my face. "You're a God among mere mortals, Zane Kingston."

I make my way to him ready to hug him, but pause when I remember the other night. I don't want to trigger him. He doesn't need his past making itself known right now.

Sensing what I want, Zane sets the bag down on the ground and guides my arms around his neck then wraps his around my waist. Pulling me close so our bodies are pressed together he brings his head down and inhales. My heart flutters as he takes in my scent like it's the only thing he wants to breathe for the rest of his life. With my elevated height I can rest my head on his shoulder, but when I do, I spot a man standing awkwardly just inside the door behind Zane.

"Oh, hi! Welcome to Abstract Dreams."

Zane turns, resting an arm across my shoulders and tucking me against his side. "Angel, this is my partner. Detective Liam James."

This detective looks like a kid. His innocent appearance is magnified by the way his mouth is hanging open, staring at the arm slung around my shoulders. Ignoring his shock, I go to step forward only to be pulled back by Zane. I elbow him in the side, causing him to grunt then chuckle, and finally step away with my hand stretched forward. "It's nice to meet you, Liam. I'm Spencer Gray."

He recovers clumsily and grasps my hand with a firm shake. "You too, Spencer," he says with a tight smile.

"Are you staying for lunch?"

Liam flashes me an easy smile that reminds me of Hayes and says, "Not today. I just wanted to get a peek at the gallery. I'm going to walk down the street to the gyro stand on the corner."

"Are you sure?"

"Yeah. I don't want to impose."

"Feel free to bring your food back here and eat. We have a huge break room in the back."

As he turns to walk out, Rio bursts through the door. "Hey, Mama! Did you miss me?" He walks right up to me and plants a tender kiss on my cheek that contrasts his obnoxious mood. "Ooo! Z! Did you bring me lunch too?"

Zane rolls his eyes at Rio, but nods in affirmation.

"Oh! You must be the new partner. I'm Rio, the best friend and roommate."

Liam cocks his head to the side as if he's trying to figure Rio out.

Good luck with that.

Liam introduces himself and shakes Rio's hand. All four of us begin chatting, ignoring the food that is going cold and get to know Liam a little. Asher eventually saunters over but hangs back by the desk. For a brief moment things feel normal, and I can pretend that all's right within our little bubble.

But those moments never last.

You know when it feels like time slows right before something big happens? A moment of complete mental clarity. A moment before your world shatters. Literally.

One minute we're talking and laughing and then comes a loud *pop, pop, pop*. Glass explodes inward across the front of the gallery.

Zane turns to me with wide, panicked eyes and moves as if to lunge toward me, but his shoulder jerks and he falls on his back.

"Zane!" I scream, but no one hears. I can't even hear myself. My shout is drowned out by what I realize is rapid gunfire.

Peering out to the street, ice rolls down my spine when I see the person driving the car with two guns held out the windows. Pierce Murphy. I knew even back when I first met him that his chilling blue eyes always held violence in them. The type of violence that would decimate anyone in its path then he'd mock the aftermath.

He gives me a slow wink and a wide smile. A smile that on anyone else would make me swoon, but on him, it's terrifying.

A scream causes me to turn my back to the windows. I start to shout at Iris to hide, but Asher is already there diving over the desk and tackling her to the floor.

"Spencer, get down!" I don't know how I hear Rio yell over the sound of bullets. It's almost like he whispered directly in my ear. When I whip around to Rio, his arm is outstretched ready to pull us to the ground, but he sinks down to one knee, his face twisted in pain.

I take a step towards him ready to save us both, but before I can take another step the wind is knocked out of me as the side of my body connects the hardwood floors.

"Stay down!" the man above me shouts. Liam. I blink and his gun is out as he spins around on his knees and returns fire. My ears are already ringing, so the sound of his gun firing doesn't affect my already damaged eardrums.

When Liam lowers his weapon, all the breath returns to my lungs. I shoot up to a sitting position as the blood drains from my face. My gaze shoots around the destroyed room unable to truly focus on a single thing.

"Z, get back here!"

My head snaps and I see Zane sprinting through the shattered windows and down the sidewalk with his gun in hand.

"Spencer? Spencer, look at me, Mama."

Two hands hold my head and turn it to the side. I try to scurry backwards, but I'm met with soft chocolate eyes and the tightness in my chest eases a little.

"Are you hurt?"

My eyes are blank and my brain isn't able to formulate words to answer him.

Rio checks me all over. "A few cuts and scrapes, but nothing serious," he lets out a breath of relief. "You're okay. You're not hurt. I'm right here."

A whimper escapes my lips and Rio pulls me into him. I settle my hand on his thigh and he lets out a small hiss. I jerk back, looking down at my hand I see smears of deep red across my palm. I realize he's hurt and I know I need to get my shit together.

"Rio! You're bleeding!"

"I'm fine, Spence. It's nothing."

"It's not nothing! You were shot!" My breaths come quickly now causing a black haze to creep into my vision, blurring the world around me.

"Hey, hey," Rio's hand lifts my chin and his other rests over my hammering heart. "I'm okay. We're all fine. I need you to breathe, Mama."

There's another boom and I flinch, this time it's the metal door leading to Clay Creations cracking against the wall with Hayes standing in the doorway. "Iris!"

Asher lifts Iris in a bridal hold and hands her over to Hayes when he makes it across the room. Hayes settles them in the computer chair behind the desk and whispers peace in her ear as she sobs.

Before long I'm being lifted into a set of thick tattooed arms and resting against a hard chest. My big guy. He doesn't offer sweet words or empty promises. He gives me what he can, comforting me with his body. Asher nuzzles his face in my neck and breaths deep.

I draw my head back when I peek over Asher's shoulder and notice a familiar beige suit laying limp on the ground covered in red.

Lance?

"Oh God," I whimper.

"Shhh. Don't look, Princess." Asher guides my face so it's nestled in his chest, obstructing my view.

Sirens are audible in the distance as we stay like that until Zane walks back through the devastation of the gallery with Liam on his heels.

"They got away, but we got a make and model on the car and Liam got one of the shooters in his hand," Zane reports.

"I saw three of them. One driver, two shooters," Liam adds.

"Same," Zane agrees.

Three people. It only took three people to destroy what I hold dear. My safe space.

Two shooters. One driver. Sixty seconds. That's all it took.

CHAPTER 41

RIO

*B*lood is going to flood the streets. I'm not just going to paint this city red, I'm going to drown it.

They robbed my Babygirl of her peace. This was her hard work, her haven, and they took that from her. They can run as far as they want, but they won't be able to hide from us, not for long.

The ambulance and police arrive three minutes too late. Good response time, but still late. They poured from their vehicles like ants. The cops recognized Zane and Liam instantly, lowering their weapons when Zane told them the assholes got away.

EMTs came straight to Lance who had been dead since the first shots, then Zane and me. Liam and Asher had to force Zane into the back of the ambulance so he could get stitched up. We were just grazed, but by Ash's reaction you'd think we had lost a limb. Asher didn't shout, but the beast within him was so angry the vibrations coming off of him were almost palpable.

Captain Williams was on the scene twenty minutes later.

He questioned Liam and Zane privately, but he didn't try to hide his anger at two of his detectives being involved in a shooting. He didn't blame them. Williams is a level-headed man, but that doesn't mean he can't be angry at the situation, it's messy. He didn't hesitate to point out that a victim in his jurisdiction should have had more protection especially if the FBI thought she might be a person of interest to a serial killer. As he walked away, he was on the phone with Asher's boss.

Spencer sits quietly staring down at her hands, shoulders slumped. She's wearing guilt like a thick, heavy cloak. She has nothing to be sorry for, but no matter how much I tell her that, she still hasn't moved.

Hayes and Iris are with her now. Iris has an arm wrapped around her and Hayes is standing sentry on Spencer's other side.

We have all given our statements to the cops on scene. Spencer was able to bring it together to answer questions, but she averted her gaze when asked if she saw anything that could help. I'll be getting that answer out of her later.

Trusting that Spencer is in good hands, I make my way to the back of the ambulance where Zane is giving an EMT grief. Walking with a bullet graze on my thigh isn't fun, but the pain doesn't faze me. I refuse to limp. It would only cause Spencer to worry, and she doesn't need that.

"I said I'm fine," he lashes out.

"You really should go to the hospital, man. Maybe get some antibiotics to make sure you don't get an infection," Liam reasons.

"Yeah, listen to Rambo," I tease.

"Rambo?" Liam questions.

"Yeah, man. Did you see yourself? The way you got Spencer to the ground and spun around on your knees like you popped out of a John Wick movie. Then you chased those guys down on foot. Definitely Rambo material."

Zane and Ash give a nod of approval and Liam beams. I don't think his smile could shine any brighter, but then he realizes he's grinning ear to ear like a little boy and quickly puts on a straight face, acknowledging our approval with a slight nod as well.

"But really Z, listen to Rambo. You should go to the hospital. Hell, I'll come with you," I say with wide-eyes hoping Zane picks up what I'm putting down.

Recognition dawns his face and he nods. "Yeah, you're right. Ash, how about you drive us."

Asher turns to Liam. "You should take off. You've earned it. Go home to your wife and kids."

Liam lowers his shoulders. "Okay, but only if you're sure you don't need me."

"Yeah, yeah. We got this."

"Okay. I'm going to go check in with Fernandez over there. Once they've cleared the scene, I'll catch a ride with one of them back to the precinct," he hesitates as he turns to walk away. "You didn't tell me you were dating her."

"It's not relevant," Zane replies.

"You know Captain won't see it that way."

"If it was your wife, would you let anyone else investigate?" Zane poses the question already knowing the answer. No man would be able to stand aside when the person he loves needs them.

"Frick," Liam mutters as he drags a hand through his hair.

Frick? Este maldito niño.

"Fine, but don't do anything to jeopardize the investigation. I don't want to get demoted just as I arrive."

Zane just nods which must be enough for Liam, or Liam

has acclimated to Zane's silence, because he turns and walks away.

Hours later, the windows are boarded up, evidence has been collected, and Spencer is tucked safely in her apartment with Hayes and Iris.

Asher is getting his ass chewed out by SSA Marreli, and he's taking the verbal beating stoically. You would never know he's ready to combust.

After he hangs up the phone he spits out, "Let's get these fuckers. I'm tired of being attacked on all fronts. It's like playing fucking wack-a-mole."

"We can't all go. Someone needs to stay with Spencer," I point out.

"We all need to be there hunting down the shooters. We're already hours behind," Asher argues back.

"Talk to Hayes. I'm sure he'll stay with her if we ask him," Zane suggests.

"*Es solo un niño*. I don't think he's ever touched a gun."

"He'll be fine. I'll talk to him," Asher says firmly.

"Fine, but if anything happens to her I'm going to rip off your arm and beat you with it."

Asher just smiles and we all turn to head upstairs. We're met with the smell of carnitas, cilantro, and lime when we walk in. Iris stands at the stove while Hayes lingers nearby and Spencer sits on the couch staring blankly at the TV, which was still off.

I break off from Zane and Asher and go right to the person I want most. Gathering her in my arms I bring her to my lap and nuzzle her hair. Her jasmine scent soothes the Devil begging to tear someone limb from limb. It's a temporary satisfaction, I know the Devil won't be tamed until he's tasted blood.

"Talk to me, Mama." I whisper, my lips pressed against her head.

"He knows. He's here," she responds. Her skin is ghostly pale.

"Who?"

Instead of answering, she repeats herself, "He knows. He's here."

"Anthony?"

She nods.

"You're safe. We're here. We'll take care of everything." I assure her as I place a gentle kiss on her forehead.

"You got hurt, Zane got hurt, and Lance—" she whimpers. Not once today has she mentioned her gallery being destroyed.

My heart warms at how much she cares. I only wish she cared about herself just as much.

"We've both had worse. I promise."

She adorably scrunches her nose thinking through my implication. "That's not comforting."

Chuckling at her endearing disposition I tell her, "We have to go, Spence."

She turns her gaze to me, full of curiosity and dread and asks, "Where?"

"We have to stop by the hospital for a checkup and get antibiotics. Zane already tore his stitches being a stubborn ass. I'm the lucky chauffeur and Asher was called into the field office."

"Oh. Okay," she nods to herself, piecing together an invisible puzzle I can't see. "I'll just see you tomorrow then."

Her dismissal feels more like a way to get rid of me and not a sweet parting of promise.

My next move may be forward, but I don't give a fuck. I reach into my pocket and pull out my keys. I removed one and hand it to her. "Here."

She takes the single key and stares at it. "Uhh. Thanks?"

"Promise me something, Mama."

"Depends," Spencer says with a side glance in my direction, unwilling to commit to any more terms.

"Promise me that if you get the urge to run again, that you'll run here instead," I request as I tap the key with my finger.

"Where is here?"

"Me."

Tears gather in her eyes, but she works double time to prevent them from falling. Her eyes are already rimmed red and puffy from crying over the last several hours. As much as I don't want to see her cry anymore, I wouldn't mind these tears shed for me.

"Did you just give me a key to your house?"

"I figured it was time."

"It hasn't even been a month since we met and we're not official or anything."

"First, we were official the moment you let me hold those perfect tits in my hands. Second, time is insignificant."

She looks back down at the key in her hand. I give her a moment to soak in my sincerity. I don't care that I'm not rational. I don't care that most people would disapprove. Fuck them. She is my everything. She's in the marrow of my bones, and I will never let her go.

Spencer brings her eyes back to mine. "I can try," she croaks out.

"That's all I ask." Resting my forehead against hers, I breathe her in and close my eyes.

One more moment of peace.

I'll give myself that much before I am unleashed on this city.

CHAPTER 42

ZANE

When I kissed Spencer goodbye, she was speechless, and a soft pink brushed her cheeks. The sight almost had me beating my chest and shouting "mine" to the world. She probably wouldn't be into that type of display, but I can always test it out next time.

Asher didn't hug her or even offer a "goodbye."

Hmm. Interesting.

Now we're on the hunt. The Devil in me smiles and is eager. The fucker is practically rubbing his hands together and bouncing off the walls. The shooters may have a head start, but that doesn't deter me. Instead, all the muscles in my body tingle, and I have to hold back a laughter bubbling inside of me.

"What's our plan of action?" Asher asks from the backseat.

"Find Hank and see what information he has. The shooters were targeting *us*. None of the bullets came close to hitting Spencer or Iris. My money's on Cain," I answer him while I speed through the dirty city streets, ignoring all traffic laws.

"It could be another favor Cain owes Anthony." Rio guesses as he rubs his chin.

"We won't have much more on that until we follow Dustin, and last I checked he was still hiding out at a warehouse in Red Hook." As soon as I was stitched up earlier, I whipped my phone out to check his location.

"Pussy," Asher mutters.

Rio grunts in agreement.

We're all feeling the itch. Patience is usually within reach, but with a storm stirring so close to our front door, patience is a concept none of us care to understand.

Rio shifts in his seat restlessly. "What about traffic cam footage?"

I grit my teeth not wanting to snap at the man who has meant more to me than anyone else since the day I met him. Thankfully Ash is the one to pipe up. "I got Berkowitz on it."

When I pull up to a stop next to Central Park, where Hank usually sells, we all hop out of the car. Normally I would tell whoever is with me to stay back while I talk to Hank, but this is different, and I know there would be no holding back Rio. Probably Ash too.

It only takes a minute to find him. They say people are creatures of habit. That is definitely true for dealers. They have to stick to a routine so people know where to find them. Some of those people might be three angry motherfuckers ready to fuck shit up in the name of a beautiful Angel.

Arms spread wide as if I'm ready for a hug, I approach Hank head on. "Hanky Boy!" I've only called him that a few times. I should have gone more subtle, but I'm eager for a chase.

Hanks eyes bug out of his face and the fucker takes off, too fast for a skinny shit his size.

295

Rio lets out a dramatic sigh. "*Mierda.*" Simultaneously we all shoot off after Hank.

We have done this enough that we have a strategy down. I take up the middle directly following the runner, Rio takes the right, and Asher takes the left.

We have a standing bet. Whoever gets to runner first, gets his drinks paid for at the Black Horse for a week. I usually win, but occasionally I throw Rio or Ash a bone and let them get the tackle first.

Hank ducks and weaves through the bushes and trees, occasionally hurdling over people who are spread out on the grass, skimming the line of second base in the evening light. My blood pumps through my veins, giving me the rush I need. I relish in the way the electricity of the hunt floods my body.

I'm toying with Hank, letting him think he has a chance at getting away, intentionally keeping myself ten yards back. I also need to make sure when I tackle him, we don't have an audience.

From the right, I see Rio veering towards Hank. Asher isn't close enough yet, but I have every intention of winning this round. When we're secluded, I dive for Hank. We roll a few times, but I end up on top and flip him over with his hands secured behind his back.

"Get off me, asshat!"

Rio and Asher sidle up to us breathing heavily while I'm riding the high. Rio's eyes are blown wide from the thrill as well. Asher is stoic, but he vibrates with the same exhilarated energy.

"We have some questions, Hanky Boy."

"You could've just asked like normal, dickface," Hank spits, wriggling under me trying to get free.

Rio squats down by Hank's face, resting his elbows on his knees and letting his hands dangle between his legs. "Now, now.

No need for name calling, *hombre*. We just need you to answer our questions and we'll be on our merry way. ¿*Sí?*"

Hank glowers at Rio, unafraid of the psychopathy seeping out of Rio's seemingly unthreatening words. He has some balls staring down Rio like that. Other men have literally been gutted for less.

Asher nudges Hank with his foot. "What do you know about a drive by shooting in Chelsea?"

"I don't know shit!" Hank has stopped struggling but is still tense.

"How about this? You tell us what we want to know, and we won't take you somewhere else for further *questioning*." Rio lets the implication hang in the air between him and Hank.

"You're crazy. You're all crazy!" Hank resumes kicking his legs trying to buck me off.

"You knew that from day one," I drawl. He still doesn't answer, and I don't actually want to let Rio loose on Hank. None of us do. So I offer the kid some honey to go with the vinegar we've been pouring down his throat. "Give us the info and we'll set your mom up in rehab."

Hank stills. He's always wanted to get his mom clean. I've offered before, but he told me to shove the charity up my ass. He's always kept score between us because he knew he didn't have anything to offer me that's worth sending his mom to rehab. But this is important and my offering rehab in exchange for the info tells him as much.

"It has to be a good one. One of those fancy ones celebrities go to. With a spa and shit."

"Done," Asher answers.

Hank lets out a sigh and finally relaxes. "Will you at least get off of me so I'm not cutting the grass for free?" Hank snarks at me.

I stand, but none of us give him the space to run again.

Dusting off his clothes, Hank gets up and folds his arms over his chest. He's posturing, but that's Hank. He'll look the scariest motherfucker in the eye and not lose a wink of sleep. "Word is a couple MS-13 have been taking on odd jobs for the right price. Anything goes. Castillo ain't got a clue though."

"Word will reach the MS-13 leader soon, no doubt," Asher states, which is true. Castillo may be a crazy fucker, but he isn't dumb. He runs a tight ship, if some of his guys are operating on the side without his say so, they'll be dead soon.

Rio takes a step forward. "We need names, Hank."

"I don't have names. Only an address," he rambles off an address in Brownsville and continues, "The idiots put in a big order and wanted it delivered for a party. They were loose-lipped when I stopped by and bragged about taking on jobs for Cain with Castillo being none the wiser."

Asher tilts his head. "What kind of drugs did they want?"

"Molly, china white, acid, bud. Anything I could get my hands on."

Rio let out a whistle and chuckled. "You really pulled through for them, *amigo*."

"That's what I do," Hank says with a shrug.

Asher nods his head. "Thanks for the info." We all turn and walk away.

"Wait! What about my mom?" Hank calls out.

"I'll get everything arranged tonight," I call back over my shoulder. I don't turn back to see if he's satisfied with my answer, he knows I'll come through.

"Let's go party with some gangsters," Rio says with a violet grin.

CHAPTER 43

ASHER

I'm ready for heads to roll. Specifically, a couple fuckers who thought they could come by and shoot up my family. Spencer may give me more headaches than my last clingy hookup, but she's important to Rio and Zane—my constant hard on around her doesn't factor into the equation.

These MS-13 fucks are lucky Spencer and Iris weren't hurt. They already have a world of hurt coming down on them, but if Spencer had been shot? We wouldn't just be hunting them down to slaughter them like the little pieces of shit they are, we would make an example of them.

In fact, maybe that's what we'll do. Make them an example. Then everyone will know that you don't fuck with Spencer Gray.

When driving through Brownsville, out in Brooklyn, your head better be on a fucking swivel. My Glock rests on my thigh and my shoulder holster is loaded with two more guns. We suited up after we left Hank in the rear view.

Rio has his knives strapped at his waist and his Beretta in hand.

That man and his knives. Never offer to hold them for him.

Zane is wearing his own shoulder holster and has a gun on each side.

We don't expect to encounter too much trouble, but you never know. Those two could have a whole armory in that rundown house.

The upside in this whole thing? The neighbors won't call the cops if bullets start flying. It's that kind of neighborhood.

We park a couple houses away. The house is white—or what once would have been called white. Now the paint is chipped and yellowed from neglect and the elements. It's a small one-story house which will make infiltration easier. The grass is a pathetic brown and the door is the same tinted white color. There's no fence around the small property which means no pets. No pets mean the guys inside won't be warned of our approach.

The sun has begun to set, in just thirty minutes it will be darker than the pits of Hell. We can let loose and *play*.

Zane turns toward me in the backseat. "How do we want to play this?"

Rio bounces his knee impatiently. "Pizza delivery?"

I groan. "Seriously?"

The smile in Rio's voice rings clear when he says, "It's my favorite!"

"I don't have any pizza boxes in my car."

"Nah. I put some in the trunk the other day. Sal gave them to me."

Letting out a chuckle I shake my head. He would. "When the fuck did you have time to do that?"

"I like to be prepared. I never know when I'll need an excuse to get inside someone's house." He's dead ass serious. *Of course, he is.* We may be crazy assholes, but Rio's mind has always operated differently. His sister's death broke something in him when he was just ten-years-old.

We sit in silence, watching the house, waiting for a signal that someone is home.

After what feels like an eternity, there's movement in the front window to the right of the door. Someone is peeking through the blinds. Zane just nods and Rio chuckles low.

Oh, you stupid motherfucker. You have no idea what's coming.

We quietly get out of the car and Rio grabs the empty pizza boxes for his dumbass ruse. The pretense isn't necessary, we could just bust down the doors or sneak in and surprise them, but Rio enjoys playing with his food first.

Zane and I take the back door. I'm always in the door first. If someone gets shot, I want it to be me. If someone tries to run, it's on Zane to chase them down. He's fast and can outrun Rio and me even on our best day.

From the back of the house we hear the doorbell ring and muffled voices. I note at least two. While they talk, I test the doorknob.

Unlocked. Idiots.

As soon as the front door opens, I slowly open the back with my Glock in hand, outstretched in front of me. We open to a musty kitchen with dingy appliances, a card table, and foldable chairs. The tiled floor has clearly seen better days.

Creeping across the kitchen, I bypass the hallway as Zane turns to go down it and clear each room. My path leads me to the living room and the next thing I know, I'm staring at the back of a tattooed head.

Rio drops the boxes and with a large grin says, "Boo."

The guy jumps back into my chest and tries to dart to the left, but I already have my arm up and around his neck, cutting off his air supply. Ten seconds later he's out cold and I let him drop.

"Zane went down the hallway. Meet up with him and make sure he's good. I'll get this one tied up and ready to go."

"I bet I was a pizza delivery driver in another life. I'm fucking good at this."

"Yeah, yeah. I'm sure." I shake my head at him and the shit that comes out of his mouth.

Just before Rio is able to close the door, tattooed fingers wrap around the edge.

"You've got to be kidding me," Rio groans.

The door swings open, banging against the wall outside, and in steps the last person we wanted to see. Gabriel Castillo, *palabrero* of the MS-13 New York cell. He has even more tattoos than Rio and that's saying something. He has a blue, folded bandana tied around his forehead and wears a large white tee with saggy, dark wash jeans. The dim light from inside the house reflects off his shaved head; three inked tear drops rest below the corner of his left eye. A gross misinterpretation as we all know he's killed more than three men. An accurate number would probably be closer to several dozen.

"Rio! *¿Qué pasa, hermano?*"

"*Dios mío, dame paciencia,*" Rio looks to the ceiling with his hands clasped together in front of him. "I'm not your brother, *puto.*"

"Right, because a brother wouldn't leave another brother behind." Gabriel crosses his arms and leans against the door frame, his demeanor shifting from friendly to deadly.

"I went to college, *compa*. Just because I didn't want to join *la mara* doesn't mean I left you in the dust. Put on your big boy *chones* and get over it. Read a self-help book or something."

Ignoring Rio's response, Gabriel turns his head to me. "What're you doing with my homeboy there?"

"We need to ask him some questions." I cross my arms over

my chest and keep my face blank. He won't get more of an answer than that.

"What a coincidence. I have some questions myself." Gabriel mirrors my stance. I hope he doesn't think he looks intimidating. Just because I can see his gun tucked in the front of his jeans, doesn't make him a badass. I could easily grab his gun that's perfectly aimed right at his dick.

"We'll drop him off to Mommy after Daddy is done." Rio gives Gabriel a condescending wink. He's pretending to be calm, but I can see his hand twitching for his knives. I don't know the entire history between them, but I know it wasn't pretty.

There's a scraping sound coming down the hall and we all freeze. I whip around with my gun in hand and aim at the hallway opening. Zane is standing there holding the ankle of the second occupant of the house. He's unconscious and bleeding.

Zane unceremoniously drops the boy's leg and crosses his arms. "What are you fucking doing here?" His question is directed at Gabriel like a dagger between the eyes. To say that Zane is Gabriel's biggest hater is an understatement. I'm not a big fan either, but for Z, the disdain runs deeper than that.

Gabriel spreads his arms wide. "I came to clean up a mess, but it seems you three beat me to it. Thank you for tying them in a nice little bow for me. You can go now. I'll take it from here."

"That's not fucking happening. We have some questions for your homeboys and then you can have what's left over." Zane spits out the word *homeboys* like it's diseased.

"I wasn't asking for your permission, *cerdo*."

"The only way you're taking them is over my dead body." Zane takes a step forward.

"That can be arranged." Gabriel gives Z a vicious smile.

In the blink of an eye Rio has his tactical karambit in his hand pressed against Gabriel's throat and his k-bar in his other hand resting above Gabriel's gun. "Say that again, *cabrón*."

"These are my men," Gabriel spits out. A trickle of blood rolls down his throat and the fucker doesn't even blink.

"Your men who are taking side jobs from someone else. They shot up my girl's shop today, and I intend to find out who the *fuck* sent them." Rio pushes his knife into Gabriel's throat more.

"I can't just let you walk out of here with them."

"Sure you can. You just stand there and we leave." I shrug my shoulders.

Gabriel signals one of his men when he whistles, and like the good little bitch he is, Diego Rivera walks through the back door. I whip around with my gun trained on him while his is on me. Looks like we're going to have a good ol' Mexican standoff.

"You've got to be kidding me." Zane pulls out his two Berettas, aiming the first at Diego and the second on someone coming down the hall.

Fucking Mateo Alvarez. I should have known. Gabriel doesn't go anywhere without his *segundo palabrero* and his other unofficial *segundo palabrero*.

"Let's make this a fun reunion. Two long lost friends working together for the greater good. We can talk to the two *mierdas* together," Gabriel suggests.

"Fine. You can follow us to our place." I lower my weapon as a show of good faith.

"No fucking way." Zane holds steady, refusing to give in.

"Z," I state, my voice even. I don't need to say more to get him to listen. He knows this is the best option.

Rio and Gabriel may be childhood friends, but he wouldn't hesitate to kill us if he had to. You don't make it to be the *palabrero* of New York, and keep the respect, without a healthy amount of ruthlessness.

Rio sheaths his knives and steps back still facing Gabriel, his carefree persona back in place. "You can pick up the pies from Sal's. I don't like working on an empty stomach."

"Do I look like your errand boy, Flores?"

"No, but you have two right there." Rio grins at Mateo and Diego, giving each a slight nod in their general direction.

"*Hijo de puta.*" Diego rolls his eyes, tucks his gun into his jeans, and walks out the door. Mateo follows Diego's lead.

"Let's get this show on the road, *amigos!*" Rio claps his hands while Z and I lift the two unconscious bodies up and over our shoulders. Rio stops on the front lawn and we immediately recognize our problem.

"Should've hijacked a car," Rio mutters.

Coming up with a solution, I bite out commands. "Rio you take Tweedle Dumb with Gabriel and Mateo. Z and I will take Tweedle Dee with Diego." Rio nods and we all part. Rio, Gabriel, and Mateo all head towards an Escalade parked right out front and the rest of us head to Z's clown car.

"You need an upgrade," Diego says with his light Hispanic accent.

"Fuck off," Zane bites back.

As we open doors to get in the car, I hear Rio tell Gabriel, "I was serious about the pies. I'm fucking starving. I do my best work on a full stomach."

CHAPTER 44

SPENCER

I swear if those three went out and did something stupid like die, I'm going to kill them. I'm supposed to be the one leaving, not them.

Leaving is supposed to keep them safe. Someone already got hurt. I can't handle any more of that happening because of me and the fucking psycho who can't handle an ounce of rejection.

I'll deal with Anthony on my own, in my own way. It worked last time. I was able to avoid him for three years. If I'm smarter this time, I'll be able to hide longer than that.

Iris and Hayes made me get in bed last night, but I hardly slept. I tossed and turned until the sun came up. I didn't realize how accustomed I had become to my two bedmates. I need their warmth, their comfort.

Like a clingy girlfriend, I ended up texting them last night. Even Asher, which is embarrassing enough as it is. I haven't heard one word from any of them.

Again, they better not be fucking dead.

The sweet aroma of pancakes is a big reason why I finally

decide rolling out of bed is a good idea. Throwing on my usual relaxation garb, I meander out to the kitchen where Iris is cooking up a storm. I don't know where she got all this food. Usually, I'm lucky if the milk in my fridge isn't expired. Somehow, she has come up with a full spread: fruit, pancakes, scrambled eggs, bacon, coffee, and hash browns.

"Hayes went to the market early this morning," she says, noticing me eyeing the food.

"Oh. Where is he now?"

"He stepped out to hang a sign that the studio is closed for the next couple days."

What would I do without Hayes?

You'll find out soon enough.

Unsure of what else to say, I shift on my feet. "Anything I can do to help?"

"Absolutely not," she points at me with her spatula. "Make yourself a coffee and have a seat."

I walk over to her and grab her hand. "Hey. I wasn't the only one there yesterday. You were too. You also need to take some time to breathe, girl."

She refuses to look me in the eye. "Cooking is how I cope. Let me do this."

Scanning her face, I concede. As much as I want her to take it easy and relax, I know better than anyone that we have to do what helps us get through the next twenty-four hours. Whether that be a run, hiding in the bathroom, blasting music, or cooking like you're feeding an army.

I nod. "Okay, but promise me if things become too much you'll tell me or Hayes?"

She raises an eyebrow at me. "Like you promised to turn to Bad Boy Rio, Daddy Zane, and Viking Hottie Asher?"

"Don't eavesdrop," I playfully swat at her shoulder. "And I only promised Rio."

She turns back to the stove. "Uh huh. But if I were you I'd run to all three of those men," she peaks over her shoulder at me and lowers her tone. "If you know what I mean." She gives me an over emphasized wink before turning her head back toward the pancakes.

Laughing, I fire up the espresso machine and I shake my head at her. "You're incorrigible."

Iris makes no effort to reply. We fall into companionable silence and eat together when Hayes returns. After stuffing ourselves full, we all venture to the couch and pull up Netflix. The buzz of the TV falls into the background as I stare at my phone, willing it to ding with a notification.

Still nothing.

Deciding I'm going to be *that* person, I start a group chat with all four of us. If they don't like it, tough. They should have replied instead of making me worry sick.

I know this is the opportune time to leave and make my way to California, but I can't leave without knowing they're okay first.

> Me: Where are you guys?
>
> Me: I'm just going to keep texting until one of you fucking replies.
>
> Me: Y'all better not be hurt.
>
> Me: Please don't be hurt.

Letting out a sigh, I throw my phone down on the cushion next to me. If I don't hear back from them soon, I'll go by their house to check on them. I just need to see that they're okay then I can make my way to Port Authority for the long bus ride ahead of me.

Hayes pauses the show and leans forward on his elbows. "I think you need to talk to somebody."

Umm. That came out of left field.

"Okay?" I don't know why it comes out as a question. I know I need to talk to a professional. Especially after Anthony. I probably should have gone to someone years ago. But as they say, hindsight is 20/20. Now I'm here after surviving a drive by shooting that I know was ordered by my ex-fiancé.

Yeah, I think I need to talk to somebody.

He fishes out his wallet and hands me a card for a counseling center. I examine it and give him a questioning look.

"I started going there after I got mugged. Remember that? They're really nice there and helped me work through everything I was feeling. I still go once a month."

His confession leaves me speechless. Iris shows no surprise. I remember when Hayes got mugged not long after he started working at the studio. It scared the shit out of me.

"Thanks, Hayes. I'll give them a call tomorrow." The lie leaves a sour taste in my mouth.

Hayes gets comfortable again with his arm around Iris and resumes the show. By the end of the third episode, I check my phone again. Still no new texts or calls.

My gaze catches Iris eyeing my phone. I lock it and set it down.

Sticking to the plan, I stand and make an excuse that I'm tired and going to lay down. Neither Hayes nor Iris gives it a second thought.

My guilt weighs heavy on me, so I give them each a hug and tell them I love them. I ignore their confused looks and casually make my way to my room, even though I'm sweating bullets.

Locking the door behind me, I snatch my bags from their hiding place under my bed and open the window. I'm halfway out with my ass on the windowsill when I hesitate.

Is this the best way? Is leaving going to make a difference? How do I know Anthony will leave everyone alone?

I shake off my doubts and shut the window. With my bag across my body and my backpack secure, I climb down the steps.

The guys kept my goodbye letters. Inconvenient as hell, but I'll just have to ask them to give the letters to Hayes, Iris, Paul, and Alma for me. A text will be shitty of me, but I can't ask them to distribute the letters in person. I wouldn't be able to go through with it and I'd end up staying.

The walk to the subway is short, but I can't rush it. I have to act natural even if it feels like my breakfast wants to make a second appearance. Trying not to wring my hands is right up there next to impossible, but this bitch can do hard things.

Strolling down the sidewalk with sweat dripping down my back, I feel the hairs on the back of my neck begin to stand. I almost dismiss the feeling, attributing it to the slight breeze blowing by.

Still going for a casual exterior, I pull out my sunglasses and slide them on. With the added barrier I'm able to scan my surroundings. No one looks suspicious or out of place. A mom is pushing a stroller, a jogger blasts their music in their ears, a teen walks their Corgi down the sidewalk.

But I can't disregard my gut, it's what has kept me alive this far.

I pretend to stretch my neck and get a look at the people behind me. A businessman with a briefcase, an elderly woman with her cane, a couple holding hands while they chat, and just six feet behind them is a man with his focus zeroed in on my head. I've never seen him before, and commit his face to memory.

Dark hair with a military cut, brown eyes, alabaster skin with freckles, and a scar running down his jaw. His shoulders aren't the kind of wide that he takes up the whole sidewalk, but wide enough to feel threatening.

Adding a little more pep in my step, I pick up speed. The subway entrance comes into view, and I risk another glance over my shoulder. My mouth goes dry.

He's closer than before.

Now at a brisk jog, I hear a pounding on the pavement behind me.

Shit.

I'm a runner, but I've never gone on my morning run with the extra weight of bags hanging from my body.

Something to practice in the future.

I pump my arms as I switch to an all out sprint. The pounding behind me gets louder and my stomach knots. When I reach the steps leading down to the platform, there's a fierce tug on my backpack, my torso is jerked back and I almost lose my balance.

This is not fucking happening again.

Turning my momentum around, I spin and duck under the man's arm. I lift my elbow and bring it down on his arm repeatedly which catches him by surprise.

I keep reminding myself the goal isn't to win. The goal is to get away.

When he lets go I aim back for the stairs, but this time he grabs my ponytail and I cry out.

I twist back around and clutch his grip with one hand and his wrist with my other. Turning so his arm is extended with his elbow contorted at the wrong angle. I crank his wrist and thrust my head forward allowing my body to follow the direction. He goes down with me and I straddle this chest. Delivering two swift blows to his head, I scramble to my feet and dart down the stairs.

My pulse is flying and air rapidly saws in and out of my lungs. My legs shake as I flee.

"Fucking bitch! You're lucky he said not to hurt you!" His voice is gravelly like he smokes a pack a day.

I slide over the turnstyle. I know it's technically stealing, but steal or get kidnapped. I won't lose sleep over stealing a few dollars from the New York government. They'll live. I may not.

Righting myself, I attempt another sprint. I'm jerked back again when my duffle bag snags on the turnstyle.

Fuck.

Glancing up I see the man, his face twisted in anger. With vigor, I tug on my bag. He's not close to me yet, but he will be in seconds.

Tug. Tug. Still no give.

"Line two approaching the platform. Stand back."

That's my train.

I plant my feet and give the synthetic fabric a firm yank. There's a tearing sound and I'm finally free.

Switching my weight, I take off just as my mysterious attacker makes it over the metal barrier.

I'm five feet from the doors and they begin to slowly slide closed. Digging deep into my reserves, I pump my arms harder and push my stride faster.

"Don't you fucking dare, cunt!"

With less than two feet of space between the doors, I jump and land just inside the train car. There's a rush of air and I know the doors have closed. Spinning, I see him standing there and his rage has reached new heights. He slams his fist over and over on the safety glass.

Thankfully, the New York subway waits for no one and the

train moves. He somewhat regains his composure and whips out his phone. Before I am able to read his lips, he's out of sight.

I plop down on the nearest seat and count my lucky stars. That was too close. Anthony is too close.

My heart still hasn't returned to a normal rate and I highly doubt it ever will.

Fucking hell.
Is this my life now?

CHAPTER 45

SPENCER

Almost an hour later, I'm off the train and making my way to the address Rio texted me yesterday.

They still haven't texted me back.

Maybe this is a sign. A sign that they don't want me anymore. Did yesterday make them realize I'm not worth all the trouble?

The thought stings, but this would be for the best. A clean break. Although avoiding me would be a shitty way of them telling me they're done, I'm not sure I can blame them.

How do you tell someone whose place of business just got a shot up that you're not interested in them anymore?

Apparently, the answer is to say nothing at all.

I make my way through their neighborhood. Kids play in the street, a pair of elderly women gossip in lawn chairs, and a man moves his trashcan to the curb, a picturesque New York residential area. It's peaceful. Laughter rings down the street.

It's the complete opposite of the turmoil going on inside me. My muscles are stiff, ready for the next bad thing to happen. My focus darts about, checking for threats.

I force myself to take calming breaths and to slow my pace. Everyone out here is enjoying their afternoon. I don't want to scare the children whose only goal is to have fun. They deserve their carefree play time.

Finally arriving at the address, I take a moment to reel in my nerves. I can't go in there with this intense, high-strung energy and then expect them to just let me leave.

Their brownstone is not what I expected. I mean, I didn't think I would find beer cans on the small lawn, but I also didn't expect to find it so cozy and clean.

I wait a few minutes, but the only sign that someone is home is Zane's Honda Civic in the driveway. They may have taken Asher's car somewhere and gone out together.

Yeah, that's probably it.

Perhaps I should leave a note on the doorstep. Let them know, I'm gone. But I don't want it to blow away.

I could leave it inside.

Is it breaking and entering if I have a key?

Glancing up and down the street, I make my way to their front door. I don't know why I'm so nervous to go inside. It's not like someone is going to jump out and say, "Hey! You can't do that!"

I unlatch the deadbolt, turn the knob, and try to push the door open but it won't budge. It's definitely unlocked so what the hell?

Shoving my shoulder into the door, there's only an inch of movement.

So that's why it's unlocked.

Using my hip I give the wood a good couple bumps. It finally opens without so much as a squeak. I stand there staring at the open doorway.

Am I really going to do this?

Apparently.

Ugh. Suck it up, Spencer. Be a big girl and just put one foot in front of the other. You're not a burglar, you're just leaving a note. You're more like Santa Claus.

I go straight for the kitchen and don't allow myself to get caught up in admiring the nice couch or gawking at the plain decor. I find a pen and a paper menu for Sal's.

God, these men and their pizza.

On the back of the paper I scribble out a note and demand my tears to stay put.

Thump.

What the hell was that?

I keep my body impossibly still, listening for the noise again. Nothing happens so I finish my note with a little heart and "Love, Spence." It may be ridiculous to add a heart seeing how their radio silence speaks volumes, but I can't end the note without some kind of indication that I still care.

Thump. Thump. Thump.

I set the pen down and follow the source of the noise. Tiptoeing across the wood floors, I don't make a sound. The last thing I need is one of the guys finding me creeping around their house.

Thump.

With ominous energy in the air, I find myself in front of a door behind the staircase.

That's not creepy at all. I should turn around and leave the way I came.

What if one of them is stuck down there and needs help?

My hand automatically wraps around the doorknob before I am able to talk myself out of it.

Oh God. I'm going to be *that* girl, aren't I? The one that goes into the eerie basement like an idiot even though she's being chased by an ax murderer. Nothing good ever happens in basements.

Dropping my hand, I take a step back, but then there's another *thump* followed by a painful moan.

My bags go to the floor softly. I steel my nerves and open the door. There isn't a light on the foreboding stairs, just a path to a nice dark pit.

Well, isn't that lovely.

My feet take slow steps downward. If an ax murderer really does jump out at me, I'll allow all of Hollywood to say, "I told you so," because they've literally tried to warn me with all the scary movies they have produced.

When I get to the halfway point a few voices float up my way.

"He doesn't know anything."

"*Hijo de puta!*"

The second voice is Rio, but the first I don't recognize. It's accented and deeper than Rio's.

A new voice interrogates, "Who sent you? Who told you to shoot up Abstract Dreams?"

That is definitely Zane, but who the hell are they talking to? Did they find the shooters? Why are they here and not at the police station?

"*No te diré ni mierda.*" Another voice I don't recognize.

"Let's just get it over with and kill them. I'm bored." Another unfamiliar, accented male voice. Does Rio have brothers I don't know about? How many people are here?

I land on the final step and grunts of pain meet my ears. I peak around the corner, but don't dare to come out of the shadows.

My hand flies to my mouth to keep in the gasp ready to slip out.

What the hell is happening?

There are two savagely beaten men tied to chairs. Rio is squatting by one of the men and whispering something in his ear while he traces a knife down the man's arm. Zane is standing with his arms crossed and his back to me. By the way his muscles are tense in his back, I can tell that his mood is foul.

Off to the side are three more men. All tattooed and a little scary looking. One has a passive look on his face as he twirls a knife around his knuckles, I'll call him Bored Dude.

The second man wears a scowl like it's permanently etched on his face and he has no interest in changing that, he's dubbed Angry Man.

The third looks annoyed, but there's amusement in his eyes. It's as if he's entertained by what's going on. He's officially Creepy As Fuck Guy.

I look back to the men tied to the chairs and silently gulp. My stomach churns as I take a mental inventory of their injuries. Both of their eyes are swollen shut, dried blood sits under their noses and coats their lips. They have bruises all over and their shirts have been cut down the middle, barely hanging on their shoulders. The guy currently not receiving Rio's special attention is shaking like a leaf.

Did Zane and Rio do that? Where's Asher? Does he know what's going on?

Rio adds pressure to his knife on the man's hand and I simultaneously add more pressure to my hand covering my mouth.

"Okay! Okay! His name is Cain. We met him at Euphoria."

Zane drops his arms and takes a step forward with his fists clenched. "You saw him?"

The man in the chair pants while speaking. "Not really. He passed us notes."

"You took a fucking hit job via a note like you're some schoolgirl passing notes in class? Are you fucking kidding me? How dumb are you? You could've been set up." Creepy As Fuck shakes his head at the guy like he's disappointed.

Disappointed rather than disgusted? Seriously? Who is this guy?

"They're useless." In a flash Creepy As Fuck whips out a gun I didn't notice and shoots each tied up man in between the eyes.

My mouth gapes open in a silent scream and arguing ensues between him and Rio. My hands quiver as I bring them to my sides.

Step by step, I back away from the scene before me. Without looking behind me, I run into a wall I wasn't there seconds before.

No.

Not a wall.

A person.

Before I can scream, a large hand clamps over my mouth and an arm hugs me around my waist.

"Now, where do you think you're off to, Princess?"

❦ ❦ ❦

The Devils of New York story continues in *Tainted Truth*. Preorder your copy on Amazon.

Want more of Rio, Asher and Zane? Get an exclusive bonus scene by scanning the QR code below.

ACKNOWLEDGMENTS

This is all still very surreal. I can't believe I did it. I published a damn book. I would not have made it this far without the love and support of some very important people.

Zach, my love,

You are a rockstar. Thank you for encouraging me, telling me how proud you are and pushing me to keep going even when I wanted to quit. You are my inspiration. You are my home, my touchstone and my safe harbor. When shit hits the fan, you calm me and comfort me. We've made four beautiful kids together, adopted an energetic pitbull, celebrated eleven years of marriage, and watched the Hobbit and LOTR more times than I can count. I can't imagine doing any of it with anyone else. I love you and will love you forever.

My ride or die, Emily,

I don't know how you put up with me sometimes. Thank you for matching my crazy and loving me through every stumbling block. Your love and loyalty know no bounds and I am beyond blessed to have both. I love you so damn much.

My siblings,

Remember, Mom and Dad don't know about this. If you tell them, I'll deny it until my dying breath.

Alpha/Beta Readers,

Wow. Y'all are amazing! Thank you for the vital feedback. This book would not be what it is without your input. Your comments and suggestions went a long way to building this story. Thank you for hyping me up and getting excited with me about Spencer and all her crazy. Love y'all!

Jenn,

We fucking did it! We're published authors! Thank you for talking me through all my breakdowns, helping me learn the ropes, encouraging me from literally day one, and always being someone I can turn to when I need to vent or be lifted up. Thank you for telling me to take my power back from those who have stolen it. I love that you're my reading mirror. You've gotten me hooked on some amazing books and now we have matching cow mugs. I love you!

Eliza and Lilian,

Thank you for encouraging me, doing sprints with me, answering ALL of my little and annoying questions, your words of wisdom and being the people I can turn to when I feel lost and overwhelmed. My book and sanity wouldn't be what it is without you two.

Savannah,

Girl, you are a powerhouse! I don't know how you do what you do and then also have time to let me sit on your couch and write. Thank you for being a true friend, bringing me cheese puffs late at night, and doing coffee runs with me. Love you!

Lauren,

Thank you times a million! You helped me more than you know. We live thousands of miles apart, but you literally held my hand when I needed it.

Ashli,

Your honesty is a gift. Thank you for helping me battle all the bullshit that got in my head and telling me not to listen to the haters, whether they be a different person or the anxieties in my own head. Your opinions have been vital to this book and my mental health. I love you!

Britt,

Yeah, you're in here, Britt. Thank you for helping me understand why I am the way that I am and accepting me, but also showing me how I can grow. Thank you for helping me accept the darker side of my brain and understanding that the things I write don't make me a bad person.

All my ARC readers, bookstagrammers, booktokkers and reviewers,

Thank you for reading my book! You are key to this whole process. This book is as much for me as it is for you. Thank you for reading and just being interested! It means the world to me!

STAY CONNECTED

You can find Ivy in all the bookish places...
- Website
- Newsletter
- Ivy's Spicy Harem (Facebook Reader Group)
- Instagram
- Goodreads
- BookBub
- Amazon
- Pinterest
- Threads

ABOUT THE AUTHOR

Ivy King was born in California and raised in Texas. She now resides in the beautiful mountains of Idaho with her husband, four kids and adorable pitbull.

When she's not busy writing, she can be found potting plants, playing with her kids or going on an outdoor adventure through Yellowstone National Park. She also enjoys listening to true crime podcasts, "rescuing" plants from local stores and hanging out with her close friends.

Printed in Great Britain
by Amazon

49307804R00188